A

Week Like Any Other

Novellas and Stories

by Natalya Baranskaya

translated by Pieta Monks

The Seal Press

© 1989 by Natalya Baranskaya
Translation Copyright © 1989 Pieta Monks

This U.S. edition first published in 1990 by The Seal Press, 3131
Western Avenue Suite 410, Seattle, Washington 98121.
Published by arrangement with Virago Press, London.

The cover art is a detail from the painting "Old Muscovite"
(1988) by contemporary Soviet artist Elena Romanova. Our
thanks to International Images, Ltd. for making this art available.

The stories in this collection first appeared in the following journals
in the USSR: "A Week Like Any Other" in *Novy` Mir*, 1969;
"The Purse" in *Souvremennik*, 1981; "The Petunin Affair" in
Molodaya Gvardia, 1977; "Lubka" in Molodaya Gvardia, 1977; "A
Delicate Subject" in *Zvezda*, 1973; "The Woman with the
Umbrella" in *Souvremennik*, 1981; "At Her Father's and Her
Mother's Place" in *Novy Mir*, 1986.

Library of Congress Cataloging-in-Publication Data

Baranskia, Natal'ia.
    [Short stories.   English.   Selections]
    A week like any other: novellas and stories / by Natalya
Baranskaya.
        p.   cm.
    Translations from Russian.
    Contents: A week like any other — The purse — The
Petunin affair — Lubka — A delicate subject — The woman
with the umbrella — At her father's and her mother's place.
    ISBN 0-931188-80-6 (pbk.). — ISBN 0-931188-81-4 (cloth)
    1. Baranskaia, Natal'ia—Translations, English.   I. Title.
PG3479.R27A6   1989
891.73'44—dc20   89-34486
                                                              CIP

Printed in the United States of America

First printing, February 1990
10 9 8 7 6 5 4 3 2 1

Seal Press
P.O. Box 13
Seattle, WA 98111

Contents

A
Week Like Any Other

Monday

I'm in a rush. I rush on to the second floor landing and bump into Yakov Petrovich. He asks me into his office and enquires about my work. He doesn't mention my lateness. I'm fifteen minutes late. Last Monday I was twelve minutes late. He had a chat with me then as well, but that was later on in the day: he wanted to know which American and English journals and catalogues I was looking at. The exercise book which we use in the laboratory for clocking in was lying on his desk and he looked at it now and then but said nothing.

Today he reminds me that by January the tests on the new plastiglass must be finished. I tell him I know. 'We'll be placing an order in the first quarter,' he says.

I know. How could I forget?

Yakov Petrovich's dark eyes shine out from the depths of his soft, rosy face; he catches my eye and says: 'So, Olga Nikolaevitch, your tests won't be late?'

I flush, and remain silent, confused. I could, of course, say: 'No, definitely not.' It would be better to say that. But I say nothing. How can I promise?

Yakov Petrovich continues in his quiet, even voice: 'Taking into account your interest in this work and, hmm . . . your talent, we promoted you to the vacant post of junior research assistant, we included you in the group working on this interesting problem. I will not conceal from you the fact that we are rather worried, hmm . . . astonished by the fact

1

that your attitude towards your work does not seem to us suf-
ficiently rigorous . . .'

I say nothing. I love my work. I value my independence. I
work willingly. It doesn't seem to me that I am unrigorous.
But I'm often late, especially on Mondays. What can I say? I
hope that this is just a little lecture, nothing more. A little
lecture for being late. I mutter something about the icy paths
and snow drifts in our unfinished new housing estate; about
the bus that arrives at the stop already full to overflowing;
about the terrible crowds at Sokol Station: and, with an
anguished sick feeling, I remember that I have said all this
before.

'You must try to be a bit more organised,' concludes
Yakov Petrovich. 'Do excuse this little talk, but you're just
beginning your working life . . . We have the right to hope
that you'll value the trust we have accorded you as a young
specialist . . .'

He unbuttons his lips and a smile appears. This artificial
smile upsets me more than anything else. I apologise in a shrill
voice, unlike my normal one, and promise to be more organised. Then I leap into the corridor. I rush, but at the laboratory door I remember that I haven't combed by hair, so I turn
round and run down the long, narrow corridor of the old
building, a former hotel, to the toilet. I comb my hair, placing
the grips on the wash-basin under the mirror, and hate myself.
I hate my tangled, frizzy hair, my sleepy eyes, and my urchin's
face with its big mouth and nose, like Pinocchio. It seems to
me like a man's face.

I comb my hair half-heartedly, tug at my jumper and walk
out into the corridor: I must calm down. But the talk with
my head of department goes round and round in my mind like
a tape on a spool. All sorts of things, individual phrases, his
intonation, each separate word, seem to have a sinister significance. Why does he say 'we' all the time? 'We trusted', 'we
are worried'? That means that there has been talk about

me – with whom? Surely not the director? Had he said 'it worries' or 'it astonishes'? 'Astonishes' is worst. And that reminder of the vacant post: Lidya Chistakova wanted it. She had priority as far as length of service went, but they chose me because it was closer to my research topic. And, of course, my English helped; they find it very useful.

Of course, Yakov Petrovich had taken a risk when he brought me into his group six months ago and entrusted me with work on testing new materials. I realise this. He would have been more secure about deadlines with Lidya . . . Suppose he wanted to give her my work now? That would be terrible; I've done nearly all the tests.

Maybe I'm exaggerating. Maybe it's just my perpetual anxiety, my everlasting rush, my fear that I won't get things done in time, that I'll be late . . . No, he just wanted to give me a little telling off, he's irritated by my constant lateness. He's right. It's his work, after all. We know our head, he's meticulous, a workaholic. Stop! I must stop thinking about this.

I switch on to something else: today I will summarise the results of the tests we did on Friday on high and low temperature resistance. I'm not worried about the tests in the physics and chemistry laboratory, which are coming to an end, it's the mechanical testing that is our weak area. In that laboratory there is neither enough equipment nor enough staff. It doesn't matter too much about the staff, we can do a lot of it ourselves, and we do. But there was a long queue for some of the equipment. As Yakov Petrovich puts it, one has to 'keep a close eye on things' or 'barge one's way in'. I push in with my plastiglass, another group pushes in with their project – we all rush to the old laboratory assistant on the ground floor who draws up a table of tests and their order. We try friendly familiarity, dear Valya, or friendly respect, Valentina Vasilevna, we jump up and down in front of her, we do everything we can to find a crack in the order through which we can push our tests.

Yes, I must hurry to Valya. I go downstairs, I push the door open and I'm met by an elastic wave of noise. I push through it and through the glass partition. This is Valya's 'little office'. It's always crowded, but now she is alone. I ask her to squeeze me in this week, she shakes her head, but I persist.

'Try seeing me in the second half of the week.'

Then I go to the polymer laboratory – my room. In our 'quiet' room where we work out results and carry out calculations there are nine people, but only seven tables can be fitted in. But someone is always carrying out tests somewhere or away on a study trip. Today one of the tables is mine and it has been standing empty a whole forty minutes.

I go in. Six pairs of eyes meet mine. I nod and say: 'I went into mechanics on the way.'

Fair Lusya's blue eyes are worried: 'Has something happened?'

Dark Lusya's huge, fiery eyes reproach me compassionately: 'Not again!'

Maria Matveyevna warns me silently as she looks at me over her glasses: 'No excuses, please.'

Alla Sergeyevna looks at me absent-mindedly: 'Who's that? What's that?'

Shura's round eyes, always a little astonished, look even bigger than usual.

Zinaida Gusavovna's eyes for one moment reveal her sharp hostility to me: 'We know all about the mechanical – you were late, you've been told off, your cheeks are red and your eyes are anxious.'

I work with the two Lusyas.

Our director is Yakov Petrovich, although Lusya Markoyan seems to be more involved in the group's work. When I first came to work in polymers the new plastiglass was still in the planning stage. Lusya was weaving magic with analytical weights, test-tubes and thermostats, working on the composition. Everybody thought the new plastiglass had been her idea, but it turned out to have been Yakov's. I once

4

asked her: 'Lusya Vartanovna, why do people say that it was you who invented the new plastiglass?' She looked at me: 'Is that what they say? Oh well, let them.' And that was all. She once promised to tell me the 'whole stupid story', but she hasn't up to now, and I don't ask any more.

I'm entrusted with certain tests: some I do by myself, some with the workers in the laboratory where the tests take place. Then I work out and summarise the results.

Blonde Lusya (her proper name and patronymic is Ludmilla Lichova) compresses and moulds models according to strictly established specifications and helps in other ways.

We also share Zinaida Gustavovna: she is office manager of all the groups and deals with customers.

Everybody has more than enough to do.

At my table, finally! I move a box away to get at my log book of experiments, then I notice a questionnaire on the table. On the top in bold type is written: 'A Questionnaire for Women'; in the corner in pencil: 'to O.N. Voronkova'.

Interesting . . .

I look round: Blonde Lusya holds up an identical one. It's a big questionnaire. I start to read. Question No. 3: 'Your family situation: husband; children up to seven years; children from seven years to seventeen; relatives living with you . . .' I have one husband, two children, no grandparents, alas, and my other relatives live by themselves.

The next question: 'Where do your children go: the crèche; kindergarten; after-school playgroup?' Well, the crèche, and my little boy goes to the kindergarten.

The authors of the questionnaire want to know about my living conditions. 'Separate flat, amount of living space, square metres, how many rooms, what conveniences.' My living conditions are excellent: a new flat, thirty-four square metres, three rooms . . .

Oh – they really want to know everything about me. They're interested in my life hour by hour in 'the adopted time unit'. Aha, 'unit' is a week. 'How many hours do I spend (a) on housework; (b) with the children; (c) on spare-time cultural activities?' Cultural activities are sub-divided: 'radio and television; cinema-going; theatre-going; reading; sport; tourism, etc . . .'

Oh, spare time, spare time. What a ludicrous phrase – 'spare time': 'Women – fight for spare-time culture!' Sounds ridiculous. Spa-a-re ti-i-me. Personally, I like to run. I run here and there, with a bag in each hand of course, up and down, to the trolleybus, the metro, from the metro . . . There are no shops near to where we live, we've been there more than a year and they haven't finished building them yet.

So I discuss the questionnaire with myself. But the next question inhibits any desire to be witty: 'Days off due to illness: your own or your children's (number of days in the last year; please give information according to the table)'. My Achilles heel. My lecture that morning from my Head . . . Of course, the directors know that I have two children. But nobody's worked out how many days I've had to spend at home with them. If this statistic is unearthed it might frighten them. It might frighten me as well. I haven't worked it out either. How much? I know it's a lot.

It's December now. Both of them had flu in October, first Gulka and then Kotka caught it, for about two weeks. In November they had colds, really the end of the flu, which lasted about a week because of the bad weather. In September Kotka brought home chicken-pox. It worked out about three weeks because of the quarantine, I can't remember exactly . . . And, as always, the minute one got better the other fell sick.

I think: what else could there have been? Alarmed for the children and my work. Measles, German measles and mumps but, most often of all, colds and flu and more colds – from a hat badly tied, from crying on walks, from wet trousers, from

6

cold floors, from draughts . . . 'Acute respiratory infection' write the doctors on the sickness certificates – they're always in a hurry. I'm always in a hurry as well. So we send the children back to school when they still have coughs, and their colds don't go until the summer.

Who thought up this questionnaire? I turn it round but can't see any information on the compilers. I look at Dark Lusya and signal with my eyes: 'Let's go outside'. But Blonde Lusya immediately leaves the room too. What a pity. I wanted to talk to Lusya Markoyan about my lecture this morning as well as work and the questionnaire, about everything. Blonde Lusya is all right but you can't say anything in front of her, she talks non-stop and can't keep anything to herself.

Lusya Markoyan immediately lights a cigarette and, puffing out a column of smoke says, challengingly:

'Well?'

I know that this means, 'What do you think of the questionnaire?' but Blonde Lusya jumps in indignantly:

'What do you mean ''well?'' She doesn't know about it, she was late!'

'Late too,' says Dark Lusya mockingly and sympathetically. She puts a hand thin as a bird's claw on my shoulder: 'Can't you stop being late, Pinocchio?'

'Those, what d'you call them, demographers, came to see us today,' says Lusya hurriedly, bursting to be first with the news, 'and they said that they're carrying out an experiment with these questionnaires at certain institutions where women work.'

'Our institute is mainly men but we do have women working in the laboratories,' elucidates Dark Lusya.

'Anyway,' Blonde Lusya dismisses Dark Lusya's remark, 'they say that if the experiment is successful they'll use these questionnaires all over Moscow.'

'What do they mean by ''successful''?' I ask Dark Lusya. 'And what exactly are *they* after anyway?'

7

'God knows,' she answers, lifting up her sharp chin. 'Questionnaires are fashionable at the moment. What they really want to know is why women don't want to have babies.'

'Lusya, they never said that!' says Blonde Lusya indignantly.

'They did, but they called it: "an insufficient increase in population growth". You and I aren't even reproducing the population. Every pair should have at least two if not three children; we have one each.' (Here Dark Lusya suddenly remembers that Blonde Lusya is a single parent.) 'You're all right, they wouldn't dare ask you for more. Olya's OK as well, she's fulfilled her norm. But me! They'll give me a plan and then I can kiss my dissertation goodbye.'

They talk and I look at them and think: 'Dark Lusya looks like a burnt out stick, Blonde Lusya like an empty, white, fluffy cloud. But if we judge by the questionnaire then Dark Lusya is much better off, and Blonde Lusya the most unfortunate of all the four "mums" in our laboratory.'

We know everything about each other. Dark Lusya's husband is a Doctor of Science. Not long ago they had a big cooperative flat built. They're not short of money. Five-year-old Mark has a nanny. What more could they want? But this Doctor of Science has been nagging at Lusya for the last five years, accusing her of being selfish, of ruining her child's life because she lets him be looked after by an outsider, an old woman. (He won't let the little boy go to the kindergarten.) Lusya's everlastingly searching for pensioners to babysit. The 'Doctor' wants Lusya to stop working, he wants another child, he wants a 'normal' family.

Blonde Lusya has no husband. Vovka's father is a Captain, a student at some military academy. He is from another town and he didn't tell Lusya that he was already married with children. Lusya found out about it too late. When Lusya told the Captain that she was in her fourth month he

8

disappeared into thin air. Lusya's mother came up from the country. First she nearly killed her daughter. Then she went to the Captain's boss to complain about him. Then she and Lusya cried together and cursed all men. Then she settled down in Moscow. Now she looks after her grandchild and does the housework. All she asks of her daughter is to do the shopping, the main wash, and to come home at night.

We know least of all about Shura. Her son is ten. He is alone after school until his mother returns. He refuses point blank to go to the after-school group. Shura telephones home several times a day:

'What have you eaten?'

'Did you remember to turn the gas off?'

'Make sure you shut the door behind you when you go out.' (His outdoor key is tied to his jacket with tape.)

'Have you done your homework? Don't read too much, you'll strain your eyes.'

He's a serious boy. Shura's husband drinks. She hides this from us but we guessed a long time ago. We don't ask her about her husband.

I should be the happiest one.

Blonde Lusya, bursting with curiosity, has taken Dark Lusya's joke about a five-year-plan for children seriously.

'What do you mean?' she gasps, and her slender eyebrows disappear under her curly hair, 'It can't be true! Oh, you're joking!' We can hear her disappointment, 'Of course, you're joking. But, listen girls, I think there's more to this questionnaire than meets the eye. Maybe they'll give us mothers some benefits, eh? Shorten our working day; pay us for the whole time we have off when our kids are sick and not just the first three days, don't you think? Now that they're looking at it they're bound to do something.'

Blonde Lusya is getting excited: her face is red and her curls are shaking.

'And pigs might fly,' says Dark Lusya. 'That's not what

9

it's about. We don't have enough builders, our workforce is too small, that's the point. What will happen? Who will do the building?'

'What building?' asks Blonde Lusya with interest.

'All the building: houses; factories; machines; bridges; roads; missiles; communism. Everything. And who'll defend all this? And who'll cultivate the land?'

I'm only half listening. The morning lecture is still going round in my head: 'I would advise you to be more organised,' Yakov had said. Perhaps everything is already decided and my work has been given to Lidya? I'm often late, I've got slack . . . What a mess! And to add to it all he's soon going to get my 'sickness data'.

It's a shame that I couldn't talk to Dark Lusya. But she sees that something's bothering me and puts her arm around my shoulder, drawing me slightly to her. She says, drawling, 'Don't worry, Olya, they won't fire you.'

'They wouldn't dare,' says Blonde Lusya suddenly, furiously, like milk boiling over, 'with two children. Anyway, first they'd have to give you a warning and so far you've only had a talking to.'

For being late . . .

I feel a bit ashamed of myself: Blonde Lusya is so kind and sympathetic, and I hadn't wanted to talk in front of her.

'I'm frightened. I'm frightened that I won't get my tests done in time. There's only a month left.'

'Oh, don't be so silly!' interrupts Dark Lusya.

'What do you mean "Don't be so silly!"' Blonde Lusya interrupts in turn. 'Can't you see the woman's worried? You should say, "Now, take it easy, relax . . ." It's true Olya, honestly, it's a waste of time worrying. Everything'll be all right, you'll see.'

These simple words bring a lump to my throat. To start crying now would really be the limit. Dark Lusya comes to my rescue.

'Listen, my beauties,' she says, slapping us energetically on the backs, 'suppose we arrange a three-way exchange? Blonde Lusya can have my flat, I'll move to Olya's, and Olya can go to Blonde Lusya's.'

'Why?' we ask, bewildered.

'No, no, that's not right!' Lusya Markoyan wags her finger in the air. 'No, this is what we should do: Olya can move to my place, I'll go to Blonde Lusya's, and she can move to Olya's. That's it.'

'You want to exchange your three-roomed flat for my one room in a communal flat?' Blonde Lusya smiles broadly.

'No, I don't want to, but needs must. I'll lose out on square metres and conveniences – you don't have a bathroom, do you? – but I'll gain on something more important. And you, Blondie, you won't lose out either: Olya's Dima is wonderful! My hubby'll be happy: Olya is younger and plumper than me. And I'll get a Granny, I need one so much. Well, what do you think? Will you help a poor woman with her dissertation?'

'Go to Hell!' Blonde Lusya shouts, 'You can never be serious about anything!'

She turns to leave us, but the door suddenly opens and she almost knocks Maria Matveyevna over.

'Comrades, you're making such a noise,' she says, 'that you're disturbing people's work. What's the matter?'

I grab Blonde Lusya's arm just as she's taking a deep enough breath to be able to relate our entire conversation to M.M. (that's what we call her amongst ourselves).

We all respect M.M. deeply. Her innocent honesty compels us to like her. But we can't really talk to her. We know in advance what she'll say. She's seen as a rather old-fashioned 'idealist'. She's somehow become abstracted from real, everyday life, she glides above it like a bird. Her life has been exemplary: she was in an industrial commune in the early thirties and was a political adviser at the front in the forties.

11

She lives alone now. Her daughters were brought up in a children's home. They long since have had children of their own. Maria Matveyevna's only interests are her work, production figures and the Party. She's at least seventy.

We cannot but admire her for her life of sacrifice.

'Well, well, what's going on here?' asks Maria Matveyevna sternly.

'We're telling Pinocchio here off,' smiles Dark Lusya, 'Olya . . .'

'What for?'

'For being late,' butts in Blonde Lusya hurriedly and foolishly.

Maria Matveyevna shakes her head reproachfully, 'And I thought you were being serious.'

I feel uncomfortable, and I can see that the Lusyas do as well. You can't be frivolous with M.M.

'Well, Maria Matveyevna, it's very strange,' I say, in all sincerity, without answering her question, 'I have two children and I'm ashamed of it. I feel uncomfortable. I'm twenty-six, I have two children, and somehow, I feel like a . . .'

'. . . throwback to pre-revolutionary Russia,' prompts Dark Lusya.

'Really, Lusya,' says Maria Matveyevna indignantly. 'Now listen, Olya, you must be proud of yourself, you're a good mother and a good worker. You're a real Soviet woman.'

M.M. speaks and I wonder why I should feel proud. Am I such a good mother? Am I really a praiseworthy worker? And what is a 'real Soviet woman' anyway? There's no point in asking Maria Matveyevna. She wouldn't answer.

We soothe M.M. by saying that I was just in a bad mood, it'll pass – of course.

We all go back in. I haven't found out anything useful about the questionnaire – when do we have to give it back and to whom? But I get a note: 'They will collect the questionnaires from us personally next Monday. They want to know what we think about it. They might have some questions. And what about us? Dark Lusya.'

Thank you. Enough about the questionnaire.

I find Friday in the log-book and write out the latest tests in it for Dark Lusya. Then I get the pile of papers as thick as a newspaper and line them up. These are to be the summary graphs of all the experiments. They will be drawn up according to our log-book data.

The first compound of plastiglass showed a high degree of fragility. We worked on the component parts. Then we began a second series of tests. Everything had to be done again: hygroscopicity, humidity resistance, heat resistance, cold resistance, fire resistance . . . I would never have imagined that such care, such meticulousness could be given to sewer pipes and roofs.

I discussed this with Dark Lusya a long time ago. I had admitted that I wanted to work in a different kind of laboratory. Lusya laughed:

'Oh, the youth of today – everybody wants to work on space projects. But who will be left to organise our life on earth?' And then she asked abruptly: 'Have you never lived in a place where dirt pours onto people's heads from old rusty pipes and the ceilings are falling in?' It emerged that we both had lived in places like this but I had never given it much thought.

The more I worked on the new plastiglass the more absorbing I found it. Now I wait impatiently for the results of all the experiments with the new compound: how will it withstand the load? How durable will it be? And then a bottle-neck, a jam in the mechanical department.

Everything else is going fine. I begin to fill in the graph with the physiochemical data – it's nearly finished. I build up the column of figures slowly, I look through the log-book:

'Water resistance. Sample No. 1 . . . Sample No. 2 . . .

Sample No. 3 . . .' The weight is in milligrams. The time of immersion '15 hrs. 20 minutes'. Time of extraction: '15 hrs. 20 minutes' = 24 hrs. Weight after extraction . . .

The fingers of my left hand hold the line on the necessary page, the right hand writes the figures, the average deduced from the results of three experiments, into the table.

I must be careful, make no mistakes.

'Olya, Olya,' a quiet voice calls me, 'It's ten to two, I'm just popping out. What do you want?'

Today it is Shura's turn to do the shopping for the "mums". That's one of our arrangements: to do all the shopping for everybody at one go. We asked to have our lunch break from two to three when the shops are less crowded. I ask for butter, milk, a pound of salami, and a roll to eat now. I won't go out, I'll work through the lunch break. I've wasted so much time today already.

Dark Lusya has disappeared somewhere – probably catching up on lost time as well. I'm right. She reappears ten minutes before the end of the lunch break. Her hair and dress smell of some sort of lacquer, the familiar smell of our compound. She's ravenous and I share my salami and roll with her; we wash it down with water from the laboratory tap.

Again I become absorbed in the graph. The second half of the day goes so quickly that I can't understand why our 'quiet' room has become so noisy. It turns out that everyone is getting ready to go home.

Again the bus, again jammed full. And then the metro, the crush of the change at Belorussia Station. Again I must rush, I mustn't be late. The others get home by seven.

I travel the remainder of the metro journey in comparative comfort: I stand in the corner by a closed door. I stand and I yawn. I yawn so vigorously that a young man says cheekily, 'Well, love, what were you up to last night?'

'I was singing the children to sleep,' I answer to stop him pestering me.

14

I yawn and I remember this morning again. Monday morning. It was still night time, dark, everybody was asleep. And then the telephone. It rang for a long time, must be inter-city. Nobody answered it. I didn't want to get up either. No, it was someone ringing at the door. A telegram? Maybe from Aunt Vera arriving unexpectedly? I rushed to the hall. The telegram lay already open on the floor, but there were no words on it, only little holes like the ones in computer paper. I flew smoothly over the dumb telegram and turned around to go back to bed. Only then did I realise that it was the alarm clock ringing and I told it to go to hell. It immediately fell silent. A deep peace reigned. It was dark, dark and quiet. A quiet darkness, a dark quietude . . .

But then I jumped up, got dressed quickly. All the hooks on my belt fell in the correct eyelets and, O wonder! even the one that fell off is sewn back on. I ran into the kitchen to put on the kettle and the water for the macaroni. And another wonder, the gas ring is burning, the water in the pan is bubbling and the kettle is whistling. It whistles like a bird: pheut-phyu, pheu-phyu. And then I realise suddenly that it's not the kettle whistling but my nose. And I can't wake up. Dima starts to shake me, I feel the palm of his hand on my back, he shakes me and says:

'Olya, Olya, Olya, come on, wake up now, or you'll be rushing like a mad thing again.'

And then I really do get up: I get dressed slowly, the hooks in my belt fall into the wrong eyelets, one of which is missing.

I go into the kitchen, catching my foot in the rubber mat in the hall, nearly falling over. There's no gas on, the matches burn out, hurting my fingers; oh, I've forgotten to turn the gas on. At last I get to the bathroom. I wash myself and bury my face in the warm, shaggy towel. I must have fallen asleep for half a second because I wake up saying:

'Damn, damn, damn everything!'

15

But that's a silly thing to say. When everything's going well, when everything's fine. When we have a flat in a new estate, when Kotka and Gulka are wonderful children, when Dima and I love each other and when I have an interesting job. Why should I say damn? It's just silly.

Tuesday

Today I get up on time. At ten past six, I'm ready, apart from my hair. I clean the potatoes for supper, stir the porridge, simmer the coffee, warm the milk, wake Dima and go in to get the children up. I switch on the light saying loudly,

'Good morning, my pets.'

But they're fast asleep. I shake Kotka, tug Gulka and then drag the blankets off the pair of them.

'Up you get!'

Kotka kneels on the bed, his face still buried in the pillow. I pick up Gulka. She kicks me and yells. I call to Dima to help me but he is shaving. I leave Kotka for the moment and pull a top on Gulka who has calmed down, put on her tights, her dress, while she tries to escape from my knees onto the floor. Something is spluttering in the kitchen – oh, I forgot to turn off the milk. I place Gulka firmly on the floor and rush to the kitchen.

'Honestly!' says the freshly-shaven Dima as he comes out of the bathroom. But I don't have time to reply. Abandoned, Gulka is crying with new passion. Her shrieks finally wake up Kotka. I give Gulka her little boots and this mollifies her. She puffs and pants as she rolls them beside her small fat legs. Kotka can dress himself now, but it takes him so long that I can't wait. I help him and then start to comb my hair. Dima has laid the breakfast table but he can't find the salami in the fridge and calls me. While I help him find it Gulka hides my comb. I haven't time to look for it so I pin up my hair half combed. I give the children a quick wash and we all sit down at the table. The children have milk and a roll, Dima eats a fuller breakfast, and I can't eat at all, I just have a cup of coffee.

It's ten to seven and Dima is still eating. It's time to put on the children's outdoor things: this has to be done quickly, both at once, so they don't get hot and sweaty.

'Let me finish my coffee,' grumbles Dima.

I sit the children on the divan, drag out all their garments and work for two: one pair socks, two pairs socks; one pair woollen tights; two pairs woollen tights; jumper, jacket, two scarves, mittens—

'Dima, where are Kotka's mittens?'

'How'm I meant to know?' he answers, but nevertheless starts to look for them and finds them in an unlikely place – the bathroom, where he flung them the night before. I pull two pairs of feet into felt boots, squeeze hats onto moving heads, I rush and shout at the children the way people shout at horses when they're trying to harness them:

'Keep still, keep still, I tell you!'

Dima joins in at this point: he puts on their coats and ties their belts and mufflers. I get myself ready. I can't get one of my boots on . . . Aha, my comb!

At last we get out. Our last words to each other are:

'Did you lock the door?'

'Have you got some money?'

'Stop rushing like a madwoman.'

'All right! And don't be late picking up the children.' (I shout this last from the bottom of the stairs.)

And we part.

It's five past seven and I, of course, must run. From our little hill, far away, I can see how quickly the queue is growing at the bus stop, and I run, flapping my hands to stop myself falling on the slippery path. The bus arrives at the stop already full. Only five people from the queue are usually let

17

on. Then some intrepid queuers from the back will fling themselves forward. Some lucky person will manage to get hold of the rail. The bus puffs and roars away leaving the odd leg sticking out of the door for a while, the odd hem, a briefcase.

Today I am one of the brave. I remember my student days when I was a runner and a jumper, 'Olya-alley-hop!' I skate along the ice, jump, hold on, and hope with all my might that someone inside will grab hold of me and pull me in. And someone does. When the dust has settled a little I manage to pull *Yunost* (Youth) journal out of my bag. I am reading a story that everyone else read ages ago. I even read it on the escalator. I finish the last page at Donskoy bus stop. I arrive at the Institute on time. I go first of all to the mechanical department, to see Valya. She is angry:

'What's the rush? I told you, the second half of the week.'

'You mean tomorrow?'

'No, the day after tomorrow.'

She is right, of course, it would be better not to try to rush people, but everybody does it, and it would be terrible to miss a chance.

I go up to my room. I ask Blonde Lusya to prepare samples for tests tomorrow in the electronics laboratory. Again I work on my graph. At 12.30 I go to the library to change my journals and catalogues.

I look systematically through the American and English publications on building materials: I always look at ours and sometimes at the scientific-technical patent ones at the Lenin Library, when I manage to get there. I'm pleased that I've kept up my English. It's enjoyable and relaxing to leaf through journals after two or three hours' work. I show anything that might be of interest to Lusya Markoyan and to Yakov Petrovich, who also know English, but not as well as I do.

18

Today in the library I manage to look through *Building Materials '86*, new issues of an abstracts' journal, and to leaf through an American building firm's catalogue.

I look at the clock: five to two. I haven't given my order for the shopping.

I run to my room, remembering on the way that I still haven't combed my hair properly. I laugh wildly. Panting and dishevelled I burst into our room and find myself in the middle of a crowd of people: the room is full. Is this a meeting? Surely I would have remembered?

'There you are, ask Olya Voronkova what her main interests are,' says Alla Sergeyevna, turning to Zinaida Gustavovna.

I can tell by their faces that a heated discussion is taking place. About me? Have I done something wrong?

'We are having a disagreement about the questionnaire,' explains Maria Matveyevna to me. 'Zinaida Gustavovna has raised an interesting question: would a woman, and, of course, we're talking here about a Soviet woman, be guided by the national interest in such a matter as having children?'

'And you want me to settle the matter?' I ask, relieved. (I thought it was something to do with work.)

Of course, I'm the main authority on having children, but I'm fed up with it. Furthermore, Zinaida's 'interesting' question is a really stupid one, even if she's asking it purely out of curiosity. But, knowing how malicious she is, and how she's always trying to catch people out, it's fairly obvious that this question is pointed, she wants to have a go at someone. She herself is at that happy age when having children is no longer a possibility.

Shura explains to me in a low voice that they are arguing about the fifth question:

'If you have no children please give the reason: medical evidence; material circumstances; family situation; personal reasons, etc . . . (please underline whichever is relevant).'

I don't know what the argument is about: we can all answer by underlining 'personal reasons'. I myself would even have underlined 'etc . . .' But it's this question that has aroused interest and even offended the childless amongst us.

Alla Sergeyevna says that it's incredibly tactless. Shura retorts that it's no more so than the questionnaire in general.

Blonde Lusya, having mulled over the part of our conversation yesterday that obviously most worried her, 'who will cultivate our land?', flings herself to the defence of the questionnaire:

'After all, we must find an answer to our serious, even dangerous, demographic crisis.'

Lidya, my rival in the competition for youngest scientific assistant, who has two adoring suitors, says: 'Let married women solve the crisis.'

Varvara Petrovna corrects Lidya kindly, gently: 'If it is a national crisis, then it concerns everybody . . . of a certain age.'

Dark Lusya shrugs: 'Is it really worth discussing the kind of short-sighted attitude embodied in this questionnaire?'

Immediately several voices are raised in protest.

Lusya elucidates: the questionnaire's compilers propose basically personal reasons for not having children, thus they acknowledge the fact that people are guided by personal reasons in having a family. It follows that no demographic enquiry would be able to exert any influence at all on this matter.

'You've forgotten the socio-economic factor,' I object.

Maria Matveyevna doesn't like Lusya Markoyan's sceptical remarks:

'We've done an enormous amount to liberate women, and there is absolutely no reason not to believe in the desire and will to do more.'

'Maybe a strictly practical attitude to this problem would yield the best results,' says Dark Lusya. 'In France they pay the mother for every child. It's probably more effective than any questionnaire.'

'Like quotas in a pig farm.' Alla Sergeyevna twists her mouth in disgust.

'Choose your words more carefully,' booms out M.M.'s masculine voice. And, simultaneously, Blonde Lusya squeals:

'It's all the same to you, anyway, pigs or humans.'

'Well, in France they've got capitalism,' says Lidya, shrugging her shoulders.

I'm bored with all this fuss. It's getting late. I'm starving. It's time for one of the 'mums' to do the shopping. And I really ought to comb my hair. Anyway, I'm fed up with this questionnaire. I raise my hand – attention! I strike a pose:

'Comrades, let a two-time mother say a word. Let me assure you that I gave birth purely for state reasons. I challenge you all to a competition and sincerely hope that you will all surpass me both in the quantity and quality of the product. But now, I implore you, please, someone give me something to eat.'

I had thought this would amuse them and end the argument. But it annoys someone and an open squabble breaks out. I only catch fragments:

'. . . turning something important into a circus.'

'If human instinct overcomes reason . . .'

'Women without children are all selfish.'

'. . . you ruin your life.'

'It's debatable whose life is ruined.'

'They volunteered to increase the population . . .'

'. . . who will pay your pension if there are not enough young people to take your place?'

'You're not a real woman until you've had a child.' And, even: 'If the cap fits, wear it . . .'

And, in all this chaos, there are just two sober voices: angry Maria Matveyevna: 'This isn't a discussion but a fish-market.'

And calm Varvara Petrovna: 'Comrades, why are you getting so excited? In the end we all choose our own fate.'

Everyone calms down. Then narrow-minded, mean Zinaida shouts out:

'Well, maybe we do. But when we have to stand in for them, trudging around factories on business trips, or sitting all evening at meetings, then it affects us as well.'

This ends our women's talk about the questionnaire and having children. I suddenly feel sorry – we could have had a really serious discussion, it would have been interesting.

I'm still thinking about this on my way home: 'Everybody chooses their own fate.' But do we really choose it freely? And I remember how Gulka was born.

Of course, we hadn't wanted a second child. Kotka was still hardly more than a baby, not yet one and a half, when I realised that I was pregnant again. I was horrified, I cried, and I decided on a termination. But I didn't feel the way I had with Kotka, I felt better, different. I said this to my neighbour in the queue at the clinic, a middle-aged woman, and she suddenly said: 'It's not because it's your second but because this time it's a little girl.' I left the clinic immediately and went home. When I got home I said to Dima:

'I'm going to have a little girl. I don't want an abortion.' He was exasperated: 'Surely you don't believe those old wives' tales,' and he tried to persuade me not to be a fool and to get the official documents for a termination.

But I believed it, and began to imagine a little girl, blonde, blue-eyed like Dima (Kotka is dark-haired with brown eyes, like me). The little girl ran around in a short skirt, shaking her funny little pigtails and rocking a doll. Dima got even more annoyed when I told him this and we argued a lot.

When we reached the absolute deadline we had a final talk. I said:

'I'm not going to kill my daughter just because she might make our life more difficult.' And I began to weep.

22

'Don't cry, you idiot. Have the baby, if you're that crazy. But you'll see, it'll be another boy.'

Then he stopped talking and studied me silently for a while. Then he banged the table and made a resolution:

'So a decision has been reached: we will have the baby. No more crying and arguing.' He hugged me. 'Anyway, a second boy is not a bad thing. He'll be company for Kotka.'

But Gulka arrived, and she was so beautiful right from the start, blonde, bright, and so like Dima that it was funny.

I had to leave the factory, where I had only worked for six months (I had stayed at home for a year after Kotka's birth, I nearly lost my diploma because of it). Dima got a second job: he taught at the technical college in the evening. Once again we had to count the kopeks, we ate cheap fish, millet, cheap salami. I nagged Dima when he bought a packet of expensive cigarettes; Dima said it was my fault that he never got a decent night's sleep. Kotka had to go to the crèche again (I couldn't manage the two of them on my own) and he kept getting sick and spent more time at home than there.

Had I chosen all this? No, of course I hadn't. Did I regret it? Not at all. The question was nonsensical. I love them so much, my funny little children.

I'm running again, to get home to them quickly. I run and my bag full of shopping bangs against my knees as I go. On the bus I see by my watch that it's already seven – they're home by now. I hope that Dima isn't letting them fill up on bread and has remembered to put on the potatoes.

I run along the paths, cut through the waste-land, and run up the stairs. Just as I'd thought: the children are munching bread; Dima has forgotten everything and is absorbed in a technical journal. I light all the gas rings and put on the potatoes, the kettle and the milk. I fling some cutlets into the frying-pan and, twenty minutes later, our supper is ready.

We eat a lot. For me it is really my first meal of the day. Dima is usually hungry after a canteen lunch. As for the

23

children, who knows what they've eaten.

The children are exhausted by the hot, plentiful food, they're already rubbing their fists into their cheeks and their eyes are heavy with sleep. They must be taken to the bathroom, plunged into a quick bath and then to bed. By nine they're fast asleep.

Dima returns to the table. He likes to drink his tea slowly and look at the papers, have a little read. I wash the dishes and then the children's clothes: Gulka's little trousers from the crèche; dirty pinafores and handkerchiefs. I darn Kotka's woollen tights, he's always rubbing holes in the knees. I get their clothes ready for the morning, and put Gulka's things in a bag. Then Dima brings in his coat – a button got torn off in the metro again. The sweeping still has to be done, and the rubbish taken out. The last is Dima's job.

At last everything is done and I go to take a shower. I always do this, even when I'm faint with tiredness. I get to bed at midnight. Dima has got our bed ready on the divan. He goes into the bathroom. I'm closing my eyes when I remember: I still haven't sewn the hook onto my belt. But I don't have the strength to get out from under the blankets.

I'm asleep in two minutes. Through my sleep I can hear Dima getting into bed, but I can't open my eyes, can't answer his question, can't return his kiss . . . Dima winds up the alarm clock – in six hours the damned thing will explode again. I don't want to hear the gnashing of the clock springs, and collapse into a deep, dark, warm sleep.

Wednesday

Everybody feels a bit uncomfortable after yesterday's outburst; you can see this by the way they are working, in a very concentrated, very polite way.

24

I take the log-book of experiments down to the electronic laboratory where Lusya is waiting for me already. She is flirting with a new laboratory worker, oohing and aahing, looking at the fearful signs:

'DANGER! HIGH TENSION!'

as if she's seeing them for the first time.

We're not in charge here, but we're allowed to be present.

Our samples, mixed the previous day in the thermostats with the given temperature and humidity, are now put into a device which determines electronic resistance. Six plates, one after the other, represent the surface resistance, and another six the volumetric.

Lusya pretends that she is still frightened, backs towards the door and disappears.

She amazes me. She works well with her hands, and remembers everything that is shown her, but she doesn't want to go fully into anything. I have tried to draw her into the calculations and have explained formulae to her. She says:

'I know that heat resistance means the pipes won't melt, and lightning resistance means the roof won't go up in flames when there's lightning.' She really regrets that she went to technical college. She loves sewing and wants to learn to cut out, but she's afraid:

'Nobody marries seamstresses nowadays.'

It's my turn to do everybody's shopping in the lunch break. It's not easy. Not only because it's heavy to carry, but because everybody behind you in the queue, even if there's hardly anybody, will curse you. You buy salami once, twice and then again . . . And the comments start:

'Opening a café, are you?'

'There she is, buying for the whole apartment block while we stand here . . .'

25

In Moscow everybody always rushes. Even those who have nothing to do. The current of haste infects everybody in turn. It's best to keep silent when you're shopping.

Looking sullen and withdrawn I buy three half-kilos of butter, six bottles of milk, three of sour milk, ten packets of processed cheese, two kilos of salami and three hundred grammes of cheese, twice, in the groceries department. The queue puts up with all this patiently, but towards the end someone sighs loudly:

'And they all complain they've got no money.'

I buy more in the semi-prepared foods department: four lots of ten cutlets and six steaks. The bags weigh a ton!

And then, dragging these bags, I turn off my road, loop the houses and come out at the glass cube of the hairdressers. I still have twenty minutes. I'll get my hair cut. It once really suited me short. There's no queue. To the accompaniment of the ferocious grumblings of the cloakroom attendant I leave my bags on the floor by the hangers, go upstairs and sit down straight away in a chair by a well-preserved woman with shaven eyebrows.

'What's it to be?' she asks, and learning that it's just a cut she purses her lips:

'Nowadays we cut it very short.'

And she's right. I look in the mirror: my cropped hair sticks out at cheek level, my head is like an isosceles triangle. I want to cry, but for some reason I give her a thirty kopek tip instead and go downstairs to get my coat.

The cloakroom attendant hums thoughtfully and, refusing my proferred cloakroom tag shouts: 'Lenya, come here!'

A young boy in a white coat appears.

'Lenya, look,' the cloakroom attendant says confidentially, 'they cut this girl's hair upstairs. Can you do anything with it?'

Lenya looks at me frowningly and nods towards the

empty chairs of the men's hairdressers. I offer no resistance – it couldn't get any worse.

'Taking the shape of your face into consideration, I suggest an urchin cut. Do you agree?' Lenya asks.

'Go ahead,' I whisper, and shut my eyes.

Lenya mutters to himself as he clips his scissors, lifting and lowering my head with light touches of his fingers, then he uses the shaver, fluffs up my hair with a comb and, finally, taking away the sheet, says,

'You can open your eyes now.'

I open my eyes. Before me I see a young, funny girl. I smile at her and she smiles back. I laugh, so does Lenya. I look at him and see that he is admiring his work.

'Well?' he says.

'Remarkable. You're a magician.'

'I'm simply a master of my trade,' he answers modestly.

Thrusting a rouble into Lenya's hand I look at my watch and gasp: it's twenty past three already.

'Are you late?' asks Lenya sympathetically. 'Next time come earlier.'

'I will,' I cry, 'thank you.'

I arrive at the laboratory puffing and panting. Of course, the Head of department has been asking for me. He is in the library and would like me to pop in. Everybody voices their admiration for my hair-do but I've no time to bask in it. I snatch up my notebook and pencil and rush out of the room. I run along the corridors and start to think up a lie for the Head in case he asks me where I've been. Then I realise that it's pointless: one look at me and he'll know.

I enter the reading room. He's sitting in front of a book and writing.

'Yakov Petrovich – you asked to see me?'

'Oh, yes, Olga Nikolayevna. Sit down.' He glances at me. He smiles:

'If one may say this about someone so young anyway

– you look even younger . . . I wanted to ask you, if it's not putting you out too much, to translate me a page from this,' he shows me a book, 'while I make notes.'

I start to explain the article in Russian, but he asks me to read the English text as well. Every now and then he asks me to repeat something. Suddenly I catch sight of Blonde Lusya behind the glass door. She's making some incomprehensible signs: she seems to be turning keys in doors, then lifting up two stretched fingers and rolling her eyes. I wave her away with my hand, it's really a bit much. Lusya disappears. But I start to worry: something must have happened. We're slowly getting to the end of the extract (and it's no page but three pages), when the Head asks me to repeat everything quickly in Russian from the beginning. I'm like a cat on hot bricks, I must get to Valya in the mechanical department to find out what Lusya wants. At last the Head thanks me, I reply joyfully: 'Thank you', and run into the old building.

Lusya is waiting for me on the landing of the ground floor of the old building. She has bad news for me: she has discovered from 'the most reliable sources' that the mechanical laboratory will be carrying out extra orders this week.

'How do you know?'

'I just do, don't ask me how,' Lusya looks mysterious, 'I know from a direct source.'

A direct source so soon, ah Lusya . . .

Nevertheless I must still get to Valya as fast as possible.

'Don't tell her,' shrieks Lusya after me.

I must try harder with Valya or we'll be really stuck. And to be stuck in December is to die a sudden death. The end of the year, fulfilling the plan, accounts, and so on. To make progress it is vital to know what the second lot of samples show – has the durability of the plastiglass increased?

In the mechanical there's a fair din. Instead of Valya, little Gorfunkel from the wood department is sitting there working in her office. No, it turns out that he's not working, he's looking for his glasses, his balding head practically on the table, his short arms burrowing through the pile of papers, like a turtle in straw. I find his glasses and give them to him. He doesn't know where Valya is. She went out.

'A long time ago?'

'Yes.'

I return to my room, looking in all the laboratories on the way. Valya is nowhere to be seen. Is she hiding?

A quarter of an hour before the end of the day people start to pour into our room. Zinaida is giving out tickets for the theatre – they're going to see *Flight* at the Ermolova.

Cultural outings – they're not for me, alas, nor for Dima. I feel sad. We haven't been to the theatre since . . . I try to remember when was the last time we went somewhere, and can't. I'm a fool – I could have ordered a ticket – Dima could have gone on his own, we'd never manage to go together anyway.

Dima's mother looks after her daughter's children and lives over the other side of Moscow; my mother is dead; my Aunt Vera, with whom I lived when my father re-married, has stayed in Leningrad, and my Moscow aunt, Sonya, is scared stiff of children.

There's no one to let us out to play – what can you do?

I leave the Institute. Snow has just stopped falling and is lying on the pavements. The streets are white. It is evening. The orange triangles of windows hang above the blue front yards. The fresh air is clean. I decide to walk part of the way. In the square by the walls of the Donsky Monastery street lamps illuminate the wild branches and abandoned benches covered in snow. Where there are no lights a slender fingernail of a moon can be seen beyond the tops of the trees . . .

I long to walk freely, with no baggage and no aim. Just to walk, to take my time, peacefully, very slowly. To walk along the wintry Moscow boulevards, along the streets, to stop at shop windows, to look at photographs, books, slippers, to

29

read posters without rushing, to think about where I want to go, to lick a choc-ice and somewhere, in a square, under a clock, to wait for Dima.

All that was such a long time ago, so dreadfully long ago that it feels as if it wasn't me but some other she . . .

It was like this: SHE saw him, HE saw her, and they fell in love.

There was a big party at the Building Institute – a party for students in their final year and those who had just finished. It was a noisy evening with funny games, jokes, charades, carnival masks, jazz, pop-guns and dancing in the hot, stuffy hall.

She performed some gymnastics: she whirled a hoop around her, jumped, bent and twirled. They clapped her for a long time and the boys shouted: 'Ol-ya! Ol-ya!' And they fought with each other to dance with her. He didn't dance but just stood, leaning against the wall, tall, broad-shouldered, his gaze following her. She noticed him: 'What an ape,' she thought. Then, passing him again: 'What does he remind me of? A polar bear? A seal?' And, going past him for the third time: 'A white seal! A fairy-tale white seal.'

He just watched her, he didn't ask her to dance. Her every movement was a response to his gaze. She felt alive and happy, she danced incessantly without getting tired.

When they announced a 'ladies' excuse me' she rushed up to him, scattering confetti from her short hair. 'He probably doesn't dance. . .' But he was a light and skilled dancer. Her friends tried to separate them and called: 'Ol-ya, Ol-Ya, come back!' And they flung paper streamer lassoos at them, but they only entwined, tangled and bound with the paper ribbons.

He saw her home and wanted to see her the next day, but she was leaving for Leningrad.

After the holidays, for the whole of February, he would

appear in the evenings in the cloakroom, waiting for her by the large mirror, and he accompanied her to her aunt's flat near Pushkin Station, where she lived.

One day he didn't come. He wasn't there the next day either. When, two days later, she still didn't find him at the usual place she was annoyed and upset. But she couldn't stop thinking about him.

A few days later he appeared by the mirror, as always. She flushed, said something to the other girls and went quickly out of the door. He caught her up on the street outside, seized her shoulders and, paying no attention to the passers-by, pressed his face to her fur hat. 'I was sent on an urgent business trip, I missed you badly, but I didn't know your telephone number or your address. Please, come to my place, or I'll come to yours, wherever you want.'

The green eye of a taxi winked on the corner, they got in and travelled in silence, hand in hand.

He lived in a large communal flat. An armchair with a torn cover stood under a telephone by the entrance. The door nearest it immediately opened and an old head wrapped in a headscarf peered out, noted her and disappeared. Something rustled in the depths of the corridor where the light of the dull, dusty lamp did not reach. She felt very awkward and almost regretted coming to his place, but the thought of the sedate order of her aunt's home, tea under the old chandelier and polite conversation at the table . . .

They got married at the end of April. She moved her things to his half-empty room with its divan and drawing-board instead of a table – her suitcase, her bundle of bed linen and her boxes of books.

In her dreams she had imagined everything differently: the marble staircase in the marriage palace, Mendelssohn's march, a white dress, a bridal veil, a well-covered table and cries of 'Kiss!'

None of this took place.

31

'A wedding?' he said, astonished, 'what do you want a wedding for? Let's go somewhere far away instead.'

They registered their marriage early in the morning: she came to the registry office with her friend and he with his. He brought her white lace carnations on long stalks. A wedding breakfast prepared by her aunt awaited them at her house. Glasses were raised to the newly-weds, they were wished happiness. Friends came with them to the bus that took them to Vnukovo Airport. In six hours they were in Alupka.

They stayed in a *saklya*, an old Caucasian peasant house clinging to the mountain-side. A path led up to it, with cut out steps to negotiate the bends. A narrow, paved yard hung above the flat roof of another *saklya*. On the low wall, made from local stone, grew vine tendrils, stretching down. There was a single tree in the yard, an old walnut, half-withered. Some of its branches, dry and grey, reminded one of winter and cold regions; on others dark green filigree leaves grew thickly. The lilac wistaria bushes, winding round the house, curled in through gaps in the narrow windows and filled the yard with a heady, sweet smell.

Inside the old house was dark and cool. The low, cracked stove had obviously not been used for a long time. The owner, an old Ukrainian woman, brought them a three-legged brazier that evening, full of baking heat – 'So that you don't catch your death'. The light-blue flames fluttered over the coals. They opened the door wide and went into the yard.

It was dark and quiet. The light from the lamps didn't reach here, the moon had not yet risen. They stood and listened to the breathing and gasping of the sea below as it fell on the big rocks. In the far distance a weak light flickered, perhaps a lamp on a fishing boat or a fire on the shore. The wind blew down from the mountains and brought to them the smell of the forests, of grass warmed by the sun during the day, of the earth.

The coals in the brazier began to ashen and darken – they put it in the yard.

A black sky spread over the old house with gaps for stars. The dark branches of the walnut tree flung their shadows on to the clay roof with its fallen-in chimney. A ravaged hearth, an alien house, now their refuge. They were together, alone with the night, the sea and the silence.

In the morning they ran down the path and had breakfast in a café, then they wandered along the shore. They clambered up onto steep rocks and warmed themselves like lizards in the sun, looking at the water boiling beneath them, and explosions of freezing foam flew up to them. There were no other people around, it was quiet and clean. She flung off her dress and did some gymnastic exercises in her swimming costume. He watched her smooth handstands, back flips and high jumps and asked for more. Sometimes, when the sea was calm, they flung themselves into the water. The cold burnt them, made them catch their breath. After a little swim they would run out onto the shore again and lie in the hot sun for a long time. Heated by the sun, they would go under the trees of Vorontsky Park, wander along the little paths under the shady arcs filled with the whistling and chirping of birds, and tell each other of their childhoods, their parents, their schools, friends, and the Institute . . .

Once or twice they went up into the mountains. There it was completely deserted. The pines stood quietly, lazily rocking their branches, their trunks, warmed by the sun, exuding tar that smelt of pine needles. From here, high up, the sea looked violet, it climbed steeply, like a wall, to the horizon.

They lay on the slope, covered in warm, dry, pine needles and looked at the fluffy clouds, whipped by the wind. Then they would leap up, scattering the needles, and try to catch each other with cries and laughter, circling the pine trunks. They slid down the slopes, slippery from pine cones, as if they were skiing, leaping between the stone gaps, crawling along the steep parts, clutching onto bushes and, exhausted, hot and hungry, they tumbled out of the thick, overgrown, hot genista onto the road. The asphalted road led them to the narrow Alupka alleys, to crowded whitewashed walls with their red-bricked roofs and with jasmine and sweetbriar below the windows.

The two weeks, culled from three days 'entitlement', three public holidays and ten days which she had got off from the Institute and he from work, suddenly ended.

Early one Sunday morning they got on the bus, carrying a rucksack and suitcase. They were leaving paradise.

That had been five years ago.

I shouldn't have walked, my thoughts strayed too far, now I'm late. I run down the escalator, banging people with my bag.

I wasn't very late, but the three of them are already munching on bits of bread. Dima looks guilty, but I don't say anything. I rush into the kitchen. Within ten minutes I place a big frying-pan with a fluffy omelette on the table. I shout:

'Quick – come and have your supper!'

The children run into the kitchen. Kotka sits down immediately, picks up a fork and then looks at me:

'Daddy, Daddy, come and look at Mummy. She looks just like a little boy.'

Dima comes in and smiles: 'You look so young, Olya, you've turned into a young girl again.'

During supper he looks at me instead of reading as usual. And he does the washing up with me, he even sweeps the floor.

'Olya, you look exactly the way you did five years ago.'

And in the end we forget to wind up the alarm clock.

Thursday

We leap out of bed at six thirty. Dima rushes in to wake up the children, I run to the kitchen to put on the milk and coffee and then to Dima to help him. It seems that we might manage to leave on time, but Kotka suddenly announces, after he has drunk his milk: 'I'm not going to the kindergarten today.'

We say in unison: 'Do as you're told.'

'Get your coat on.'

'It's time.'

'We're leaving.'

No. He shakes his small head, hunches his shoulders – on the verge of tears. I sit down next to him:

'Kotka, tell me and Daddy what's the matter. What's happened?'

'Maya Mikhailovna punished me. I'm not going.'

'Punished you? Well, you must have been naughty, you didn't listen to the teacher . . .'

'No, I wasn't naughty. But she punished me. I'm not going.'

We begin to put on his outdoor things by force, he starts to kick and cry. I keep repeating:

'Kotka, get your things on. Kotka, it's time to go, me and Daddy will be late for work.'

Dima is clever enough to say:

'Come on, I'll talk with Maya Mikhailovna and sort it all out.'

Kotka, red, sweating, wet with tears, sobs as he tries to explain:

'It was Vitka who knocked it over, not me. He broke it, but she made me sit by myself . . . It wasn't me! It wasn't!' Sobs again.

'Did Vitka break anything?'

'The flower pot . . .'

I feel like crying myself. The poor thing. And it's awful

35

having to force him to go when he's so upset. And I'm worried as well, sweating like that, he might get another cold. I ask Dima to find out what happened and to tell the nursery teacher how deeply these sort of things upset Kotka.

'OK, simmer down, they've got twenty-eight of them there, they're entitled to make a mistake now and then,' says Dima brusquely.

Suddenly, Gulka, who has been perfectly calm up to the last minute, starts crying and stretches out her arms to me:

'I want my Mummy.'

I leave them all and shout to Dima from the landing:

'Ring me for certain – OK?' I run downstairs, rush to the bus stop, I try to storm one bus, then another, I manage to get on the third.

On the bus I think about Kotka. There are, it's true, twenty-eight children in the group and maybe the nursery teacher can't be expected to notice everything or even have enough energy for them all. But if she hasn't the time to work things out properly, then it's better not to try at all, rather than punish some child unfairly.

I remember the headmistress asking me to work as an assistant there when we took Kotka to his new kindergarten, how she had tried to persuade me:

'You get paid time-and-a-half, and the nursery teacher helps to put out the camp-beds, take the bedding down from the shelves and to put on the children's outdoor clothes when they go for a walk.'

There was obviously plenty of work for two, for the assistant and the teacher. Just imagine: twenty-eight pairs of outdoor tights, headscarves, hats, fifty-six pairs of socks, boots, mittens and coats, mufflers and belts to tie up . . . And all this put on twice and taken off once, and again after the midday sleep. Twenty-eight – what kind of norm is that anyway? Who dreamed it up? I expect it was people who either don't have children themselves or who don't send them to a kindergarten.

In the metro I suddenly remember: today, in political study, we have a seminar, and I have left my programme at home; I have even forgotten to look at it. I undertook to prepare a question for it and I forgot! We have these study sessions once every two months and, of course, it's easy to forget them, but I made a commitment, I really shouldn't have forgotten, I'll be letting everyone down. Oh, well, when I get there I'll get a programme from Lusya Markoyan and, touch wood, I'll manage to think up something.

Still, my first worry is the 'mechanical'. If I can't get a spot today I'll be in trouble. I look in: no Valya. I shout:

'Where's Valya?'

At first they either don't hear or don't understand, and then *I* don't understand. At last I get it: Valya has popped out. Again! I leave a note for her in which everything, apart from one sentence, is a lie:

'My dear Valya – help! We have doubts about the durability of the completed compound. Unless we can test it everything will grind to a halt. Y.P. is getting annoyed with me. It's the second day running I've tried to get hold of you.'

They're good people upstairs. Nobody asks me why I am so late. They all want to look at my new hair-do, they didn't get a proper chance yesterday. I pirouette in all directions, turn my back to them, then my profile. Alla Sergeyevna comes in and says, smiling: 'Very nice,' and tells me that Valya has been asking for me. I bolt into the corridor, but before I go more than a few steps I'm called to the telephone. It is Dima. He tries to reassure me: he told Maya about Kotka and she promised to sort it out. I don't find this very comforting.

'That's what she said?'

'That's right.'

'And did you tell her what he said?'

'Well, I didn't go into detail, but I gave her the general picture . . .'

37

As I replace the receiver I realise that I didn't warn Dima about the political seminar – it means that I'll be home an hour and a half later than usual. And I haven't prepared anything for supper tonight. But it's difficult to get a call through to Dima's extension. I'll try later on, but now I must go with all speed to Valya before someone gets in ahead of me.

Valya is not happy. I should have come sooner:

'She pesters and pesters, and then you can't get hold of her,' she grumbles.

Today they have a production meeting. From four o'clock all the apparatus is free: if you can work it yourself you're welcome. The person who did have this time has cancelled.

From four – it's too late. Just one and a half hours. If there weren't a seminar . . . The seminar starts at 4.45 . . . I can't get out of it today as I'm a participant. That means I'll only have forty-five minutes. I try to explain this to Valya but she can't see it:

'Look, you made a request and I've given you what you wanted.'

'Couldn't I start just an hour earlier, at least on one unit?'

'Impossible.'

'What can I do?' I think aloud.

'I really don't know, but you'd better decide now or I'll give it to someone else, there's enough people who want it.'

'Who's before me? Maybe we could do a swop?'

'No, thank you. An exchange bureau here is all I need, it's like a railway station as it is.'

All right. We'll take that time. Four o'clock, that is.

I'm racking my brains, going back. What can we do? Perhaps Blonde Lusya could be excused from the seminar and carry out some experiments? It's just that every sample has to be measured with a micrometer, it's vital that this is done every time, even though it's prepared in a standard way. Would she do this? The cross section area has to be calculated as well. She isn't really methodical enough. No, forget about Lusya. Who else could we ask – Zinaida? But she's probably forgotten it all.

So, *I* must get out of the seminar.

I pore over the log-book. I enter a summary of yesterday's electrical tests, all the time my thoughts going round and round: how can I get out of everything and work in the physics-mechanical until it closes?

'Where's Lusya Vartanovna?' I ask.

Silence. Surely somebody must know? So, I'm done for. Dark Lusya must have left 'to think'. When she does this she hides herself so well that nobody can find her.

The lunch break arrives suddenly. Blonde Lusya is leaning towards me: 'Are you asleep or what? Tell me quickly what you need, it's nearly two o'clock.'

I start to work out loud what I need, but Lusya is in a hurry:

'Is that the lot then?'

'Since you're in such a tearing hurry, yes, that's the lot.'

'Don't get angry.' Lusya backs off.

I'm not angry. I just don't know what to do.

The telephone rings:

'Voronkova is asked to come immediately to the entrance to pick up a delivery from production.'

I fling Lusya two three-rouble notes: 'Buy some kind of meat.' At the door I remember: 'And something to eat now.' (I haven't eaten anything today.)

In the hall below, flung down from the pick-up, are three unwieldy bundles with the labels: 'Polymers for Voronkova'. They are the first experimental prototypes of our first plastiglass compound, manufactured in our experimental factory, roof tiles and thick, short pipes. Yakov Petrovich was a bit hasty in ordering them, after all, the compound is completely different now, they will only take up room on the shelves.

I ask the porter where Yury is, our worker, 'a nice strong young lad to help with the fetching and carrying'.

'He was here a minute ago.'

He is always 'here a minute ago' when you need him. I try to get hold of him by telephone, but don't have the time to hold on. I take one of the bundles and drag it up the staircase to the third floor. The old porter feels sorry for me and mutters curses directed at Yury under his breath. To this accompaniment I drag all the bundles, one by one, up to our laboratory. As I'm dragging the last one in, Lusya catches me up with our shopping.

'Olya, they're selling Lotus washing powder in the hard-ware department. I've saved a place in the queue, somebody can go and get powder for everybody.'

I need Lotus, oh how I need it. But I just wave her away – I haven't the time. It's past three, I have to get everything ready for the mechanical and still find time to peep at the seminar programme. But Lusya Markoyan is still not here . . . I realise that I've decided that I will go to the mechanical. I'll eat what Lusya has bought me and get to work. But Blonde Lusya has disappeared somewhere – gone after the Lotus, maybe? I rummage in her bag: two rolls and some cottage cheese, half is probably mine.

I get ready gradually. Our samples were taken down long ago. At five to four I disappear.

I start with the pendular impact machine. I measure the first bar of plastiglass, secured in place, establish the angle of impact and release the pendulum. A blow. The sample has withstood it. Now we increase the load. I'm getting excited. Gambling fever. The second version of plastiglass – will it withstand the greater impact or not? The sample does not break under the heaviest blow. Hooray! Or is it still too early to shout 'hooray'? After all, there are more tests for durability yet . . . What about the tensile strength? Compression? Firmness?

I am engrossed in this fascinating sport in which I am the trainer and the sportsmen under me are plastiglass. We have come through the first round and are preparing for the second: again I measure the thickness, the width, again I calculate a cross section area. Now a new machine and a new load.

After a while I find a soft roll and some cottage cheese on my page with calculations on it. That's funny. I've already eaten my roll and cheese upstairs. This must be Lusya's. It's so good to work this way, quickly, in silence, alone with one's work.

Suddenly I become aware that my surname is being repeatedly and angrily shouted:

'Voronkova, Voronkova! For goodness sake, Voronkova!'

I look round. Lidya is standing in the doorway.

'The seminar has started. Quick, your question is third.' After this explosion she slams the door after her.

I fling all the measured samples back into the basket together with the micrometer, the pencil, the paper with calculations on it, and place the log-book of experiments on top of the lot.

Everybody in the laboratory, about twenty people, is going to the seminar.

It is taking place in the big room next to ours. I run into our room, empty all my bits and pieces onto the table, grab a pencil and, looking guilty, go in.

Zachuraev, our boss, a former lieutenant colonel, is talking but stops the minute I open the door. I apologise and try to get through to Lusya Markoyan.

'It's really not good enough,' Zachuraev says testily, 'Sit down then, there's a free place there,' and he indicates the nearest table. 'Let's continue . . .' He pulls a handkerchief out of his pocket and wipes his hands. 'Let us look at concrete examples. Please . . .?'

There is a silence. It must be my turn to ask a question. What can I do? I stumble, hesitate, start to speak, grasping for a theme: antagonistic contradictions, non-antagonistic . . . the lack of contradiction . . . survivals from the past, i.e. drunkenness, hooliganism . . .

I flounder, pause, rise to the surface, pause, correct myself, others correct me, some expound, Zachuraev summarises . . . I listen for a couple of minutes and then my mind wanders.

It's awful, I still haven't warned Dima about the seminar. What will he do with the children? What will he give them to eat if I'm not there? I wasn't able to prepare anything for supper this morning. And what about poor little Kotka and his trials and tribulations? I cannot be sure that Maya Mikhailovna 'sorting things out' hasn't made things worse . . .

The seminar ends. I rush to our room, grab my bag and run to the cloakroom.

The clock in the hall says a quarter past seven. I could get a taxi, not all the way home of course, but at least to the metro.

But I can't find a taxi, and I run to the trolleybus stop, and then down the escalator to the metro, and to the bus stop . . . Panting and sweating I burst into the flat at about nine o'clock.

The children are already asleep. Gulka is in her cot, undressed, but Kotka, still fully clothed, is asleep on the sofa. Dima is sitting in the kitchen at a table covered in dirty crockery looking at sketches in a journal and eating bread with tinned aubergine. The kettle is on the stove puffing clouds of steam.

'Well?' says Dima coldly.

I tell him briefly about my day, but he doesn't accept my explanations, I should have phoned him and warned him. He is right. I don't argue.

'What did you give the children to eat?'

He gave them black bread with aubergine, which they liked very much, 'They ate a whole jar-full', and then milk to drink.

'You should have given them tea,' I remark.

'How am I meant to know?' he snaps back and returns to his journal.

'And what about Kotka?'

'As you can see, he's asleep.'

'I know that. What about the kindergarten?'

'Everything's OK. He didn't cry any more.'

'Let's undress him, then, and put him to bed.'

'Couldn't we at least have something to eat first?'

All right, I give in. It's pointless arguing with a hungry man. I kiss Kotka and cover him up (he seems white, his cheeks a little sunken). I go back to the kitchen and make a big salami omelette. We eat it.

The house is a real mess. Everything has remained where it was flung in this morning's rush. And beside the sofa on the floor are a pile of children's clothes: overcoats, boots, hats. Obviously Dima is making a protest about my being late.

Dima thaws a bit after the omelette and some strong, hot tea. We undress our son and put him to bed together. We put away the children's clothes together. Then I tidy up the kitchen and go into the bathroom to tidy up there and to wash and rinse clothes.

I get to bed about twelve-thirty. At two-thirty we are woken by loud cries from Gulka. Her tummy hurts, she has diarrhoea. We have to wash her, change her clothes and her bed linen, get some medicine down her and give her a hot-water bottle.

'That's your aubergine and milk for you,' I snarl.

'Never mind,' says Dima comfortingly, 'she'll be all right now.'

Then I sit beside Gulka, holding the hot-water bottle next to her, and hum sleepily:

43

'Bye-baby-bye, under the bush we lie . . .'

My head is pillowed in my free arm, my hand on the edge of the bed. I get back to bed about four o'clock and it seems that I have hardly shut my eyes before the alarm goes off.

Friday

All morning they have been putting me through the mangle for not preparing my question, and thus prolonging the seminar. I listen submissively to all the complaints and apologise. I'm thinking about the children. We took Gulka to the crèche, but she should have stayed at home. She doesn't need a certificate for one day, but Dima and I do. And if we had called a doctor we would have to tell what had happened. Because it concerned the stomach the doctor would have to send off for an analysis, and that would have meant waiting several days – so, we sent Gulka back to the crèche.

I am quickly forgiven. Even Lidya softens. Maria Matveyevna announces, 'strictly between ourselves', that from the New Year we will have a new boss, a specialist in philosophical science.

We start work. Friday is the end of the week and we all have an enormous amount to do. Bits of work have to be finished, books and magazines have to be signed out of the library, we have to make business appointments for Monday, personal appointments for the weekend, to have a manicure or our shoes heeled. We 'mums' also have the main shopping to do for the weekend ahead.

And then there is the questionnaire. Everybody has questions that seem to have been waiting for this last day, and everybody wants to see personnel to know about their days off sick. It has been decided to do this in an organised way. Lusya is ordered to help with the calculations.

I know that nobody will have had as many days off sick as me.

But I haven't the time to think about this. Like everybody else, I've got a lot to do. I have to process what I did yesterday in the 'mechanical'. All my bits and pieces which I flung on the table yesterday are still there. It's annoying that I wasn't able to use all the time that Valya had offered me. I just hope that Blonde Lusya's information about the extra orders isn't true – it'd give the green light to all the laboratories. Or at least let it take place a little later. According to the timetable for that week we have the mechanical for a whole day. Three of us will work together: me, the laboratory worker and Lusya. Maybe we will get everything done. Maybe we will have enough time.

I write down the results of yesterday's experiments in the log-book and I put yesterday's samples in the box. I tear off and fling out my rough calculations. Blonde Lusya and I unwrap the bundles of samples. We place a few bits of plasti-glass pane and some short bits of different pipe sections on the stand for observation. I write out labels for them. Now I can work on the graph and bring it up to date, so that only the new experiments have to be added to it.

But where is it? I didn't work on it yesterday, but the day before I put it in the drawer, under the log-book. I pull everything out of the drawer onto the table: the graph is not there. I go through all the heaps of paper – nothing. I say to myself: 'keep calm', put everything that is on the right side of the table, bit by bit, on the left side. Nothing. Did I bring it into the mechanical yesterday together with the log-book? I run to Valya. No, she hasn't seen it. I can't have lost several days' work!

My mind freezes, I sit and stare at the wall. I see nothing, my mind is blank. Then I notice the calendar – I focus my eyes and see that today is Friday, 13 December. It seemed only yesterday I was saying to myself that December had begun, and now here we were in the middle of the month, and in two weeks I will have to give my report. Can I do it in fourteen days? No, twelve, no, eleven? Finish the experiments in the mechanical and in the electronical laboratories, summarise the results, do a new graph and write the report . . .

I sit, doing nothing when I should have been looking for the graph, and I think: 'I can't do it.'

I feel a hand on my shoulder. Dark Lusya bends towards me and asks:

'Where are you, Pinocchio? Have you lost yourself or something else?'

Lusya! That's good. I touch her hand softly with my cheek. She understands everything. I have lost myself, in the pile of work and worry, in the Institute and at home.

'I've lost my summarising graph of the results of all the experiments, a table that big . . .' I show her with my hands how big it was, 'I've looked everywhere, I just don't understand . . .'

'This isn't it, is it?' asks Lusya, touching a white piece of paper lying in the middle of the table.

I pick up the piece of paper, unfold it and it turns into my graph. Laughter bubbles up inside me. I shake with laughter. I cover my mouth with my hand so that no one will hear me and laugh until tears come to my eyes. I laugh, I can't stop. Lusya grabs my hands and drags me out into the corridor. She shakes me and says:

'Now stop that this minute!'

I stand, pressing my back against the wall, tears rolling down my cheeks, and I groan quietly with laughter.

'Olya, you're completely crazy,' says Lusya, 'I congratulate you, you're having hysterics.'

'You're crazy yourself,' I say affectionately, breathing jerkily. 'Anyway, hysteria isn't fashionable nowadays. Today we talk of "stress", it's shorter, and it's just as effective. I'm just laughing because I have a very amusing life. One thing

46

after another slips past. My thoughts and feelings are all mixed together, like a cocktail. I'm not crazy. Just look at yourself, those dark circles under your eyes – still not sleeping? You're the one who's really crazy.'

'I know, but I've been crazy for years, and I'm six years older than you. And you know that things are always a bit tense at home. But you mustn't give in, you're young, healthy, and you have a wonderful husband.' She squeezes my hands between her thin fingers; her long finger-nails hurt me, but I don't complain. She looks at me piercingly, straight into my eyes, as if trying to hypnotise me. 'You're clever, capable, full of energy . . . Oh, well – ' Lusya lets go of my hands, 'let's have a cigarette. Oh no, you don't smoke.' She presses a cigarette between her teeth, clicks a cigarette lighter and inhales. 'You ought to, it helps. No, I expect it's best not to start if you've resisted up to now. Look, in the lunch break we'll do our shopping together and you can tell me all about it.'

So we walk and I tell her all about my problems with the mechanical and Valya, my talk with the departmental Head, Gulka's tummy, and about my time limit for experiments and my fear that I won't be able to get everything done in time.

Lusya listens and nods her head, sometimes narrowing her eyes, then opening them wide, and saying, 'yes, yes-yes . . .' Or flinging in a melodious, 'rea-all-yy?' It makes me feel better already. We walk in silence for a little.

'Pinocchio, do you remember asking me who invented our plastiglass and I promised to tell you?'

'Yes, you said you'd tell me "the whole, stupid story".'

'That's right. But it's not even a story really, more a joke. It was my idea, and I gave it to Yakov. Not because I was rich at the time, but because I was pregnant. I'd already decided that I would have a second child. Don't think that Suren had finally got to me. No, I'd made up my mind that it would be better for little Mark. Then I wouldn't have been able to work for a long time, I knew that. I thought, let them do with without me. And I gave it to him.'

'And?'

'And what?'

'What happened to the child?'

'What child? I cried off at the last minute. I had an abortion. I kept it a secret from Suren, like I always do.'

'How?'

'I went on a research trip for five or six days . . .'

I find Lusya's hand and hold on to it. We walk in silence together.

In the shops there is a bigger crush and rush than usual. We fill up four bags and start back at three o'clock. I carry mine quite easily, but Lusya seems to be breaking under the weight of hers. Then we see Shura.

'I thought I'd come and give you a hand.'

I ask her to take one of Lusya's bags, Lusya says to take one of mine. In the end we put Shura in the middle and carry four bags between the three of us. We have to get off the pavement, and then we have to keep stopping to let the cars pass.

'Can you carry us as well, darling,' shout two young men coming towards us.

'We've got little boys of our own,' I reply. I feel happy because it's a sunny day, because we're blocking everybody's way, because there are three of us.

Because I'm not alone.

The moment we get back Blonde Lusya appears with the calculations of our 'sick days'. Of course I head the list, as I had thought. I've lost seventy-eight days, almost a third of my whole working time, in sick days and certificates. And all because of the children. Everybody copies out their days and so can see what everybody else has got. I don't understand why I feel so awkward, even ashamed. I shrink, avoid looking at people. Why? I'm not guilty of anything.

'Have you filled in the questionnaire?' asks Lusya, 'let's have a look.'

We don't know how to calculate the time, to work out what goes on what. The 'mums' get together. We decide that we must indicate the time spent on travelling: we all live on new housing estates and spend about three hours a day travelling. Nobody can apportion 'time spent with the children' either. We 'spend time with them' while doing everything else. As Shura says: 'Me and Serezha spend the whole evening together in the kitchen: he misses me during the day and so he won't let me out of his sight when I come home.'

'Well, what shall I write about the children, then?' says Blonde Lusya, perplexed.

'What week are we meant to work out, a particular one, or an average one?' asks Shura.

'Any,' says Dark Lusya. 'Aren't they all the same?'

'But I don't go to the cinema every week,' says Blonde Lusya; more problems.

'What's the point in racking our brains,' I say, 'I'm going to take the questionnaire home. They just want a week like any other.'

Stupid questions, we think. As if you could calculate time spent on different things at home, even if you spent the whole week with a chronometer in your hands. Lusya Markoyan suggests that we put down all our free time, left over from work and travelling, and then list what this time is spent on. We are astonished: it turns out that we have from forty-eight to fifty-three hours a week at home. Why isn't it enough? Why do so many unfinished tasks follow us from week to week? Who knows?

Who really knows how much time family life needs? And what is it, anyway?

I take my questionnaire home. Dark Lusya does the same. We have to rush through certain things before the end of the day.

It isn't easy getting home today. Two heavy bags in my

49

hands – I've got everything except the vegetables. I have to stand in the metro, one bag in my hands, the other between my legs. There's a crush. I can't read. I stand and work out how much I've spent. I always think I've lost some money. I had two ten-rouble notes and now I only have bits of silver. I'm missing three roubles. I start to add it up again, mentally going through the purchases in my bag. The second time it works out that I've lost four roubles. I decide to forget about it and look at the people sitting down. A lot of them are reading. The young women have books and journals in their hands, the respectable-looking men have newspapers. There is a fat man there in a pudding-basin hat reading *Krokodil**. He looks gloomy. Young men look to one side, closing their eyes sleepily, anything not to give up their seats.

At last my stop, Sokol. People jump up and rush up the narrow steps. But I can't, I have milk and eggs in my bags. I flounder at the back of the queue. When I get to the bus stop there's a queue big enough to fill six buses. Should I try to get on to a full one? What about my bags? I try to squeeze onto the third. Because of the bags in both my hands, I can't hold on, one leg falls down from the high step, my knee gets badly knocked and hurt. At this moment the bus starts to move off. Everybody cries out, I shriek, and some old man, standing by the door, grabs me and drags me in. I collapse on top of my bags. My knee hurts, and I've probably got scrambled eggs, but at least someone gives me a seat. Sitting down I look at my knee: my tights have holes and there is blood and dirt everywhere. I open the bags and discover that just a few eggs are broken and one packet of milk squashed. It's awful about the tights, they cost four roubles a pair.

As soon as I open the door they all run into the hall – they've been waiting for me. Dima takes the bags from my hands and says: 'You're crazy.'

*A satirical magazine.

I ask: 'How's Gulka's tummy?'

'Fine, everything's OK.'

Kotka jumps on me and nearly knocks me off my feet. Gulka immediately demands a 'norange' which she's already noticed. I show them my knee and limp to the bathroom. Dima gets out some iodine and cotton wool. Everybody is very sorry for me. I like it.

And I like Friday evenings. We can sit at the table longer, we can play with the children, they can go to bed half-an-hour later. I don't have to wash any clothes, I can have a long bath . . .

But after my sleepless night last night I have an over-whelming desire to sleep. When we've put the children to bed we leave everything in the kitchen the way it is.

I'm in bed. Dima is in the bathroom. My body is already heavy with sleep, but suddenly I'm sure that Dima will put the alarm on from habit. I thrust it under the sofa saying: 'Sit down and be quiet.' But its ticking pierces the thickness of the sofa. So I carry it into the kitchen and shut it up in a cupboard with the crockery.

Saturday

We sleep late on Saturday. We grown-ups would sleep even later, but the children get up just after eight. Saturday morning is the best morning: we have two days of rest ahead of us. Kotka wakes us, he runs in to us, he has learnt to let down the side of his bed. Gulka is already jumping up and down in her bed, demanding that we come and get her. While the children play head-over-heels with their father, squealing loudly, I prepare a huge breakfast. Then I send the children off with Dima for a walk while I get down to business. First of all I put the soup on to cook. Dima tells me that the soup in the

51

canteen never tastes nice, the children don't say anything, but they always eat up my soup and ask for more.

While the soup cooks I clean the three rooms, I do the dusting, wash the floors, shake the blankets on the balcony, (that's not really a good idea, but it's quicker), sort out the underclothes, soak mine and Dima's in Lotus, collect things up for the laundry, and leave the children's things for tomorrow. I prepare the meat for cutlets, I wash the dried fruit and put it in a pan for *compote*. I clean the potatoes. We eat at three. It's a bit late for the children, but at least at the weekend they get a proper walk. We have a long meal, we don't hurry. The children should really have had a sleep, but they're past it now.

Kotka asks Dima to read him *Aiybolit**, which he knows by heart, and they settle down on the divan, but Gulka crawls up to them, starts to pester them and make a fuss, and tears the book. I'd better put Gulka down for a nap or none of us will get any peace. I sing her a lullaby and she goes to sleep.

Now I must get to grips with the kitchen, wash the stove and clean the gas rings, tidy up the cupboards with the crockery and wipe the floor. Then I must wash my hair, wash the clothes that are soaking, iron the children's clothes taken down from the balcony, wash myself, mend my tights, and I *must* sew the hook back on to my belt.

Dima has to go to the laundry. Kotka won't let go of him, so he has to go too. It's not really a good idea, there'll be a queue, it'll be stuffy, with dirty linen, but they're taking the sledge with them, they can have another walk on the way back, breathe in some more fresh air.

This means that I'm left on my own and can get on with cleaning the kitchen and things like that. At seven the 'men' come back and demand tea. And I remember that Gulka is still asleep – I'd forgotten all about her. I wake her up and she

---

*A Russian children's story.

starts to cry loudly. I give her to Dima so that I can get on with the supper. I want to get everything done a bit early today because the children have to go and bath. Gulka grumbles at the table, she doesn't want anything to eat, she's not hungry yet. Kotka eats well, he's had a good walk.

'Tomorrow I'm going to spend the whole day at home,' he says, looking at his father and me.

'Of course, tomorrow is Sunday,' I assure him.

Kotka is rubbing his eyes now, he's tired.

I fill the bath and wash Kotka first, but Gulka is screaming and crawls into the bathroom, leaving the door open.

'Dima, come and get your daughter!' I shout.

And I hear his answer: 'Maybe I've done enough today? I want to read.'

'And I don't?'

'Well, that's up to you, but I have to.'

'And I don't, I suppose.'

I carry Kotka off to bed myself (normally Dima does it) and see that in the 'study', which is what we call the single, separate room with a writing desk, Dima is sitting in an armchair reading a journal – he really is sitting and reading. As I pass by I say loudly: 'Incidentally, I've got a degree as well, you know, I'm just as highly trained as you are.'

'Congratulations,' Dima replies.

This seems to me extremely nasty and hurtful.

I'm washing Gulka with a sponge when I notice my tears splashing into the bath. Gulka looks up at me, shrieks and tries to climb out of the bath. I can't get her to sit down so I give her a slap. Gulka is deeply offended and wails piercingly. Dima appears and says angrily: 'There's no need to take it out on the children.'

'You should be ashamed of yourself,' I shout, 'I'm tired, do you understand, tired.'

I feel very sorry for myself. I'm crying out loud and

reciting everything that I've done and all the things that I should have done and haven't managed to do, and how it's always like that and how my youth is passing, and I haven't sat down for a minute all day.

There's a loud shriek from the children's room: Kotka is standing up on his bed in tears, repeating: 'Don't hit Mummy.'

I pick him up to comfort him. 'There, there, don't be such a silly-billy. Daddy never hits me, he's a good Daddy, a kind Daddy.'

Dima says that Kotka has had a nightmare. He caresses and kisses his little son. We stand with the children in our arms, pressing close to each other. 'Well, why is she crying?' Kotka asks, passing his hand over my wet face.

'Mummy is tired,' Dima answers, 'and her arms hurt, and her legs hurt and her back hurts.'

This is the last straw. I thrust Kotka into Dima's other arm, run into the bathroom, grab a towel and covering my face with it, cry so hard that I shake. I don't even know why I'm crying – it's everything all mixed up together.

Dima comes in and puts his arms around me, pats me on the back, strokes me and mutters: 'There now, that's enough, calm down, I'm sorry . . .'

I do calm down, just letting out the odd sob now and then. I already feel ashamed at having made such a scene. What happened? I don't understand.

Dima doesn't let me do anything else. He puts me to bed like a child and brings me a cup of hot tea. I drink it and he tucks me in and I fall asleep to the sound of noise from the kitchen: the splash of water in the sink, the clink of crockery, the rustle of footsteps.

I wake up and don't know what time it is – morning, evening – or even what day. A lamp is lit on the table with a newspaper covering the top of the lampshade. Dima is read-ing. I can only see half his face: the curve of his forehead, his light hair, already thinning, a swollen eyelid and a thin cheek – or is it just the shadow from the lamp? He looks tired. He turns the page silently, and I see his hand with its sparse reddish hair and his index fingernail, bitten to the quick. 'Poor Dima,' I think, 'he's got a lot on his plate as well.' And again I feel the tears welling up inside me, 'I feel so sorry for you, I love you . . .'

He straightens up, looks at me and asks, smiling, 'Well Olya, how are you? Still in the land of the living?'

I bring my hand out from under the blanket and silently stretch it towards his.

Sunday

We are lying in bed, doing nothing. The top of my head nestles under Dima's chin, his arm is round my shoulders. We are talking about everything and nothing. About the New Year and getting a tree for it, about getting the vegetables today, and about why Kotka didn't want to go to the kindergarten.

'Dima, do you think that love between a husband and wife can last for ever?'

'We don't last for ever ourselves.'

'You know what I mean – can it last for a very long time?'

'Starting to have doubts already?'

'No, come on, tell me what you think love is.'

'Well, it's when two people get on well together, like me and you.'

'And when they have children together?'

'Yes, and when they have children together.'

'And when they mustn't have any more children?'

'That's life. And love is part of it. It's time we got up.'

'And when there's never time to talk?'

'There's more to life than talking.'

'That's right. I expect our stone age ancestors never talked at all.'

'All right, let's talk. You begin.'

I'm silent. I don't know what I want to say. I just want to talk, and not about vegetables, either. Maybe I want to talk about my thoughts.

'We've only got five roubles left in the box,' I say.

Dima laughs – was this what I was getting so upset about?

'Why are you laughing? It's always like this; we only ever talk about money, shopping and the children.'

'Come on, we talk about lots of other things.'

'For example?'

'It's time to get up.'

'What else do we talk about?'

Dima didn't answer for a long time and I thought with malicious glee: 'A-ha, he can't think of anything,' but he was just going through our conversation themes in his mind before conscientiously listing them, to me:

'We talked about Harrison, the procurator, remember? We often talk about space travel, and we've discussed figure-skating, whether it's an art or a sport, we've talked about the war in Vietnam, about Czechoslovakia, about getting a new television and the fourth channel. When *are* we going to get a new television?'

We need an awful lot of things: Dima needs a raincoat, I must get a new dress and shoes, the children need things for the summer. We've got a television already, an old KVN 49 which Aunt Sonya flung out.

'We'll have to wait for the television, our savings aren't growing quickly enough.'

'Why not?' answers Dima reproachfully, 'We made a decision not to spend any of it on food.'

'Well, I don't know . . . We don't get anything special, but there never seems to be enough money.'

Dima says that if we go on like this we'll never have enough money for anything. I reply that the only thing that I spend money on is food.

'In that case you spend too much.'

'In that case you eat too much.'

'I eat too much! Oh, that's interesting, now we all have to work out exactly how much each of us eats.'

We were no longer lying down now, but sitting bolt upright, facing each other.

'All right, I mean we eat too much.'

'And what am I supposed to do about that?'

'Well, what am *I* supposed to do?'

'You're the housewife, aren't you?'

'All right, just tell me what I shouldn't buy and I won't. What about milk, shall I stop buying that?'

'I think we should stop this stupid conversation. If you can't manage your affairs you just have to say so.'

'*I* can't manage? So now I'm stupid, and I make you have stupid conversations! Just as long as I know.'

I leap up from the bed and march into the bathroom. I turn on the cold tap and wash my face, saying fiercely to myself: 'Stop it! Stop it now!'

Maybe a shower will cool me down. Why have I got so upset? Why? Is it because I'm always worried about getting pregnant? Am I taking too many pills? God knows . . .

Or perhaps I don't need this kind of love any more?

This last thought makes me sad. I feel sorry for myself and sorry for Dima, and my sadness and the hot water has the effect of refreshing and invigorating me.

The children are squealing and laughing, playing with Dima. We dress them in clean clothes. 'Don't you look beautiful now!' I say, as I call them into the kitchen to help me lay the table while their father has a wash.

During breakfast we plan what we have to do during the day: someone has to get the vegetables, the children's clothes need washing and everything needs ironing.

'To hell with it all,' says Dima, 'Let's go for a walk, it's so nice outside.'

'Mum, oh Mum, come with us, it's so nice outside,' pleads Kotka.

I give in and put off my tasks till after lunch.

We take the sledge and go to the canal where we can slide down the hill. We all take it in turns, except Gulka, who slides first with me and then with Dima. The hill is steep and worn smooth. The sledge races down and powdery snow rises up from under our legs. All around us the iridescent, shimmering snow blinds us with its whiteness. Every now and again the sledge tips over and the children squeal and we all laugh. It's nice. We return home hungry, happy and covered in snow. I decide to feed Dima first, before he goes out. I boil some macaroni and heat up some soup and rissoles. The children immediately sit down at the table and watch the gas under the pans. I feel much better after our walk. I send the children off for their nap and Dima out for the vegetables. Then I begin: I fling all the children's underwear into a bucket, wash the dishes, cover the table with a blanket and get out the iron. Then I think, 'I'll shorten my skirt. Why should I go around like an old woman with my knees half-covered?' I quickly steam out the old hem and am working out how much to turn up and how much to cut off when Dima walks in, lugging a full rucksack on his back. 'See how much better you feel after a good walk,' he says.

He's right, I feel much better. I finish the tacking-up and try on the skirt. Dima looks me up and down, grunts, and then laughs, 'It'll be twenty degrees below tomorrow and you'll have to let it down again. Still, you've got the legs for it.'

I switch the iron on to do the hem. I'll just have to sew it properly and it'll be finished.

'Can you do my trousers while you're about it,' says Dima.

'Oh Dima, can you do them yourself? I want to finish this.'

'It won't take long. You've got the iron out already.'

'It will! Look, Dima, be a pet, I want to get this finished. I've still got all the children's things to wash and all the ironing from yesterday.'

'Then why bother with all this nonsense?'

'Let's not start. Just do me a favour, iron your own trousers, and let me get this done.'

Then he says suspiciously, 'Where are you going tomorrow, anyway?'

'To the Lord Mayor's ball, where d'you think?'

'I just thought you might have something special at work . . .'

'Well, maybe I have,' I concede vaguely. If I can just get a bit of peace and quiet to finish my skirt. If I can just avoid doing those trousers. 'Do you remember I told you about the questionnaire? I've got to fill it in today and the demographers are coming round tomorrow to collect them and to talk to us.'

'I see . . .'

(Oh, Christ! Now he thinks that I've decided to shorten my skirt just because of this meeting.)

As I sew I tell Dima that they're adding-up all the days that we've had off work because of illness, and mine comes to seventy-eight days, nearly a whole quarter.

'Well, Olya, maybe it's better to give up work altogether. You spend nearly half the year at home as it is.'

'And you want me to spend all of it here? Anyway, we couldn't possibly live on what you earn.'

Dima looks round the kitchen, at the rucksack and the iron. 'If I didn't have all this to bother about I could probably earn more, 200–220 roubles. And, in actual fact, if you add up all the days you don't get paid, you probably only earn about sixty roubles a month. It's not worth it.'

No, No! 'Dima,' I say, 'You want me to do all the routine stuff, while you do your interesting work, because you think my work isn't worth it. You're just a rotten capitalist.'

'Maybe I am,' says Dima with an unfriendly smile, 'but it's

59

not just a question of money. It would be better for the children as well. The kindergarten is bad enough, but the crèche is even worse. Gulka hardly gets out at all in the winter, and she's always got a cold.'

'Dima, do you really think I don't want what's best for the children? You know I do, but what you're suggesting would kill me. What about my five years at university, my degree, my seniority, my research? It's easy enough for you to dismiss it all, but if I didn't work I'd go mad, I'd become impossible to live with. Anyway, there's no point in talking about it. There's no way that we could live on your salary and at the moment you really haven't been offered anything else.'

'All right, Olya, all right! I was wrong to mention it. I just had this vision of a different, ordered kind of life. If I didn't have to fetch the children all the time I could work so much better, I wouldn't feel so constrained. Maybe I'm being selfish, I don't know. Let's drop it.'

He goes into the kitchen. I watch him going and want to call him back, to say, 'I'm sorry'. I don't.

I hear his shout from the hall: 'Hi there, hally-gally, time to get up!' It's our special cry. He gets Kotka and Gulka up and they have some milk. We think about going for a walk and decide not to. If we did go out there'd be nothing left of the evening and I still have lots of things to do and Dima has practically walked himself into the ground already.

Kotka settles himself on the floor with his building blocks. He likes building things and makes houses, bridges, streets and huge conglomerations which he calls 'high palaces'. But Gulka's a trouble-maker. She crawls up to her brother, wanting to destroy his buildings, and she snatches cubes to take them away and hide them. Kotka calls out intermittently, 'Mum, tell her! Dad, tell her!' But words have no effect on Gulka. She just looks straight at us with her clear eyes and says frankly: 'Gulka wants to hit house.' Then I make her a little 'daughter'. A little daughter is made by

60

filling a small, hooded play-suit with rags. I put a little cushion wrapped in white in the hood and draw a face on it. Gulka doesn't like dolls but she'll drag a 'daughter' all over the place with her and have long conversations with it.

Sunday evening is quiet and peaceful. The children play, Dima reads, and I do the laundry and make the supper. I keep repeating to myself: 'I mustn't forget to sew the hook on to the waistband.' And that'll be the lot, won't it? Oh no, I still have to fill in the questionnaire, but I can do that after the children have gone to bed.

The children have supper and then play a bit, not wanting their Sunday games to come to an end. But eventually they gather up the scattered cubes, including those that Gulka has hidden under the bath and in my boots in the hall. We wash their hands and little faces, brush their teeth. We tell Gulka off when she breaks away shouting, 'Gulka wants dirt!'

At last we get them to bed.

There is still some time left. Should I read, watch television maybe? Oh, the questionnaire! I sit at the table with it while Dima peeps over my shoulder making critical remarks until I tell him to stop. I want to finish it. There, that's done. Now for a book with my legs up on the sofa. But which one? Maybe *The Forsyte Saga* at last? Dima gave it to me on the birthday before last. But I won't be able to get through it, how can I carry a book that size around with me? I'll leave it for the holidays. I choose something lighter – Sergei Antonov's stories.

A peaceful Sunday evening. We sit and read. After about twenty minutes Dima says: 'What about my trousers?'

We decide that I'll iron his trousers and he'll read aloud to me. But Dima doesn't like Antonov and picks up the latest issue of *Science* which we haven't looked at yet. He begins to read Ventsel's article on operational research, but it's difficult for me to follow the formulae by ear, so Dima goes into the kitchen and I'm left alone with his trousers.

I'm already in bed and Dima is winding up the alarm clock and turning out the light when I remember – the hook! I still haven't sewn it on. Damn it! But I'm not getting out of bed now!

I wake up inexplicably in the middle of the night. I feel uneasy. I get up quietly so as not to wake up Dima and look in at the children. They too look uneasy in their sleep: Kotka has flung off his blanket; Gulka has slid right down from her pillow and her legs are sticking out of the bed. I straighten them out and cover their heads. I feel their foreheads – have they a temperature? The children sigh softly, making munching sounds with their lips and swallowing succulently. They fall fast asleep again, peaceful and secure.

What is the matter with me?

I don't know. I lie on my back, my eyes wide open. I lie and listen to the silence. The central heating system gurgles. The wall-clock in the flat above ticks. The pendulum above beats out the time evenly and the alarm clock, simultaneously, grindingly, chokingly, bursts into life.

And so another week, the week before the last one of the year, is over.

The
Purse

The paper was of excellent quality. The ballpoint pen new. The silence in the flat complete. And I had a story. Through the window I could see the distant green of Timirazevsky Park. I pulled out the telephone plug to guarantee complete peace and sat down to write. The story was working. It began in the park with a half-hidden gate behind an old house: the house had turrets and a clock-tower with a bell.

I wrote. Suddenly I heard a knock. Or rather an avalanche of knocks. Somebody was beating out a dancing march on my door with their knuckles. I opened the door: there was a familiar figure, gangling, broad-shouldered, with hair like the bristles on a nail brush.

'Good God! Igor!' I said and immediately thought: 'There goes my day and my story.'

Igor and I had been in the same class at school. An old friend. We thought much but saw little of each other.

'Ludka, why are you locked up like the princess in the tower? Inaccessible by phone, deaf to knocks on the door. Outside the sun is shining; there is a gentle breeze, and she is incarcerated ten floors up. This is no time to work.'

'I've just started a story.'

'What about?'

'About . . . about . . . I don't know what it's about yet, I've just started. It's about a woman who's lonely, with sad eyes.'

'Good God! Sad eyes! Ludka, you forget about those eyes. Look out of the window.' He put his arm around my shoulder and led me to the window. As if I needed him to show me what was out there.

'Look: the sun, a breeze, summer! Can't you think of anything happier?'

'Look, you cheeky so-and-so, stories don't grow on trees, you can't just pluck off the one you want.'

'You're right, everything's already covered in the classics.'

I could see that I wasn't going to get any work done and began gathering up the pages covered in writing.

'You may say that stories don't grow on trees, but I've just found one for you, about a purse.'

'You've found a purse?'

'No. I'm giving you a story. A happier one. Someone like me, say, finds a purse . . .'

'With thirty kopeks in . . .'

'Why be so mean? Let's say it's got a hundred roubles in.'

'Nobody walks around with a hundred roubles in their purse.'

'Ah-ha – the dead hand of naturalism strikes again. All right. Is it OK to carry ten roubles in your purse? So, we have a purse with a tenner in it.'

'And you call this a happy story? Well, firstly, it hardly constitutes a story, and secondly, this purse was probably lost by a woman hurrying into a shop on her way home from work, rushing to pick up her daughter from the kindergarten. She flings her purse into her string bag which, unfortunately, has a hole in it. When she gets home she will notice that it's missing. She'll keep on looking for it and get upset. That's a happy story?'

'Why invent a woman, let alone one with a small child. The purse was lost by some young hooligan. He'd managed to drag himself home with a terrible hangover only by keeping his eyes glued to the pavement to make sure that his feet didn't part company with it. He felt in his pocket for a handkerchief and—'

'He wouldn't have had any money left in his purse. What he did have was the key to his flat. So he can't get in. He has to wait outside for his mother to come home from work. He falls asleep on a bench. His mother, poor woman, gets very upset and gives him a terrible telling off.'

'Serves him right. No point in feeling sorry for him. It'll do him good, he'll give up drinking. "To hell with drink," he'll say, "I think I'll spend the time reading instead." So, you see, our story acquires a happy ending.'

'He gives up drinking? Just like that? You think that's possible?'

Igor and I have quarrelled all our lives. It began at school. We became friends and started quarrelling. He developed an unrequited love for me. When he married I realised that I loved him, but by then he had fallen out of love with me. Then I married. The years passed. His life worked out well – mine didn't. I'm separated from my husband. I have a little boy. We live with my mother. Igor and I no longer talk of love, but . . .

'I give up,' Igor said, 'Anyway, this purse is getting boring. You'll have to work it out for yourself. Ludochka, my dear, I have come to carry you off. Do come for a walk with me. It's my day off; I've just finished some work, I want to relax, and I've been missing you.'

Well, if he was going to put it like that I'd give up. I combed my hair, put on my outdoor shoes and picked up my handbag. Igor watched me. He said: 'Why are you so thin? Don't you eat properly?'

The park wasn't far. As we walked we talked: about life, work and our temporarily absent children. Igor's eldest was on holiday in a pioneer camp, his youngest was with his wife in the Crimea. My son was at our dacha. We stopped by an

65

ice-cream kiosk. Igor wanted to buy me three chocolate ice-cream cornets. I objected. The ice-cream lady laughed. Igor bought three ice-creams anyway. He said we could eat them between us.

We licked our ice-creams and walked and talked in the young park. A pond sparkled in front of us, circled by a wall of trees. The leaves were as fresh as they are in spring. The breeze softly rippled a pattern on the water. Orange and sky-blue boats smoothed the surface of the pond.

'Look, boats,' said Igor happily. 'Let's get one. The queue's quite small, and it's a magnificent day for a sail with the sun and the breeze.'

'And it's summer!' I prompted.

We stood in the queue. It was small but it moved slowly. We could smell the algae, the silt and the wet sand in the water. Three white gulls, wheeling up and down, circled the pond. They must have come from the lake. They often flew here. Why only three?

'Come on, we'll have to get a boat some other time.' Igor suddenly broke into my thoughts. He grabbed my arm and pulled me out of the queue.

I didn't know what was the matter. Why was he looking so annoyed?

'I've lost my bloody wallet. It must have been by the ice-cream kiosk.'

I suggested retracing our steps. Maybe the ice-cream lady had it. Igor just shrugged his shoulders. Then I opened my handbag: 'I've got some money. Let's go on the boat. It's our turn next.'

'Go on the boat!' said Igor furiously, 'Go on the boat! Look, I couldn't care less about the ten roubles, it's my keys I'm worried about. I had to put them in the wallet, of course! I'm such fool. And we've got two safety locks. Damn! Damn! We'll have to break everything. And the locksmith is always drunk. It'll be a real job even finding him. And I've got no money!'

I gave Igor all the money I had on me – twelve roubles. I poured small change into his cupped hands and went with him to the bus stop.

Igor was silent and scowling as we waited for the bus. His presence now depressed me. 'What a good thing I didn't marry him,' I thought.

I suddenly felt an irrepressible and irresponsible urge to laugh. Luckily just then a bus came.

'Bye then,' I said, 'give us a ring sometime.'

'Goodbye,' said Igor, pumping my hand in a business-like way.

'It's a nice, happy story,' I shouted after him as he stood on the inside step of the bus. And I waved my hand. And then I couldn't help it, I began laughing. Igor watched me through the glass. He said something which I couldn't hear. Then he wrote on the glass with his finger: 'A little topic', and laughed as well. I watched the bus go and thought what a nice laugh he had.

'Maybe I should have married him after all,' I thought as I went home.

By and by I stopped thinking about Igor. The lonely woman with sad eyes rematerialised. She went through the gate into the park. She had a book in her hand and wandered along the avenues looking for an empty bench. I knew what was going to happen to her, and I couldn't alter it. And what about my life?

I answered myself: 'A writing table, paper of excellent quality and a pen. Forward march!'

The
Petunin Affair

The lads in the editorial office always called it simply 'that Petunin business' or 'that silly affair', while older colleagues, and those nearer to the Head, called it the 'Petunin Story'. But the interesting thing is that there was no Petunin story at all and there was absolutely no reason to call this affair by my name. I was not the central character in this story – someone else's name would be much more appropriate.

Incidentally, at the moment I do consider myself to be rather important: I want to understand what kind of a person I am. And I have plenty of time to think about it: I have been sent on a work assignment of several months duration to a remote town. It is autumn now, soon we'll be in the depths of winter.

So, I decided to write this story. I cannot bear these evenings in an empty hotel, and the bright light in my white room that looks like a hospital ward. One could go crazy in these white, empty evenings. At least writing occupies me. Also, it seems to me that if I recall everything in order I will see the events unfold as if on a screen and in the running of this film the kind of person that I am will become clearer to me.

I remember how the Old Man himself had called me a 'positive hero' when he gave me the job two years ago. He said it with a sly grimace, having read my short curriculum vitae. There were only a few lines: born 1941; left school with high marks; served in the army – got some medals; Young Communist League member in charge of local literacy; external student in the faculty of journalism at the university; passed my finals.

I was called a 'positive hero' again quite recently – by Nina. Her soft voice sounded quite spiteful. I had brought in some new 9 × 12 photographs for her, carrying out the new boss's orders to have all staff photographed in the same way. I had never aimed at being any sort of a hero, and I was really the most ordinary sort of person in our office. She annoyed me. If externally I resemble the image of a 'positive hero': blue eyes; ginger hair; white teeth; broad shoulders; strong arms; height – 6ft; weight – 13 stone, and even a dimple in my chin – well, it's *really* not my fault.

So, this opus will be called '*The Positive Hero*' in quotation marks.

THE OLD MAN

I had been working freelance on the local paper for three years before I was taken on to the permanent staff as an editorial assistant on the Letters' Page. When I started the third year of my correspondence course I was temporarily transferred to the Department of Culture and Everyday Life, DCEL for short. It wasn't bad going for someone of my age.

While the Old Man was there my work went well. Everything in the office worked smoothly. I liked my work, all of it. I started a new story with pleasure and finished it with pleasure, glad to relax when it was done.

The Old Man would praise me (unusual for him). He would say in a fatherly way: 'That young Petunin is a great lad'. Almost since my first day at the office I had been called 'that young Petunin'. My colleagues seemed not to take to Anatoly – my given name. I didn't mind being called 'young Petunin' – it was affectionate and not offensive.

The events which led to my being here started with the retirement of the Old Man – our boss. He probably would have gone on working – after all, sixty-five isn't old nowadays. We only called him 'Old Man' out of respect. He was well liked. He wasn't autocratic, didn't poke around into every nook and cranny, didn't nit-pick, and didn't make us shoulder the responsibility for his mistakes. On the other hand, if somebody did make a serious mistake, he didn't mince his words either. There was that case, for example, when Fedka Fedorovich, typesetting an article on a leading poultry farm in a village called 'Swanage' included a bit at the bottom from a review of a touring company's production of *Swan Lake*.

But the Old Man hadn't been well since the previous spring. He began having fits of depression and complaining about his heart. People started speculating. Sometimes he wasn't at work for two or three days. Some people said there were upsets in the family, others that the Old Man had fallen out with the local Party who thought we were behind the times. They said the paper was not active enough in leading the fight against old, pre-revolutionary habits and, in particular, against alcoholism.

Finally it was rumoured that they were removing the Old Man, offering him another post, but that he had decided to take early retirement.

And at the beginning of summer they began to talk about the new boss. It was learnt that he was a young Muscovite, who had once worked on a factory newspaper with an enormous circulation. Different rumours flew around: that he had been the Director of a large Palace of Culture; that he had worked in the civil service in a senior, practically consultative post; that he had established trading links with an African state. It was even rumoured that he had traded fur on the international market.

We couldn't work out what was true and what was invented. But we were surprised that he had been sent from Moscow to a provincial town of no significance.

There was nobody to explain this to us. Although

71

everybody knew *something* there were none amongst us who had the full range of information. However, the more talk there was about the new boss, the more details emerged. He was a high-flyer, very modern, very energetic, would make us jump to it; he was handsome, so watch out girls! Facts were revealed that could only have been known by his wife, although it was also discovered that he was a bachelor. There was plenty of talk, plenty of gossip. And the more gossip there was, the more impressive one imagined the appearance of this new head would be, with lights, drums and chariots . . . But it was nothing like this. It all happened very differently.

One July morning a young, insignificant chap in a dark suit attended an editorial staff meeting with the Old Man. He stood up. The Old Man introduced him.

'Allow me to present the new Editor-in-Chief of the paper, Comrade Anatoly Yurevitch Petrayev.' At this point lots of the lads looked at me. Well, what was so funny about it? Anatoly Petrayev and Anatoly Petunin – what was the big deal? Incidentally, my patronymic, as it happens, is Petrovich. Later the lads said that they'd looked at us because we were alike. Perhaps. It's not for me to judge. I had a good look at him as well, of course. He was about my height, but a little more solid. He was also fair, but had less hair than me, in fact he was very slightly balding. He had blue eyes as well, but they had a kind of intensity. No one could have called his nose classical, but it was straighter than mine. I suppose you could have called Petrayev handsome; personally, I didn't like the look of him. He seemed somehow strained and wooden. But once he started to talk this impression disappeared. He spoke simply and with restraint; he hoped that we would have a happy working relationship; he was pleased to see so many young people among the editorial staff – that was very good; he liked volleyball. His final comments moved many people deeply: he would like to maintain the high standards that had been attained under the 'many years of Ivan Vasilevitch

72

Makhov's wise leadership'. Personally, I thought he sounded false, and I noticed that the Old Man didn't like it. He was frowning.

This was our first meeting with Petrayev. For the following week he came into the office promptly, at the beginning of the working day, went straight into the Old Man, and sat in his office for a few hours. Well, it could hardly be called his office any more – the Old Man was handing over his affairs. Then Petrayev visited other departments. He would come into a room and stand over somebody and watch them, or he would walk up and down the room, as if measuring it in feet: he would cast frowning glances at the walls and ceilings, knitting his brows. Then he would leave. We had no idea what he was thinking about. He didn't *seem* to be very pleased. Talk started: perhaps he'd been sent here from Moscow as a punishment for some misdemeanour.

The Old Man said goodbye to us all at a full editorial staff meeting, and then went round the departments shaking our hands, with a word for everybody. I remember clearly what he said to me:

'Think, Petunin, you must think more!' I didn't understand him at the time but I was sure that he hadn't said it lightly. Anyone else would have said: 'I wish you success in your studies or as a journalist.'

The Old Man was really something! I don't know why I say 'was' – he's still alive.

The next day Petrayev held the editorial meeting. Everybody noticed that he had changed a great deal in one day. He was as clean and smooth as if he had just come out of a barber's shop. He was wearing a new light-grey suit of a rather fashionable cut. He looked satisfied and well-fed, as if he'd just eaten something very tasty. Most interesting of all, he seemed taller.

'It's time to start work,' he said significantly.

Everybody knew, of course, that he wasn't talking about

the editorial meeting here today, but about work in general. As if there were a dividing line: up till now we hadn't worked and now we were going to start.

'Our first task,' continued Petrayev, 'will be to rebuild our newspaper, to move it on to different lines. And we must do it in such a way that far from lessening our productivity we will increase it, increase the speed and power of the collective . . .'

He talked for ages. He went well over the time allocated for these meetings. Old Mrs Sash, who runs our errands for us, couldn't believe her eyes and kept peering into the office: when would the copy for typesetting be ready? But Petrayev went on and on. He sketched for us a distant future with 'electronic computerised and self-correcting machines'. He underlined the importance of a 'sociological study of many questions' in particular that which must be tackled first (and here he glanced at me), 'the question of the widespread partiality of our people to alcohol'.

Then he announced that he must start with many 'organisational details, no less important than ideological matters and just as decisive in determining the direction of our work and the image of our paper.' I have put this in quotation marks as I noted it down in full to practise my shorthand.

The meeting had been going on for over two hours now, the situation was becoming critical. By now we should have sent at least half the current copy to be typeset, should have worked out who was going to do the typing, the corrections and who would look through the latest post. But we were hypnotised by this speech. We were deflected and entertained by the pictures, each one more interesting and beautiful than its predecessor, of the future of our newspaper. We liked listening to him; faces glowed with girlish enthusiasm.

But all this poetry and romance was interrupted by the head of the agricultural correspondents, Shilov. He stood up and grunted in his hoarse, deep voice: 'I have a lot of copy to write and we are late with the paper.' He moved to the door, his artificial leg scraping the floor.

Petrayev was silent until he got to the door, only then did he say:

'I will not detain you then.'

And he continued with his speech, as if nobody, except for Shilov, had any copy to write for the following day's newspaper. We didn't know what to do; we exchanged glances – what *should* we do? But nobody had the courage to say that it was time we got back to work.

Our unease finally communicated itself to the Chief (I would like to say that since his very first day the name 'Chief' stuck firmly to Petrayev). He began to round off his sentences and after about ten minutes announced that the 'editorial meeting' was closed. It had lasted not the usual twenty minutes, but over two hours.

Everybody jumped up and rushed towards the door.

The Chief said loudly: 'Would Comrade Petunin please stay behind?'

THE TASK

He was standing behind a table with a mountain of files. 'Sit down, Anatoly Petrovitch,' he made a flowing gesture with his arm. It was only then that I noticed two armchairs placed on one side of the table. They had not been there before. He sat down as well.

'You are taking a correspondence course: what year are you in?'

I told him.

'You live alone with your mother; your father died during the war?'

I nodded. What was there to say? He already knew

75

everything. He must have looked at my personal file, it was there along with all the others. I was also late with my copy. I began to fidget in the armchair.

'I see you are in a hurry,' the Chief said, 'please, don't let me detain you. I would like to have a serious talk with you, but we can postpone it till tomorrow. Pop in after you've finished your copy.'

His voice had the self-assurance of a boss who has no reason to ask a subordinate whether a particular time is suitable or not.

The next day began in an unusual way. It was as if there had been a hurricane in the night. In some rooms tables were piled high: some had their drawers to the wall, some had no drawers, and others had drawers which didn't belong to them. We had difficulty in even discovering who had lost their galley proofs and who had lost their plimsolls. Everybody was swearing and in a foul mood. In other rooms there were no desks at all and here they were already beginning to whitewash the ceilings. Two young men with a notebook and tapemeasure were proceeding along the corridor. The editorial meeting started late. Petrayev opened it thus:

'You will have to be patient. All re-building demands extra resources including the re-siting of tables . . .' And he smiled at his witticism. I realised that this was the first time I had seen him smile in all the time he had been here. His smile made him look extremely unpleasant. It stretched mechanically, like elastic, while his eyes remained cold. Petrayev spoke of the maintenance work as 'an overdue necessity to move from prehistoric times to the middle of the twentieth century'. It was a month before we appreciated the full meaning of these words.

Our serious conversation took place at the end of the working day. On that crazy day the paper had been put to bed very late. We had had no time for proper lunch; we ate ice-cream and bread.

Petrayev said that independence and initiative were very important for a young journalist starting out on his career and, backed by energy and enthusiasm, could bear 'tremendous fruit'. An energetic young worker could cover in two to three years what might take others ten (he was undoubtedly referring to himself). I waited for him to get to the point. But he began to talk about the dangers of alcoholism for the growth of the national economy and consequently for the basic political tasks facing society. It was funny: nobody had ever spoken to me about my work in the style of a newspaper editorial. In the Old Man's time any high-flown rhetoric in the office was known as 'cock-a-doodle-doodling'.

Petrayev crowed some more on the dangers of alcoholic drinks and then, suddenly, in a matter of fact voice, asked: 'Do you drink?'

'Er, no, not very often . . . Well, I don't really drink at all. Do you?'

'Only dry wine,' he answered meaningfully.

And having clarified, as it were, whether or not he could trust me, he got down to business at last.

'I want you to draw up a plan for a series of articles in our paper on the fight against alcoholism. I don't want the standard, trite kind of articles: I want you to think up something fresh and original that will attract widespread attention, that will move people deeply. For example – why aren't you taking any of this down?' he asked, astonished.

I was even more astonished. It was perfectly clear; I had been asked to draw up a plan for a series of articles. I understood this and I could remember it. What did he want me to take down? He said he believed that some of his thoughts might be useful to me. I thanked him and said:

'I'd like to have a go with my own ideas first.'

'Oh well,' he said, offended, 'let's try it that way, then. I'll give you a day to think something up.'

I was already at the door when he stopped me.

'Have you applied to join the Party yet?'

'No.'

'When are you thinking of applying?'

His voice was ominously businesslike. And why begin such a conversation at the door jamb? 'I'll have to give it a bit more thought,' I answered earnestly.

This was roughly the truth. Even if somebody else had asked me – the Old Man, or our Party organiser, Shilov, or Fedka, one of our crowd, not someone new and unknown to me like the new Head – I would have answered the same, though perhaps in a little more detail, perhaps adding 'I need more time to think about it: one should think carefully before taking such an important step.'

It's a strange thing: I can always find time for work, for study and for food. I can even stretch to volleyball, skiing and the cinema. But there is never any time left for thinking at all.

'Well, well, I won't keep you any longer,' said Petrayev coldly.

He didn't seem to like me. As a matter of fact, I didn't like him either. For the time being we left it there: not for one day, as he'd said, but for ten. That night I developed a sore throat. My temperature soared to forty degrees. I'd been undone by eating ice-cream instead of a proper lunch. It took me ten days to recover. I went back to the office. But where was the plan for the fight against alcoholism? It didn't exist. What's worse, no ideas existed either. While I'd been sick with a high temperature my head had been splitting. When my temperature dropped my arms and legs wouldn't work and I was consumed by tiredness. Well, I had thought a little, but not about the fight against drunkenness. I had thought about the drunkards and lady drunkards – 'the concrete bearers of evil'. I recalled those whom I had known personally.

Our neighbour, Old Vasya, was a lorry driver, and a terrible liar when he wasn't simply talking rubbish, although he was nearly fifty. He was an orderly drinker – he always drank on Saturdays. He would come home late. His wife and daughter would hide from him. He would start to twirl the knobs on the television and roar: 'I can't see anything, fools, scoundrels . . .' etc . . . Then he would fall off his chair with a thud and go to sleep on the floor.

The disabled shoemaker Onufriyev was another one – he lost his leg in the war. He was a hard drinker and would go on a bout every four to six weeks.

The third one was young, a tool-maker, Zhorka. He got married not long ago. He has a small daughter and a wonderful wife, Zina. He works on machine tools as well. He gets drunk on pay days. He comes home late and starts to shout.

Alcoholics – 'winos' – are despicable people. Why, then, do we feel sorry for them? I've tried to work it out: why do they drink, what for? But I can't.

That was the full extent of my 'thoughts on the plan', and with this I went back to work – in other words, with nothing.

'DO YOU WANT A CHAT OR DO YOU WANT A PLAN?'

News awaited me. Innovations.

I approached the old building with its turrets, the same oak door, the same black and gold sign. To the right, the newspaper *Lopatinskaya Pravda,*[*] to the left, the Department for Cultural Affairs. Each has its floor in the building that was formerly a provincial high school. Through the door I saw the same wrought-iron staircase with its ornate patterns. I ran up to the second floor and froze in stupefied amazement. Instead

*Invented name of the newspaper on which Petunin works. Every small/big town will have its own *Pravda*.

of our old upholstered door with a bronze sign was a thick glass window along the whole wall, fixed below with metal. And, wonder of wonders, through it I saw not the long corridor with the plush red-green strip of carpet, but a large, light room. There were low blue, yellow and green chairs and three-cornered tables standing on a floor chequered like a chess board, as if they were pieces in an unfinished game. Between them stood large containers of many different shapes with sand, cacti and pebbles in sea blues and greens.

I really was stunned. It was like looking into a giant aquarium, but I couldn't work out where this underwater kingdom had come from. It twinkled with a greenish light which, I suppose, was natural enough. And then a golden fish swam into the aquarium – old Mrs Sash, with her habitual worried and preoccupied look, carrying a heap of galley proofs. The ends of her faded red plaits swayed gently on her neck like little swimmers.

Suddenly a small figure emerged from the end of the truncated corridor, which now resembled a shallow pool flowing out of a lake. It came towards me at a run. It was only when the figure plunged into the aquarium that I recognised Petrayev. When he saw me behind the glass he stopped, and we both stood for two or three seconds without saying anything, studying each other. He didn't seem to recognise me. I should have greeted him, but the glass that made everything so clearly visible also made everything inaudible, and, for some reason, inhibited me. It was as if I was seeing Petrayev for the first time: the glass revealed him to me. I examined him thoroughly, as I would something in a shop window. I had never noticed before that he was in perpetual motion: even standing in one place he shuffled his shoulders and elbows just a little, bounced his knees – in, out – and nodded his head. All this was almost imperceptible, like the vibrations from a running engine.

The pause was long drawn out. In the end I broke it by

stepping towards the glass. It was only then that I realised that I didn't know how to penetrate through to the editorial office. The wall's surface was smooth. There was no handle in sight. I became confused. Petrayev smiled condescendingly and pushed the glass. The pane turned perpendicularly, the entrance was revealed, and we both said:

'Morning!'

'We haven't had time to put the . . . ahem . . . handles and the . . . ahem . . . sign on yet,' he said. He was pleased by my confusion.

'It's incredible,' I said, 'everything is unrecognisable. Where did this room come from?'

'They just took down the wall of the proof-readers' room.'

I wonder where the proof-readers sit now, I thought.

Petrayev asked after my health and then disappeared behind the door of his office. This door had also changed: formerly it had been covered in oil cloth, now it was a board of light-coloured wood with a sign in raised black letters which read:

'Editor-in-Chief: A.Y. PETRAYEV'.

In our room I found some low armchairs with sloping backs, new tables with open shelves instead of drawers and, on the tables, black lamps with swan-like necks.

Fedka Fedorov wasn't at his table. I had no one to ask about all these wonders.

I was still marvelling when the telephone went. Nina's clear voice asked after my health and then informed me in a business-like way that the chief requested my presence in his office with my plan in an hour's time.

Nina . . . I haven't said anything about her yet, although she's very important. She is secretary to the Head. She held this post on a temporary basis when the Old Man was here. Our secretary had a car accident and was put out of action for a long time. Nina hadn't really wanted this job, but eventually she was persuaded.

She's a proud and beautiful woman. One usually says,

'beautiful, but proud', but I feel like saying, 'proud and beautiful'. This combination causes me a lot of suffering – in secret. I can't discuss her with anybody else. Perhaps it is not yet love, but it's certainly more than the mere sporting interest that a pretty girl often arouses in a man. Everybody who's tried to get near her has been given the bird. Of course, they shrug it off, pretend they don't mind – and then wait to see who'll be next. In her first year here a gambling fever gripped our office. But it died down, we got used to her. She's quite friendly, just a bit secretive. The girls from the typing pool and the print room thought at first that she really fancied herself. But that isn't true. Nina is graceful, quick and slender and she has no affectations of any kind. Everything in her is natural and endearing. But she is stern. Maybe she is a little too stern.

Her beauty is simple. Light brown eyes, furry eye-lashes, soft eyebrows that look like mink. Her complexion is a dark rose, her mouth is large. She rarely smiles, but when she does two dimples appear in her cheeks and make her look like a little girl. But the loveliest thing about her is the way she moves. It's impossible to explain, you have to see it. Whenever she is doing anything I watch and admire her. Her hands are small, slender and quick. Even the way she opens an envelope is indescribably lovely. Until that office excursion and that business with Valya, the typesetter, everybody thought that Nina was cold. But then they realised they were wrong. Valya's true saviour was not the two who dragged her out, but Nina. From the moment they carried Valya onto the shore until the day she got married, Nina spent all her free time with her. And now? Valya is a happy wife and mother.

Nina has no real friends amongst the girls here, let alone the lads. Probably because she's shielded herself with a cold, supercilious cover. I think there must be some reason for this, she's been hurt, it's connected with her principles, there's something behind it.

I should have spoken about Nina before. She is relevant not only to my story but to me, personally. I feel like thinking about her now. I started to describe her and became involved in my memories of her. How have I described her? As dry and cold. Should I have written that? There is something very good and very real in her, not immediately apparent. But what's the point of saying all this here? I realise now that I love her.

We should return to the office, to the empty room with new tables and swan-lamps.

The chief expected me in an hour's time. I sat at the table with a sheet of paper in front of me. There was only one word written on it: 'Plan'.

I still had no ideas. It seemed perfectly feasible to create a plan for the newspaper's fight against alcoholism until I actually had to work with those words: 'alcoholism' or 'alcoholics'. Then I began to think of Old Vasya, Onufriyev, the cobbler, Zhorka and others and somehow got lost: what should I do with them? So I sat at the table and thought. I thought most of all about how I was no good at thinking. I took a sheet of paper, I took a pen and I said to myself: think! A clock ticked away, it distracted me. Of the hour that had been given to me, fifteen minutes had already gone. All that occurred to me were questions. In the remaining forty-five minutes I composed a questionnaire:

1. Should the sale of strong drink be forbidden?
2. Should sales be limited?
3. What should be done with the unsold stock from the distilleries?
4. Does vodka create more profit or loss?

And this was where I stopped. Each one of these questions gave birth to new ones. The questions multiplied. It turned out that thinking was interesting. It would have been nice to discuss it with someone clever, like the Old Man.

I glanced at the clock. I was three minutes over the limit. I seized my sheet of paper and went to see the chief.

On entering the door marked 'Chief' you immediately found yourself in Nina's room. She was sitting at her desk. She gave me a nod and seemed – or did I imagine it? – to look a little anxiously at me. It was a searching gaze from under her thick eyelashes. Then she lowered them. She was writing, probably answering the letters that lay before her in a tidy pile. She had changed in some way. But how?

'Well, is it ready?' asked Petrayev, hardly giving me time to close the door of the office behind me. He was writing in a thick, elegant notebook and he didn't even glance up at me. 'Sit down. Go ahead.'

So, his hour of triumph has come, I thought. Why 'triumph' I don't know, but I felt that this was how he would see my defeat.

'I haven't got anything, it's not ready yet,' I mumbled. 'I've been ill.'

'Well, give us the draft, then.'

'I haven't got one.'

Petrayev lifted his eyes and looked at me attentively, even with curiosity: 'So, you are not as independent as you thought,' he grinned, 'Perhaps I could ask you to note down *my* plan?'

It was really true. He was pleased at my failure.

Well, I deserved it. I fished my notebook out of my pocket and got ready to write.

He stood up and paced up and down. It was then I noticed his new office. Replacing the old, darkened, writing-table was a new one with a thick top of light wood. The long, narrow 'conference table' with its velvet tablecloth and the leather divan by the wall had disappeared. Little tables and shallow, light armchairs had taken their place. There were little ceramic ashtrays on the tables and a big narrow jug, like a stork, together with two smoky-lilac coloured glasses, on one of them. The old rust-coloured curtains had been replaced by a

84

blue, lightweight material. I liked it, it was clean, bright and pretty.

Petrayev stood for a full half-minute by the window and then said:

'So, write: "The *Lopatinskaya Pravda* Newspaper's Plan for the Fight Against Alcoholism, August, 1965.

' "First: organise letters of protest from children about the behaviour of their drunken fathers: (a) a letter from 10–11-year-old schoolchildren, confirming the fact that their alcoholic fathers are causing them to fall behind in their studies: (b) a letter from the kindergarten children at the machine-tool factory about the bad atmosphere at home –" '

To my surprise I found myself saying: 'And (c) a letter from the babies in the crèche of the sewing factory . . .'

'Not a bad idea,' agreed Petrayev, 'but three letters is probably a bit much.'

There was not so much as a flicker of an eyelid. Didn't he understand, didn't he wish to understand my sarcasm?

' "Second:" ' the chief continued with his dictation, ' "organise a vanguard movement of workers under the slogan: 'Drink But Know Your Limit'." '

'Why should we say "Drink" when we want them not to drink?' I said quickly.

'Do you want a chat or do you want a plan?' asked Petrayev cuttingly, and his eyes were as hard and sharp as nails. 'Well, understand this, I am not disposed to chat with colleagues who have no ideas of their own and who, in a ten-day period, are unable to complete a task for which one day should have been sufficient.'

I flushed but said nothing. It was true, I had no ideas and I had not completed my task.

'So, write,' he continued calmly. ' "Third: prepare an interview, to take place in the editorial office, between those individuals who drink systematically and doctors and teachers.

Work out a conversation plan. A certain quota of individuals should be attracted. The broadcasting and televising of this event should be organised through local radio and television stations." '

'The successful completion of this plan rests with the Department for Culture and Everyday Life – with you, Comrade Petunin. Is that clear? Have you any questions?'

I sat silent and confused. Petrayev's Plan seemed to me like the ravings of a madman. I had no questions.

As I was leaving the office Nina again looked anxiously at me – or did I just imagine it? Something had changed in her appearance – but what?

It was only when I got to my desk that I realised: her luxuriant chestnut hair, usually rolled in a loose bun at the nape of her neck, was now raised up high on her head, and hair by hair, formed into a neat, shimmering helmet.

Once again I sat hunched over a piece of paper, but this time it was covered with writing. I gazed at it listlessly: Petrayev's Plan – shameless self-promotion. But I was the one who had to do it.

Fedka Fedorov flew in through the door.

'Aha – you've come back!' he yelled, 'At last! We lost the last game of volleyball to the executive committee because you weren't here . . . Well, what do you think about all this?' He glanced around the room. 'Are you impressed? Between you and me our chief has a superfluity of energy, enough for two power stations!'

Without a word I moved the paper in his direction.

'What's this?'

'Read it.'

He read it, and made a surprised sound, probably at the kindergarten letter. Then, 'But it's wonderful! An interview with drunks.' I never knew when Fedorov was joking and when he was being serious.

'This sort of thing has never been done before.'

86

'Mmmm, well if it hasn't . . .'

I said to him that this extravagant plan made me feel sick. Fedka tittered: 'I'd like to see you round up all these winos.'

I reassured him: we would be rounding them up together. After all, he was my colleague.

Then I stood up, pulling the piece of paper out of Fedka's hand: 'I'm going to see Shilov.'

Our Party Organisational Secretary has a good head on his shoulders. I wasn't going to him to complain but to confer.

'He's not here. He's touring the area. The elections have started – while you were ill. Well – why the long face?' thundered Fedka, 'You're not the only one who'll be involved in this and it won't be your responsibility. We're little people, we do what we're told.'

'That's a good idea, you go and be a little person, I don't feel like it.'

'Listen, we've got to talk,' said Fedka, abandoning the serious stuff, 'there's a game going on with big stakes. Petrayev has started to chase Nina Boiko. Will he be successful or not? A man like him should succeed. After all, look at what he's accomplished here in two weeks – turned everything upside down – what energy!'

This was the last straw. I was stunned by this blow, but didn't want Fedka to see. 'You mean he changed all the furniture around out of love for her?' I asked, just to say something.

So that was the reason for her new hair-style. Probably Petrayev liked that kind of hair-do. And Nina, with Petrayevan hair, seemed lost to me for ever.

'Hey, let's go out to the court and have a game!' I shouted, giving Fedka a nudge with my fist. I rushed out and along the corridor. On the way I popped into the typing pool.

'Good morning girls!' I thundered, although there was only one 'girl' there, Rita; the other two typists were near to forty.

'Young Petunin, you've come back! How are you? How do you like our new quarters?' Rita began.

But I didn't answer, I was already sliding down the banisters to the yard, to the volleyball court. I had to do something physical.

I thumped the ball furiously, as if it wasn't a ball but him, our new chief, that handsome lady-killer, Petrayev.

PERESTROIKA

'Well, you must admit, he's good looking . . .' It was a phrase that was now frequently heard. We noticed that the women began to pay special attention to their appearance. One darkened her brows, another put on long eyelashes, another put mascara on, and a fourth dyed her hair red. New stockings, shoes, dresses and bags appeared. But the most incredible transformation was that of our librarian, Angelina Adamovna. She'd never before emerged from her outsize black satin overalls. Now she suddenly appeared in a completely transparent nylon blouse, through which vague shapes of light-blue, violet and pink were visible.

Did the object of all this attention notice anything? I don't think he did. He was absorbed in his work. Having changed the appearance of the newspaper offices with staggering rapidity he started on the face of the paper itself: he ordered new two-tone blocks for the newspaper's title and for the permanent headings. Typographical workers were constantly scurrying to and from his office on urgent summonses: the zincography shop superintendent, the print shop, or the whole of the typesetting department.

Nina was constantly juggling two telephones: connecting him to the Head of the Regional Committee; the Head of the District; to a chemical laboratory where they were doing an analysis of a new kind of ink, and to a transport agency – there was something, new typefaces or a new machine, expected from Moscow.

Maybe Petrayev's feelings for Nina were more than comradely, but if so they seemed to dissolve in all this furious activity. I never noticed anything, but then I didn't want to.

The day of the 'Round Table Interview' drew nearer. Our paper's plan for fighting drunkenness was examined at an editorial meeting (and was immediately dubbed 'Operation P' – a reference to Petrayev's and my surnames – by our office wits). Invited representatives from the District Health and Education Authorities were also there to consider the plan.

They praised us. I listened to the speakers – I was wrong, my attitude towards Petrayev's plan was in error. At that editorial meeting my opinions were changed to such an extent that I was impatient to begin.

A day was appointed: Thursday, 26 August – 6 p.m. To do it by then would demand energy and speed.

The following day I got down to work with the necessary enthusiasm. I toured many different organisations, including trade union committees, announcing the sort of material we needed. I made a list of the drunks who interfered with the fulfilment of the five-year plan, who were destroying their family life and having a bad influence on their children. I visited some of their homes and looked at how they lived and what they ate. I collected hundreds of living impressions. I began to see the form the programme would take and the scenario of the interview.

I began to enjoy it. It was something new. Not exactly a sketch, more a television film. Anyway, it was certainly new. I wanted it to be successful and worked all out on it. Now I was being helped not only by my own department (Fedka) but also by some Young Komsomols allocated to me by the paper. One of them was Nina Boiko. How she had managed to extricate herself from the Chief's telephone conversations I do not know.

The most difficult thing was to get enough people. It was easy to make arrangements with non-drunkards. An

89

'Honoured Teacher of the Russian Republic' agreed to appear, as did the director of our drama theatre, the directors of two factories, a psychiatrist, a pediatrician and a major from the police department. All of them were meant to paint a moving picture on the theme: 'Alcohol is the Ruin of Man'.

As far as the drunks were concerned, it was presumed that the most conscientious, and conscious, amongst them would repent and say a few words in reply. Or perhaps they would simply give a solemn promise to give up drinking. I managed to get five of them to agree to this (with a few in reserve). Old Vasya was one of them; when he learnt that he was going to appear on television he glowed happily, but I must admit that I was a bit doubtful: could one really trust Old Vasya? But his wife went on and on at me, 'Let the old devil give his word in front of the whole district – maybe that will make him him stop drinking.' We also made sure that those being 're-educated' would appear in a proper state: sober and with a tie on.

At last I got through all the material, a scenario had been written, copies of which were made at lightning speed. I was ready. I went with it to Petrayev.

SOBERING UP

My hour of triumph had arrived. I'd done my work well. I'd also had some thoughts of my own: I'd decided to make a small documentary film and had spoken to my friend, Yasha Feinstock, an amateur film maker. We had wandered around the town together and captured a few 'sights': a Saturday crowd of men around a beer stand; a picturesque group nearby. We unearthed a colourful gentleman at the bottle exchange bank: he had a black eye, a bandaged cheek and a string bag with empty bottles in it.

On Sunday we swooped on the square by the grocer's.

We were sworn at and threatened with a beating up, but we still managed to record a couple of bodies dead to the world. Yasha also filmed the exact moment of a vodka bottle being shared into three parts in a side alley.

And the scene with the 'Daddy' was good too: he was taking his son to the kindergarten, or, more exactly, his son was taking him, holding him up.

We edited the material we had filmed into an introduction lasting for six to seven minutes. It was quite powerful.

The interview prepared by me had the following format: first an introduction by Petrayev: a plea to society to stamp out drunkenness. Then our little film. Then some words from the District Health Authority and the doctors. Then the teachers, for the defence of children and the family, followed by manufacturers on the collapse of the five-year plan, accidents, fights and absenteeism. Then the police on the theme: 'Alcoholism – A Fertile Soil for Criminality'. I had agreed with the theatre director that he would talk about the role of art as a moral force, but we had had to leave this out: a few days ago there had been an unfortunate event in the theatre. During a love scene the principal man had fallen asleep and started snoring. There was no point in reminding people of this. The whole film was meant to culminate in the solemn promise of three of the drunkards to give up drinking.

Petrayev was very pleased with it. He praised me for my initiative and efficiency and said that the documentary film was 'excellent'.

He kept on saying, 'Oh, that's good, that's very good.'

And it's true that I thought then: 'He's really not so bad, I've been too critical.'

'But let's just make one small addition: after the personal appearances I'd like to come in again, to explore the issue in a little more depth, and, of course to remind people about our paper again, we must repeat our adherence to new ways of working, encouraging initiative . . .'

I asked how much time he would need. Why did I ask about time and not about what he would say?

Twenty minutes – it was a lot. I had already worked everything into an hour, the television channel wouldn't give us any more. Perhaps his second appearance needn't be broadcast? No, no, it must be fitted in. We compromised on fifteen minutes. I would have to shorten the doctors and teachers.

Petrayev had another look through the scenario, mumbled something and said:

'You know, there's just one thing missing.'

'What's that?'

'Mothers.'

'Uh?'

'There aren't any mothers taking part,' he said chidingly, 'It is vital that we get a mother's story, told with feeling, even with tears. That she reveals how she is tortured by her drunken son. It would get through, don't you think? Touch people's hearts, as it were?'

He said all this in a calm, business-like way, drumming his fingers on the table-top.

And suddenly I sobered up from the intoxication of the last two weeks, from all my gutter journalism. 'Operation P' stood before me naked. 'Shameless self-promotion', as a fairly intelligent young man had once said.

I suddenly imagined my own mother, her face covered in tears, upset. The way she is once a year, on 12 August, the anniversary of my father's death, when she reads his old letters. I saw her standing under the bright arc of light from the lamp with red eyes and trembling lips, old and pitiful.

'And where would you like me to get this mother from?' I asked rudely.

'That's not my problem,' Petrayev snapped back. 'You're quite capable of finding suitable material, as you've shown,' and he slapped his hand on my 'scenario'.

'I won't do it,' I said, and stood up. Everything was

shaking inside me; let it shake. There are certain things that you cannot do, whatever the consequences.

'Did you hear how he spoke to me?' said Petrayev to someone behind my back.

I turned round. Nina was standing by the door. I hadn't heard her come in; I didn't know how much she'd heard.

'Petunin, you can go,' said the Chief angrily, waving his arm. 'Nina, you can organise this.'

As I went past I gave her a furious look. She looked back at me and then lowered her eyes. I thought that I caught a flash of warmth from under her long, thick eyelashes – or was it just my imagination?

THE JUG MADE FROM CZECHOSLOVAK GLASS

Three days later, on Wednesday, 25 August, we had a rehearsal of the 'charade' as I now called the round table discussion. I was still furious. I still felt as I had in the office: that the whole thing was dirty and dishonest, superficial and sensationalist. But I did everything according to Petrayev's plan and my organisation and preparation, done while I, Anatoly Petunin, was in full possession of my faculties and stone-cold sober. It was true, I possessed all my faculties, and yet I continued to work on it, to do everything that the scenario demanded.

They had been dragging chairs and tables into the aquarium all morning. In one corner they'd erected a kind of stage, but instead of our usual committee table with its scarlet cloth they had placed little tables and chairs, like in the television programme 'Blue Light'.

'I wonder if Nina found her "television mother"?' I thought, as I tugged and pulled at the furniture.

Petrayev was directing everything himself, rushing round

the auditorium, jumping effortlessly on and off the stage, in constant motion, constantly adjusting, constantly commanding.

'Where's the water? We must put some water out!' he shouted from the auditorium.

Our assistant manager, Amerigo Vespuchin (his surname is real, the other is a nickname) brought in a cut-glass decanter without a stopper and an aluminium slop-basin. The Chief hurled the slop-basin to the floor and put down the decanter (he decided not to smash it), and roared: 'What is this rubbish? Are you mad?' gently tapping the decanter with his foot. 'Go to my room – No, not you – ' (to Vespuchin), 'but you,' (to me), 'and bring me the Czechoslovak jug together with the glasses. Fill it up with water at the same time' (this to my retreating back).

I placed two of the glasses in my pockets and carried the decanter in both hands. It was a pretty jug, made from a smoky-lilac glass with light veins and resembling a stork.

I hoped that it would break.

I was eaten up with spite – against myself, against Petrayev and against Nina. She wasn't in the office today. She was probably rushing around trying to find a mother for our television spectacular.

My spite fixed on anything and everything. That was why I wanted to break the jug. I banged it against the edge of the basin as I filled it with water, but it remained whole. Then I carried it balanced on the palms of my hands – the jug swayed, splashing me in the face with water, but it didn't fall. I wanted to smash it, but the fear that I might must have been greater.

Walking along the corridor I heard Angelina's voice behind me: 'Comrade Petrayev, I've found this leaflet for you . . .' Then she noticed her mistake and said in obvious disappointment, 'Oh, it's you . . .'

The television crew arrived a bit before three – a whole

94

army. Cameras, television lamps. The clang of iron, the rustle as they crawled around with the cables. The priming of technology.

We stood in for the participants in the following day's broadcast. We sat in our designated places and the camera operators aimed their lenses at us as the television lamps lit up. The director of the broadcast was Astra Pavlovna, a peroxide-blonde in green stockings. She told the camera operators what to film and when to alternate close-ups with long shots. She watched the screens of three monitors and shouted abrupt, incomprehensible phrases: 'Third camera – the right corner is collapsing!'; 'A bit fuller!'; 'Put on the *contre-jour*!'

The rehearsal went smoothly except for one small thing: a 500-watt bulb exploded while filming. Somebody gasped, the girls shrieked, and there was general pandemonium. Astra rebuked us: whatever happened during the transmission we must keep calm and keep quiet. She gave us two examples of the stoicism demanded from us: the composer, Sigismund Katz, continued to sing even after a glass splinter from a lamp had fallen into his eye, and the writer, Irakly Andronnikov, did not break off his story or even shudder when a 150-lb television camera collapsed onto his legs.

'The most important thing on television,' said Petrayev, responding to Astra, 'is to be relaxed. It is absolutely vital to be 100 per cent relaxed.'

THE TELEDRAMA

The interview day looked as if it was going to be hard work. In order to get out the following day's issue of the newspaper we arrive at eight in the morning instead of eleven. Petrayev too.

We had to go and get the participants at about three o'clock. Petrayev insisted that we brought them in early.

By four o'clock a television van was already parked outside our offices. Two lads were adjusting aerials on the roof of the van. Passers-by stopped and raised their heads to watch them work.

'Is it a fire?' one old lady asked another old lady carrying shopping bags. Little boys were scurrying around shouting out the day's big sensation: 'They're going to show drunks on television!' The crowd in front of the building grew.

Petrayev was fussing nervously around, flinging out orders to everybody and anybody who happened to be in the office. We must get through to the local police-station, we need a policeman to keep everything in order; we must reach an agreement with the other occupants of the building about the closing of doors (people were slinking through to the stairs and a gang of little boys was already standing on the landing pressing their sweaty hands and damp noses against our wonderful glass).

They rang the meteorological offices several times in order to get the most precise weather forecast. Petrayev was afraid there might be a storm and that this would interfere with transmission. There hadn't been any rain for a whole week. The portrait that didn't fit into the television picture must be re-hung and, conversely, the television set that did come into the picture must be removed. They'd forgotten to hang up a screen for our film. After the little boys had been chased away and the landing door locked there was a sudden realisation that another door, the one leading to the yard, would have to be opened. It was, in fact, behind this very closed door that I and Old Vasya (who had just had a small drink to give him courage), were standing, in the heat of the sun, and had been for quite some time.

Fifteen minutes before the start the auditorium was filled to overflowing. Everybody was in their places. All the tipplers we had signed on had turned up and everything seemed in order. The lads from the television studios, in their narrow-toed black boots, had taken up their battle positions. Yasha Feinstock was setting up the projector.

I went to get Petrayev, but Nina wouldn't let me in: he was getting ready for his television appearance and had asked not to be disturbed. He would be punctual.

'So, where's your "mother" then?' I couldn't help asking rudely.

'My mother died ten years ago.'

'I mean the programme . . . He asked you to . . .' I felt a bit embarrassed.

'That's cancelled, I talked him out of it.'

'I'm sorry.'

I wanted to apologise for my rudeness in thinking that she could have done something like that. I wanted to show her my respect and gratitude. But she made me feel shy. I liked her more than ever.

'Ah, well, time to go,' I glanced at my watch, 'five minutes to blast-off.'

Nina looked briefly into a little pocket mirror and got up. The office door opened and Petrayev came out.

His hair had been carefully smoothed down. He'd managed to change his open-necked shirt for a white, starched one and he was wearing a bright tie with a large pattern on it. But his face looked rumpled and tired.

It was extremely stuffy in the aquarium. The windows had been shut to cut out street noises and the air was getting very warm from the bright television lamps.

I and Petrayev took our places behind one of the little tables in the centre of the stage, near to the doll-like prettiness of the announcer, Inna. Hot, blinding, white lights were pointed at us.

Petrayev put a sheet of paper in front of him, covered all over in little beady handwriting. Astra looked round at every-body, lifted an arm and waved it: 'Shoot.'

'Comrades,' began Petrayev, 'according to the traditions

97

of our newspaper we are gathered here together around a round table—' (our table was triangular in shape). 'When important things have to be discussed, a live exchange of opinions is more important than any other form of intercourse. We are gathered here today to discuss an unpleasant question which presents difficulties for industry, the family and our community as a whole, both in the town and in the country. This is why the whole district is listening to and watching us today. We are talking about that disgusting relic of pre-revolutionary life which is dragging us backwards, is hindering our rapid transformation to communism. About the partiality to wine, about the misuse . . .'

'Why is he spinning it out,' I thought, 'repeating himself, going into purple prose? He should say straight out, it's about drunkenness.'

They turned out the lamps. We breathed deeply and wiped the sweat off our faces. They turned on the film projector. The familiar scenes flashed by to the accompaniment of music from a tape recorder. Every now and then something between a laugh and a croak was heard in the auditorium. The film ended and the damned lamps lit up again.

The personal appearance started. Everything was going precisely to plan. The only one who deviated at all was the psychiatrist, Dr. Konaev. He linked his speech to the pictures in our little film. He spoke simply and convincingly. The workers from the District Education Authority, on the other hand, did not deviate by one word from their written text, which had been looked over and corrected by myself and Astra. They spoke flatly, monotonously, as if they had learnt it off by heart. And the police were offended by our documentary film: Major Kuzetsov took it as an accusation of inactivity, 'Our young comrades on the newspaper have overgilded the lily somewhat.' But overall things were going well.

Until Petrayev asked whether any of the comrades would like to speak who'd had personal experience of the harm that alcohol can do.

Again there was a strange sound resembling a groan. Petrayev looked at me angrily, as if I had done it.

We had agreed to have two speakers: old Karasev, the carpenter from the machine tool factory who'd been cured of alcoholism a year ago, and Old Vasya. But Karasev wasn't at any of the tables, he had managed to slip out of sight. I nudged Inna, we exchanged glances, and she proposed that Vassily Ivanovich Khalibov say a few words. Old Vasya was in his proper place but he looked a bit dazed. The heat was making him tired. We had rehearsed his short speech twice. He was to admit that his love of vodka was a personal defect and to make a solemn promise to give it up.

But when he saw the cameras bearing down on him he became confused and was rendered speechless. I kicked him under the table.

'What are you doing? Leave off!' muttered Old Vasya in a hoarse falsetto. However, after a loud bout of coughing, he suddenly began:

'Well, you see, ladies and gentlemen, drunkenness is a very bad thing. It's worse than thieving. The way I see it is that you're stealing from yourself, you're stealing your own health away, with your own hands –'

'He's a born orator,' I thought. Inna moved the microphone a little bit away from him. Old Vasya dried up for a minute and then went on just as vivaciously and just as loudly:

'So, what do I want to say? Well, vodka only causes unpleasantness, it makes life at home very difficult. Say, for example, that I come home pissed. My wife says: "You bloody old bastard, you've been drinking again –", and I say to her, "I drink because of you, because of your nagging –" '

My eyes met Astra's – a sign, 'cut', was made to the sound operator. On the monitor we could see that the audience was livening up, some were beginning to smile. Old Vasya stared fixedly at the screen:

'Fools,' he muttered, 'swine, you can't see a damned thing on it.'

The public appearances of the repenters was cut short. Petrayev tapped the programme soundlessly with his finger – a sign to Inna to 'move on'.

Inna lifted her wondrous eyelashes and enunciated clearly:

'I would now like to introduce Comrade Petunin from the editorial board of *Lopatinskaya Pravda*.'

I shuddered: two blunders in a row – wasn't that a bit much? Astra raised her index finger and, frowning, indicated Petrayev to Inna. Inna lowered her eyes to the text and her cheeks turned scarlet. Petrayev looked at me furiously. What did I think I was up to? He'd obviously decided that I was making my bid for glory. But it was just a typing error. Inna calmly corrected herself:

'Excuse me comrades, the Editor-in-Chief, Comrade Petrayev, will speak on behalf of the newspaper.'

Just a small slip, but it had frightened us, and my heart was beating so loudly that I thought everybody would be able to hear it through the microphone.

Petrayev poured himself half a glass of water from the beautiful jug. I was very thirsty as well, but it didn't seem right for everybody to go for the water at once. I could wait, but he drank thirstily, gulping it all down.

His face looked strange; was it angry, confused? Surely there hadn't been another mistake? What could it be? No, he was just choking a little, trying to overcome a cough. The pause lengthened. Aha, at last, he was going to speak. But why was he so red? Probably from the tension, it's not easy to stifle a cough. Three blunders in a row, that must be bad. Never mind, he seemed to have got his breath back. He said:

'Dear comrades, I would like to sum up. We have gathered here to indicate where possible ways of overcoming harmful and sinful pre-revolutionary ways, which are obstructing the path to our bright future, just as a boulder that has tumbled down from a mountain top will close the road to a traveller who—'

('What is he going on about?' I thought, and began to feel awfully hot. But Petrayev wisely discarded the traveller half-way on his journey and started a new sentence.)

'Alcohol was the ruin of many talented and remarkable people who lived in Tsarist Russia . . .'

(He rolled his eyes at his piece of paper.)

'. . . the talented musician, Mussorgsky, the talented artist, Fedotov, the talented writer, Balzac . . .'

(Dear Lord, what was he babbling on about?)

'. . . of Tsarist Russia . . . The conditions in Tsarist Russia pre . . . determined, pre . . . arranged . . . Tsarist conditions presupposed drunkenness . . .'

(No, he must be feeling ill, he had gone quite white.)

'. . . slipped down until they were men-like apes . . .'

(Astra! Do something!)

Unexpectedly Petrayev raised his voice: 'My dear ladies and gentlemen! Our Soviet furs are first-class, from the little cat to the minks . . . We have on sale a set of Astrakhan –'

Here the Chief hiccuped and slid quietly to the floor.

'You're a man-like ape yourself!' shouted out a hoarse, deep voice.

But the discussion was no longer being televised.

The round table was ended ten minutes early.

A message appeared on the monitor: 'This transmission has been cut short for technical reasons.'

There was uproar, shouting, and a rush for the door. Major Kuznetsov demanded that the room be cleared. Somebody cried: 'Is there a doctor in the house?' and 'Call for a doctor!' Doctor Konayev bent over Petrayev's body as we fussed around him. Nina poured out water from the jug. Angelina shrieked: 'Aspirin, quickly.' And then Konayev said calmly: 'It's nothing serious. We must take him out into the fresh air.'

Fedka, Konayev, Vespuchin and I lifted Petrayev up. Just as we were about to move him I noticed Nina's eyes looking anxiously at me and heard her surprised exclamation: 'It isn't water!'

In the wonderful Czechoslovak jug which I had filled with water only the day before was – vodka! Who had done this? When? How? As we carried the sick or, rather, drunk man to his office these were the questions on everybody's lips.

Petrayev was laid down on the sofa and Doctor Konayev together with Angelina stayed to keep an eye on him.

Everybody was crowding into Nina's room and overflowing out into the corridor. There was a deafening hum of voices:

'Petrayev drank vodka instead of water.'

'What rubbish, how could half a glass of vodka make him sick?'

'What about the heat?'

'Yes, and it was so stuffy . . .'

'After all, he hadn't eaten anything all day.'

'Yes, and he was so nervous.'

'Still, a chap's not going to collapse after half a glass of vodka, is he?'

'Suppose it was mixed with something else?'

'Stop gossiping.'

'We've got to analyse what happened, don't you see?'

'Give us the jug.'

'Where's the jug?'

'Go and get the jug.'

'That's right, why waste it. We can finish it up.'

'You may laugh – it'll be a scandal throughout the whole district.'

'But they didn't show it . . .'

'He never drank vodka. He said so himself.'

'Enough chatter, bring the jug and we'll have a sniff and see what's there.'

In the end they went to the aquarium to get the jug. But the jug had disappeared. It was finally discovered on the floor at the end of the corridor. It was empty and clean.

Doctor Konayev and Angelina came out of his office.

The doctor announced that the editor-in-chief was feeling better.

Angelina whispered, rolling her eyes, that he was feeling a bit nauseous.

At last we all went our separate ways home. We had something to think about.

I, however, was not thinking about the jug, or about the mysterious transformation of the water into vodka. I was concerned about something else: when had Nina disappeared? She'd slipped away unnoticed. I couldn't remember when her intent, thoughtful gaze had ceased to meet my eyes. Surely she couldn't have slipped into his office to look after that . . . care for that . . . I just couldn't find the right word, a word that would ease my heart. I despised the Chief. Not even, perhaps, because of his stupid plan, his pompous, self-publicising firework display, but because he didn't know how to drink vodka. What a puny specimen, yes, that was the word, puny.

SABOTEUR PETUNIN

The next morning I got into the office early. So did a lot of people. There was a crowd in the aquarium. Conversation centred around two main themes: the disintegration of the television programme and the vodka in the jug. One theory was that the programme's debacle had been planned, as had the vodka in the jug. Another asked ironically, how the 'saboteur' who had smuggled in the vodka could know that Petrayev would be the one to drink it? And how could they have foreseen that he would get blind-drunk after three mouthfuls? Another insistent voice enquired repeatedly: 'Why

103

would anyone want to destroy the broadcast?'

Nobody had any answers to any of these questions.

I was hanging around aimlessly, like everyone else, listening, shrugging, tut-tutting and exclaiming. But soon I became aware of a strange chill around me. A kind of cool emptiness. I was in the middle of a crowd but I felt alone. And inside there was also an unpleasant coldness. Nobody accused me of anything. But the feeling of emptiness and loneliness increased. I realised that they suspected me. Stealthily, silently, dishonestly. Some sympathised with me, also silently, or half-silently, and this also seemed to me dishonest.

'Don't worry, old chap,' muttered Fedka, touching me on the shoulder.

'Cheer up, young Petunin,' whispered Rita the typist affectionately.

So they thought I was the 'saboteur'. Without a doubt, as if it were perfectly obvious.

From the conversation in the aquarium I learnt three important bits of news: the local party branch had been in conference for an hour already; Petrayev had risen from the dead; after a night spent at the office he was once again hale and hearty, and Shilov had arrived that morning.

I looked round for Nina – she wasn't in the aquarium, she must be in her office, guarding the conference.

I wanted to see her very much. I could ask her about something, but I would prefer just to look at her. The corridor was empty. I got to the door with the sign 'A.Y. Petrayev' and opened it a chink. There was nobody in Nina's room, but her typewriter had some paper in it. She must have gone out for a minute. I decided to wait for her. I could hear voices from behind the door of the inner office – several speaking at once. It seemed to be a stormy meeting. I tried to remember who was in the local Party branch that I knew. Shilov, Angelina, Vespuchin, someone from the typographical department, Skradnov I thought, was. I couldn't remember who else. I thought the Old Man used to be in it. Somebody's shrill, thin tenor (I couldn't make out whose), was crying: 'Sacking is too good for him, he should go to prison, I say to prison.' Were they talking about me? And again I heard a cry: 'Call in Kuznetsov, let him investigate.' I decided it was time for me to go. I hoped that later they might invite me in, but for the time being I'd better go. I decided to leave a note for Nina, asking her to pop round and see me. I went to her desk. A piece of paper lay beside her typewriter, half covered with writing. I picked up a pencil but then caught sight of my surname and I read through everything that was written there. Here it is, word for word:

In large writing: 'Nina, this is urgent, please type it immediately.' Then there was a heading: 'A Scandalous Occurrence'. It ran:

'An employee on the paper *Lopatinskaya Pravda*, comrade A.P. Petunin, who was entrusted with the organisation of a round table discussion on the fight against alcoholism, relayed on local television, arrived at the scene of the discussion in an inebriated state which led to general disarray and the breakdown of the programme. The editorial board apologises to our viewers and our readers. Strong steps will be taken with regard to A.P. Petunin. Signed, Editor-in-Chief, A. Petrayev, 27.8.65.'

Then, in his handwriting, in red pencil was added: 'Get this typed and give it to the printers for the next edition. A.P.'

And below that in blue pencil: 'I will not do this. It's not fair. N. Boiko.'

It is difficult to describe my state of mind. I stood looking at Petrayev's note, reading it over and over again. At last I tore my eyes away from it. I had an urge to take the piece of paper and stuff it into my pocket. Why? I don't know. I probably realised even then that it would be useful later on. But I didn't take it. The thought flashed through my mind that while Nina had the note she would support me, if I took it she wouldn't.

'Nina, my good comrade and friend,' I repeated to myself, and these words made me feel better.

They continued to quarrel behind the door. I heard a booming bass – Shilov must be speaking. The tenor was having a quiet spell, but Petrayev's piercing squeal was also highly audible.

For some odd reason I was feeling more cheerful. There wasn't any reason for me to. Really, after everything that I had heard today, especially after what I'd read, I ought to be feeling extremely depressed.

But I didn't, and that was a fact: 'The evil alcoholic and saboteur, A.P. Petunin, was not depressed.'

And I went out without leaving a note for Nina. I went out without anybody having seen me.

THE ACCUSER AND THE ACCUSED

An hour later I was called into the office. Shilov was sitting in Petrayev's seat. His eyes were red and his face was tired. He had travelled through the night and had probably had no sleep. The ashtray was full of cigarette ends and the room was thick with smoke, for which the window was too small an outlet. Angelina Adamovna, Vespuchin and Skradnov were seated; Petrayev was walking rapidly back and forth. When I entered he stopped as if stumbling and cried in a high-pitched treble:

'Here he is! The promising journalist! Tell us about your artistry! You'd better come clean, or it'll be the worse for you. But whatever you say you'll still have to answer for the disruption of an event of political importance.'

Shilov halted him:

'Sit down and calm yourself. Comrade Petunin, could

you please tell us which of yesterday's failures at the discussion were your fault?'

Petrayev snorted and leapt out of his chair:

'Ask him how he got the vodka into the jug.'

'Comrade Petrayev, once and for all, will you please calm yourself. Go ahead, Petunin.'

I said that I was responsible for two of yesterday's failures: Karasayev's slipping out of my sight and the typewritten error in the programme text; I had proof-read it after the typist and had not noticed that my surname was there instead of Petrayev's. Then I turned to Petrayev and said:

'I did not fill the jug with vodka.'

'I met you in the corridor with the jug,' butted in Angelina, 'before the discussion. Perhaps you could explain how the vodka got into the jug?' There was a distinct note of accusation in her voice.

'Now wait a minute,' said Shilov, 'this is turning into a criminal farce. He has already said that he didn't fill the jug with vodka.'

'But he was the one carrying the jug,' shrieked Petunin, 'everybody saw him.'

'I filled the jug with water, carried it to the table, placed it on the table, and I didn't touch it after that.'

'You ought to know how he,' Petrayev pointed his finger at me like a pistol, 'felt about this event in general: he skived off work, argued, refused to do things . . . All this must be taken into account, and then it will be clear who disrupted the discussion. Do you know that this member of the Young Communist League still doesn't know whether he wants to join the Party or not? He smirks in a supercilious way and says, ''I need to think a little more . . .'' That is his true face, and once you have seen it . . .'

I leapt to my feet. I was choking with fury. The rotten sod, the way he was twisting my words! I opened my mouth but nothing came out. I took a step towards Petrayev.

'Sit down!' roared Shilov.

Petrayev continued his speech:

'– and then these algebraic equations, who took the jug, who carried it, who filled it, would not be necessary. You are right Petr Zakharovich,' (to Shilov), 'it's not the jug that is important but fundamental attitudes towards the matter in hand. You said that he was a "capable journalist", but he has no thoughts of his own, and when you offer him an idea he doesn't want to listen. He spent ten days messing about with a plan, and the result was – nothing. He's not capable of organising two men to take part—'

'He's lying fluently,' I thought.

'– you see, he couldn't bear not having a place in the programme and so he put in his name, hoping somehow to get on television . . .'

'You swine!' I shouted, and began to hammer his miserable face with my fists. 'You're a worthless demagogue, you're completely unscrupulous! You judge everybody by your own standards, you're a damned blockhead!'

But all this was only in my head. In actual fact I was sitting despondently and mumbling through my nose: 'It's not true, it's not true . . . You must prove it . . . you're twisting my words . . . How dare you, that's slander . . .'

'I'm convinced that he's been in contact with those drunkards that he chose. They acted together to discredit . . .'

'You're lying,' I shouted, unable to restrain myself any longer, our voices merged, we were both shouting together now, 'you think that just because you're the boss you can do anything. Just prove one of your accusations—'

'Enough!' barked Shilov, and banged his fist on the table so hard that the cigarette stubs and ash flew up into the air and then resettled around the ashtrays, 'Will you both sit down and calm down. The Party branch must clarify in an objective way all the circumstances. Are there any more questions for Comrade Petunin? Any questions in general?'

'I have a question for Comrade Petrayev,' said Skradnov, 'this little note here, which you brought into the printing shop this morning,' he pulled a bit of rough copy from his pocket, 'what is its basis? It says here that Comrade Petunin appeared at the event in an inebriated condition and that this was the reason for the disruption of the programme. Is there any confirmation of this?'

'I can confirm it,' said Angelina. 'Comrade Petunin was acting very strangely that day. I saw him walking along the corridor with the jug. He was unsteady on his feet, in fact he was staggering.'

'That was the evening before,' I objected.

'But on the following day Petunin was still a bit strange,' continued Angelina, 'he seemed very agitated. He looked at me, stared at me in a rather unpleasant way.'

'OK, that'll do.' Shilov sealed this exchange of views by slapping his hand on the table. 'Now we would like Comrades Petrayev and Petunin to leave the room. Please ask Nina Boiko to come in. As far as that rough copy goes, we'll go into that in more detail later. At the moment we would like to talk to some of the other staff.'

I left the room first. Nina was at her desk, she looked pale and pinched. I wanted to say something nice to her, to express my gratitude, but Petrayev was hard on my heels.

'They want you next,' I said, nodding towards the office.

Going out into the corridor I heard Petrayev speaking quietly, conspiratorially: 'Nina, my dear, I am relying on your discretion. I beg of you, after all, it really has nothing to do with—'

I was already out of earshot before the end of the sentence.

I sat at my desk and drew imaginary circles, squares and triangles on it with my finger. Fedka was there.

'If you don't want to talk, don't,' he muttered, 'but it's not just curiosity.'

I didn't feel like talking. I wanted to know what had happened to Petrayev's libellous note.

'Where's the paper? Have you got today's?'

I looked at page four – nothing. Page three – nothing. Two – still nothing. Page one? The note wasn't on the first page either. Then I had a brainwave: if it was only handed in this morning it would only have been in time for the last few thousand editions, and the office always kept the first ones. I asked Fedka to pop into the printing shop, telling him briefly what it was all about.

Fedka swore and rushed to the printers. He returned with an edition which contained the note – on the first page. He said that the note had only got into a few hundred editions – they'd stopped the machines especially to remove it. The printers didn't know who'd given the orders for this: there'd been a phone call from the editorial office and the head of the printing shop, Lapin, had told them. He was very angry about the print run being held up.

'So it's a collector's piece,' Fedka joked, 'don't lose it.'

I didn't feel like joking. I was working out how to kill Petrayev. To kill . . . It would have given me enormous satisfaction to place a bullet inside him. It was a shame that we no longer had duels. Now people shoot from behind corners, from a window, a dark warehouse, from the roofs of high buildings, from a safe distance in short. Or, under cover of darkness they put a knife in you. It's cowardly to shoot from a hiding place. People should fight bravely, in the open. One should attack in the open and defend oneself in the open.

But I wasn't cut out for duels, really. What was I? A broken reed. I'd felt ashamed in front of Shilov, a brave soldier, a real man, an honest Communist.

A LENGTHY WORK ASSIGNMENT

The next day I didn't go into the office. I just didn't go in. I didn't want to see any of them.

Fedka came rushing over to see me at lunch-time: 'What's the matter? Are you ill, or crazy or what? He's just waiting for you to skive off.'

'He' was, of course, the boss. He had asked about me, but the lads had covered up for me, saying that I'd gone to check something in a letter.

On the way to work Fedka told me the rest of the news: the Party branch had been in conference that morning as well, the boss had gone to the local Party committee, Nina seemed to have been crying.

I passed a few very depressed days. We all worked, the paper got printed, but somehow everybody was a bit quiet, there wasn't the usual banter in the office. People talked in corners in hushed voices. They didn't talk much about the television programme. A new topic of conversation had developed: the condemnation of Petrayev. He should never have ordered a note like that to be printed. He should have stopped after the first mouthful. He could have restrained himself, not drunk any more. And what was the point of the television programme, anyway? We were a newspaper. There'd never been anything like that before, and quite right too. It was probably one of those inebriates who had filled the jug with vodka for a joke. Why should Petunin have done it when he was so closely involved in the organisation of the round table discussion? Or perhaps there was a conflict between the 'P's'? Perhaps this was a case of *cherchez la femme*?

It was Fedka who, from the best possible of motives, passed all this on to me. Petrayev was not working on the paper at all. He was as energetic, speedy and bustling as before, but this activity was directed elsewhere. He was rarely in the office.

The office secretary, Voznook, returned from sick leave and Nina's job reverted to him. Nina went back to Shilov's department.

On the tenth day, counting from that ill-fated Thursday,

I was summoned in to see Shilov. He was morose and seemed tired. He spoke, at first, in a formal way, calling me Comrade Petunin. He proposed that I should go and work on a rural newspaper for a few months in order to improve the country press.

I asked if this represented a delayed dismissal.

'No, I told you that your place and salary would be kept for you,' he said angrily, and then added, more gently, 'It would be better if you went.'

How did he think I should respond to the note in the newspaper, shouldn't I take legal action for libel?

'Legal action?! What next,' growled Shilov.

He explained that Petrayev's note was being discussed 'higher up'. As I understood it, he considered the note to be a weighty document in my favour. Then he added something which I didn't understand till a long time afterwards but which, nevertheless, cheered me up a great deal. 'I don't know how all this would have ended if it hadn't been for Nina Boiko. She's steadier than you.' He didn't consider this episode completely closed, but thought that I had nothing serious to worry about.

Then Shilov asked me to tell him how the idea of the round table discussion had arisen, who had thought of calling in the television cameras, what exactly my part in it all had been and what my attitude to it was.

'I'm asking for personal reasons,' he added, 'I watched the whole spectacle, you know.'

It turned out that this was why he'd left; the 'performance' had aroused anxiety. Not the farcical end, but the essence.

'These discussions which study serious problems do nothing but harm,' he sighed.

We parted warmly. 'Spend the winter there, like a bear in its lair. There's not a lot to do there in the winter, but study life at first hand, get to know the people there. It will help you and perhaps them as well.'

We parted on this note. A day later I left Lopatinsk. I didn't see Petrayev again.

LONG EVENINGS

I arrived here in September. It is now the end of October. I live in a hotel. I've been here for a month and a half.

The last few days I've been feeling depressed. It is cold and raining. The evenings are long and empty. I brought my textbooks with me, and set myself certain goals, but I can't concentrate. The time went quickly while I was writing this story down. I keep going back to my notes and now it's turning into a diary, into fragmentary impressions. This little town goes to bed early. It is dark and quiet. Through my open casement window the only sound is the bark of a dog and the occasional stutter of a motor bike.

A bare light bulb hangs from the ceiling. There is a square table covered with a white cloth, two beds along the walls, two night tables and two chairs. White curtains cover only half the windows. It is clean and empty, like a hospital with only one patient – me. I'm nannied by Mrs Glasha – the head doctor. The manager of the hotel is Glafira Stepanovna. There are no guests – it's out of season.

I sleep badly. I lie in bed and smoke and think: 'Why did I leave Lopatinsk?' Shilov said it would be for the best. All right, I believe him. But best for whom? They said get on a train and go, so I did, without thinking. Once again I had let someone do my thinking for me.

The local paper has a small but full complement of staff. I'm like a fifth wheel there, I only get in the way. I once suggested a slightly more lively way of doing something. They were terrified: 'We don't do things like that, what would they say at the local committee?' After that I didn't try to change anything. At the end of September I visited some local collective farms and wrote two articles. Now the bad weather has set in, the roads are impassable.

Sometimes I think that everybody's forgotten me. My mother is the only one who writes regularly. In September I got a letter from Fedka saying that he was surprised not to have heard from me. But what can I write? He told me that everything was OK at the office.

I have the feeling that I will live here, in this very room, under this bright light, smoking, learning German, washing my socks in the sink in the corridor, drinking tea morning and evening from the old kettle, and eating tinned ox tongue in tomato sauce every evening, for a very long time, for ever, without understanding what I am doing here.

When I lie in bed at night I think about our newspaper office, its hustle and bustle, its panics. My work and the people with whom I worked. My friends, Nina. Especially Nina. I seem to see her more clearly, now that I am far away, from her fluffy eyebrows to the tips of her toes peeping out of her sandals. Just as she was beginning to open out to me, during those difficult days, I was torn from her, and now she is far away. I try to imagine what Petrayev could mean to her. Surely there couldn't be anything between them? Not even the tiny beginnings of something, not even unconsciously? I recall her new hair-style, her glance in the mirror before entering his office. She wanted him to like her. She'd been able to dissuade him from the sorrowful mother number, so she had a certain influence with him. And there was her anxiety at the end of the hapless 'discussion'. And his ingratiating voice saying: 'My dear Nina, I beg of you . . .' All this indicated a relationship closer than that of mere office colleagues. This thought upset me so much that I then had to argue the other way.

She had refused to type Petrayev's note or give it to the print shop. Not only had she refused but she had condemned him. What else? She'd been steadfast in something that had acted in my defence. A warmth crept into my heart. Even more than understanding her I wanted to see her, to take her hands in mine, to pull her to me and to hold her tightly.

My heart began to beat so loudly that it deafened the ticking of the hotel grandfather clock. What an idiot I had been. Why hadn't I tried to overcome the barrier that she placed between herself and other people? I'd been aware of it and had let it repulse me. What caused it? Pride? No, something else, I was sure.

And now she was further away from me than ever. The thought that I might never see her again plunged me into despair.

Sometimes in the evening I go to see a film. There is a cinema here with two screens. On Sundays dances are held in one of the auditoriums. On Saturday and Sunday evenings people also gather in the town centre, a square where two main roads intersect. The post office, the restaurant, and the cafeteria, open till ten at night, are in the square. It's the main attraction.

The entrances to the shops are lit up. The windows, with their pyramids of bottles and tinned food, shine out. There is always a lot of noise inside. You can meet friends and acquaintances here, have a chat, a joke, get-togethers . . .

The most important department of the grocery store is the wine section. It's called 'Bottles'. Its manageress is a lively, quick, garrulous woman called Klava. She's an intrepid follower of fashion, her hair dyed, always brightly adorned, like a Christmas tree, with bracelets, earrings and rings on her plump fingers.

On Saturday evening I was overwhelmed by a terrible despair. The rain was drizzling down. An Arab film in two parts was on at the cinema. I don't like melodramas. I decided to go for a walk. But not to the monastery, not to the bright Prakha stream, which hums on the shoals like a hundred spinning-wheels. It would be dark and damp and muddy there now. I wandered along the streets, under the sparse street-lights, past lighted windows, all with the curtains drawn, past closed doors and gates. Until my legs led me to the grocery store.

I was cheered by the lights and the people, I needed crowds, their noise and movement, like on Lopatinsky main street in Moscow. I was drawn to the people. I went into the shop. It was crowded and noisy. Old Prokhor was causing some amusement because he couldn't remember whether he was coming from or going to work on the night shift. Women were buying sausages and reproaching their husbands for being unable to face the weekend without a bottle. The buyers exchanged pleasantries, knew each other's names, asked or talked about mutual acquaintances. In general the discussion centred upon alcohol: business-like answers from men, reproaches from the women, good-natured banter, sly asides. I discovered unexpectedly that I was completely indifferent to the main subject. This chance collection of people radiated good-will, and it seemed to me, in my petrified loneliness, that it was warm and alive in here.

NINA – AND NOT ONLY . . .

'Nina, you can't imagine how much I need you! I was a fool not to have talked to you before I left. And an even bigger fool to have thought that you were with Petrayev and not me. Because you were with me; you rejected his sordid scheme to place a sorrowing mother in front of the cameras. And then you wouldn't type his lying little note and you explained (of course you did), with the words, "this is wrong". And you were probably with me later, probably talked to Shilov about things that Petrayev had begged you not to. And, even if you didn't, you were still with me, and not with him.

'I love you. I mean it. I can't go on without you. I can't

116

go on living so far away from you, knowing nothing about you . . .'

I didn't finish the letter because I went to Lopatinsk to see Nina.

I'm writing it all down so I can relive it, because I am again in this small town, alone in this hotel room. But I no longer feel the same anguish.

I got to Lopatinsk Friday afternoon, in a mood of excited, happy and nervous anticipation. I rang the office to talk to Nina about a time to meet. A male voice said, 'She's on sick leave', and hung up. I didn't know where she lived exactly, just the street. I didn't even know which block she lived in. She didn't like people seeing her home. I waited twenty minutes at the enquiries booth to get her address. There was an enormous queue for taxis. I didn't know which buses or trams went there. I decided to start walking and catch a taxi on the way. I was out of luck and had to get a trolleybus. I asked where to get off and the whole of the trolleybus answered in concert. And then I was there, at Kalininskaya Street, the second on the right was Nina's street. A quiet street, with small apartment blocks. At last I got to No. 20. I went up to the third floor. My heart was thumping, I was breathless. Why hadn't I bought her anything? Flowers or chocolates? Well, perhaps it was better this way, I'd look silly holding a bunch of flowers when she opened the door.

On the landing I smoothed my hair and did up my coat buttons. Then I rang the bell. A neat-looking old woman with a spotted kerchief round her head answered the door. I asked for Nina. 'She's not back yet. She'll be here soon.'

'Do you mind if I wait?'

'Who are you?'

I explained. Unwillingly, she let me in. I took off my coat and followed her into the room.

I saw a little boy of about three sitting on a rug on the floor building a house with blocks. When he saw me he

117

started to get up and the house fell down. The little boy took one step towards me and then another, and asked: 'Can you build a house?' I sat down beside him and we built a tower. It was the Moscow television tower and so it had to be very high.

He leant trustingly on my knee, breathing warmly into my ear. He had funny little tufts of hair at the nape of his neck. His hair was dark and his eyes brown, like Nina.

We finished the blocks and built a pyramidical top of coloured, wooden rings. The tower was so tall that it swayed. I heard steps in the hall and then a familiar voice, but unfamiliar in its gentleness, say, 'Peter, love, where are you?'

'I'm in here, Mummy. We built a tower. Look, but you mustn't move.'

Nina came in, I saw her out of the corner of my eye. I was afraid to move as well. I said quietly, 'Hullo, Nina.' I was petrified by the thought that she might say, 'what do you want?' But she said, 'Hullo, Pete, are you back, then?'

Peter looked at me and asked her, 'Is this my Dad, then?'

We didn't say anything. I looked at Nina. I didn't want her to say 'No'. I took Peter's hand and did a little jump, the tower collapsed. I flung the little boy up in the air, caught him, gave him a hug and said: 'We'll build another tower, even higher.'

'No,' he said, 'you carry me now and I'll watch the parade.'

'What parade?'

'The celebration one. You carry me, and I can watch. I can watch because I'll be very high.'

I understood; it was the dream of every small child to have someone hold them up to watch the parade. All right, we would play at parades. And I carried him from window to window.

I said, still holding on to little Peter, 'I've missed you so much, Nina. I wanted to see you. I love you. Don't say

118

anything. I wrote you a letter, but I didn't send it. I decided to come and tell you, so here I am.'

I spoke with an incoherent passion. I had to get it all out as quickly as possible, before she had time to think.

I was trying to think if I'd left out anything important when Petya, frightened by my passionate speech, wailed and started kicking and trying to get out of my arms.

'There's nothing to cry about,' said Nina softly. 'Let's have lunch, shall we? You're probably hungry, Pete. Petya, show our guest where to wash his hands while I lay the table.'

After lunch Nina put her son to bed for a sleep. We sat next to each other without speaking for a long time.

'Why did you keep him a secret from us?'

'I didn't. I just don't like talking about myself. People did know about him, Shilov, for example, Valya, old Mrs Sash. Some people knew. Soon he'll be three. He'll go to the kindergarten. Up to now he's been at home with my old nanny, Martha Ivanovna.'

I wanted to know everything about Nina, but I didn't want to ask. Luckily, she began herself.

'Perhaps I'm bad at choosing people. I can see clearly now. The man I loved, Petya's father, was a bad man. We didn't get married. I decided that I didn't need anybody. I didn't want anyone to pity me. I don't want you to pity me either.'

'I don't pity you,' I interrupted. 'I need you. Very much. And Petya makes you twice as wonderful.'

At last she smiled.

'I've always dreamed of having a son, and I certainly would have called him Petya, in honour of his father.'

'You're a good person,' Nina said, and sighed.

I decided not to talk to her any more about love. I started to ask about the paper, the office; whether any decision had been reached on the 'Petunin affair', or whether the 'affair' had died a natural death, and did she know how much longer I was going to be stuck in the provinces?

119

Nina told me everything she knew. She didn't know much about the 'Petunin affair'. It seemed that Petrayev was still trying something with the town Party committee, but Shilov was providing resistance. It was Petrayev's remarks about me that were now at the centre of the investigation rather than me myself.

'By the way, where is the document itself? I mean Petrayev's autographed copy?'

'Have you seen it? Shilov has it.'

'Did Petrayev ask you to hide his note? I heard him say as I was leaving the office, "Nina, please, I beg of you . . ." '

'No, that was about something else,' Nina's face darkened. She didn't seem to want to talk about it.

I was sorry I'd asked so many questions.

She began asking me about my life in the little town, and I tried to describe it in a humorous way, but I couldn't have been very funny, because she suddenly pressed my hand and said: 'Just be patient a bit longer.'

For this I was willing to stay there, in that little town, another year. I began to say goodbye: I wanted to take away with me in good order everything that I had acquired that day.

FRAGMENTARY NOTES

Now I go to Lopatinsk at the end of each week and spend Saturday evenings with Nina and Petya. I can feel her becoming warmer and more trusting. Petya and I are great friends. And when our play gets too loud or our antics too boisterous, we sometimes both get it from 'our Mum', as Petya says, and for these words I love him even more.

Nina told me that before this 'business' Petrayev had propositioned her. He didn't say he was in love with her, but that he thought they were 'well-suited'. Nina told him that she had a son. Petrayev replied, 'This changes the position substantially, allow me to think it over.'

'And what happened when he had thought it over?' I asked fiercely.

'He's still thinking,' she answered. We looked at each other and both laughed.

She has such a glorious laugh. Wonderful dimples appear in her cheeks. I kissed her, I couldn't help it. She didn't push me away, but looked at me bleakly. So I controlled myself.

Last Saturday Petya called me 'Dad' again. She didn't correct him, as she has done before, and no shadow appeared on her face. In fact the remarkable thing was that she hardly noticed it.

I got ill on Wednesday and so couldn't go on Saturday. It must have been flu. I would have gone, even though I was sick, but what about the little boy? It didn't occur to me to send a telegram. Anyway, I had a temperature of nearly forty degrees.

She arrived on Tuesday, pale after a sleepless night on the train. She was worried and angry: why hadn't I asked her to come? My dearest, my delight, my joy . . . We parted on Wednesday. It was difficult to say goodbye but she had to go.

We spoke seriously about the round table discussion for the first time. She agreed that it had been sensationalist and self-seeking. In general, she said, we needed less words and more action. Also, it would be nice to be more independent. 'So,' she said to me, 'go to it.'

'With you?' I asked.

She told me that Petrayev had asked her not to talk to Shilov about the brandy. Apparently he was drinking before the programme in his office by himself for 'courage'. Nina had bought him the brandy at his request. He had asked her to buy the most expensive there was.

'How many stars?' I asked, just for something to say. I wasn't really interested: he and his brandy could go to hell.

'I don't remember how many stars it was, but I do remember that I paid five roubles for it, and do you know why? He never paid me back.'

We laughed.

'He's a real louse,' I said.

'Cockroach, cockroach, big ones, spindly-legged ones,' said Nina, quoting Chukovsky.

'He's a cockroach, but are you a sparrow?', I thought, remembering the end of the poem, 'no, you're certainly not a sparrow.'

But I didn't say this aloud.

Lubka

The evenings were drawing in. Soft flakes of snow fell from the low, dark clouds, settling on the heads and shoulders of the women huddled on the cold benches in the square. Wrapped in their warm clothes and muffled in their head-scarves, the old women were motionless. In the middle of the square there was a statue of a man sitting in a low armchair, with his cast-iron, booted feet flung forward. Sparrows sat on his boots and turned their heads to study the old women who, from time to time, would drag a piece of bread out from their pockets and crumble it onto the trodden snow for the pigeons. The pigeons wandered amongst the felt boots of the old women, pecking hungrily, tearing at the bigger pieces. The alert little sparrows went for the crumbs further off and squawked as they fought over them. The old women waved their mittens at them:

'Kish, kish, not for you, fly away, fly away . . .'

The birds were a welcome distraction for the women, who were getting bored with their long, repetitious conversations, rubbed thin like an old spindle. So they sat silently, looking at the quarrelling sparrows. Suddenly one turned her whole body round and, nudging her neighbours, said:

'Look, here comes Lubka from work.'

And, turning heavily, moving their felt boots slowly and clutching onto the bench, all the rest said in a chorus: 'Lubka . . . Where's Lubka? Ah, there she goes.'

A young girl hurried past the cast-iron fence, moving lightly, her bony knees showing above her high boots, and then she disappeared into the snow flakes.

123

They had already talked about Lubka today, as they had yesterday and the day before. Her whole life had been pounded, worn down, sifted through and aired. And still the talk began again. Today they felt like talking about Lubka.

'The hearing's still on for tomorrow, then?'

'It's the second time they've announced it so it must be.'

'If she doesn't come this time it'll go to court.'

'I'd like to see her not turn up.'

'She'd be condemned and put in jail.'

'Put in jail, and not before time.'

'People like her should be drummed out of Moscow. What are they doing here? They just upset people.'

'Well, she's had a good run . . .'

'She's had her fun . . .'

'She's got her come-uppance.'

There were a lot of people in the long, squat building, the local housing department club in the middle of the courtyard. A single bulb under a glass lampshade lit up the red lead of the painted door and the announcement stuck to its plywood panel: the announcement invited everybody who so desired to an open sitting of the club's comrades' court, 'regarding an appraisal of L.I. Sapozhnikova's behaviour in the light of her disregard of internal house rules and her immoral behaviour . . .'

There were many who did so desire to watch and to listen. They began to arrive at six and by half-past the creaking of the door as it opened and shut was almost continuous.

The announcement had only been hung in the club that day because the twenty announcements pasted up in individual homes a week ago had been torn down and completely covered and defaced with writing. In fact, somebody had already scribbled some obscene words in the corner of this announcement, as if they were part of the agenda.

Gradually the room filled with people. The first two rows

were filled with activists in the housing department and people invited by the chairman and also by Lubka's neighbours, who were the plaintiffs.

An elderly man whose black hair was yellow and balding at the edges, as a responsible rent-payer and the only man left in the flat after the war, was the head of the tenants' collective. Virepnikov was a bookkeeper, business-like and an expert in writing statements and complaints and sending them out to the right places. To his right sat a plump woman, heavily powdered, in a fur coat, Rosa Iosofna, a retired dentist. To his left, fidgeting uneasily, sat a sanctimonious, aggressive-looking woman, pale both from her unhealthy work (she was a dry-cleaner) and her spiteful character. Her name was Effalia Nikodemovna. Breathing heavily beside Effalia sat Matrena Spiridonovna, or Old Motya as she was known, a former lift attendant now enjoying a well-earned rest and grown fat through her passion for tea and fritters.

They were all legal tenants in the five-roomed flat in the old house where the fifth and biggest room belonged to Praskova Egorovna Sapozhnikova and her daughter Lubka.

The plaintiff-neighbours sat uneasily, waiting to see whether Lubka would turn up or not. Before leaving the flat they had peeped and eavesdropped: were the Sapozhnikovs getting ready to come or not? They could hear nothing from their room, they didn't appear in the corridor. Please God – they'd forgotten. The plaintiffs didn't want Lubka to turn up because then it would go to court, which was much more serious.

Still, they were prepared for Lubka coming, they'd agreed beforehand who would say what. They must work together, push together, in order to finally rid themselves of this plague, this poison, this damned nuisance – this Lubka!

Lubka's neighbours were worried. Each had their own, dark, illicit secret, and they were frightened that it might be discovered here and lead to serious admonishments.

And they also thought: supposing they didn't get rid of Lubka and had to go on living with her – it would be very awkward if they were at daggers drawn. And then there was that gang, that gang that got together at Lubka's: boys with long hair, looking for trouble, drunkards; and painted, shrieking girls. Everybody knew that this gang took its revenge. The women were frightened of Lubka's gang. But they were also frightened of Virepnikov, who had ordered that no one should remain silent – Lubka's behaviour in its everyday form and social effects must be revealed to the court.

So, all in all, they had plenty to be nervous about. Old Motya, her coat unbuttoned, wiped her face repeatedly with a big handkerchief; Rosa Iosofna felt stealthily in her bag for her 'nerve' pills.

The benches began in the third row, behind the chairs. The people perched on these had come just to pass the evening, to see what would happen to the notorious Lubka; they were mainly retired, elderly people. On the furthest bench, in the corner, the young people assembled, a few long-haired boys in short jackets and two young girls. One was so small as to be almost a dwarf, with a beehive of bright red hair. On top of her beehive, like a flag, fluttered a printed scarf as she twisted her head sharply round, looking at the room. The other was as skinny as a bean-pole, her shoulders hunched and her face hidden in her coat-collar as she looked fixedly from under her eyelashes, heavy with mascara, at the opening door. This was Lubka's retinue. They had come to watch Lubka deal with this circus. She would think of something, he could do it!

Three people, the comrades' court of the local housing department, sat on the platform behind a table covered in red calico. In the middle sat the chairman, small, thin, with a yellowish face and a short-back-and-sides haircut. Ivan Kornevitch Zalomin was known and respected by all. He'd worked voluntarily for the local housing department in various capacities for eight years and helped people to the limits of his power.

Zalomin was going through the papers in his file. He was not so much reminding himself of this business as thinking it over again, and thinking about how to conduct this meeting. There were grounds for refusing a review and just handing the whole matter over to the courts. His colleagues had advised him to do this: it fitted a criminal category, it was only necessary to collect some material and two or three police statements. But Zalomin had not recommended this to Lubka's neighbours and had insisted on a comrades' trial. This business has an educative side, he had said, especially for young people. The present crowd proved that he'd been right. Raising his head, Zalomin looked through his glasses at the room and saw there weren't many young people there. But he'd foreseen this and had taken his own precautions. He glanced forward, seeing the two girls near the stage, and gave them a slight nod.

Zalomin had not predetermined the decision of the court. It depended on many things, on what witnesses said, on the behaviour of the law-breaker, but she was already late and that in itself was a black mark against her.

An elderly woman with blonde hair sat to the right of the chairman. Wearing a blouse with a lace collar, pierced by a brooch, she was leaning over the table and discussing something with someone in the first row. To his left sat another woman, skinny, with grey hair combed back smoothly, wearing glasses. She kept looking at her watch and shaking her head at the two empty chairs standing a little to one side.

Zalomin had chosen both these judges himself, considering them to be the most suitable. Lidya Fominichna Rogacheva (the one in glasses), was a former schoolteacher, had pedagogical experience and was known for her strong principles. In fact, Rogacheva believed that strictness was both the basis for teaching and a fundamental of life. Maria

Ignatevna Fedorchuk (the one with the brooch), a former trade union worker in a clothes factory, had acquired the knack of smoothing over everyday squabbles, and although she fussed a bit and tended to chatter, she was known for her goodness and gentleness.

The chairman lifted his head, coughed, preparing to say something, when suddenly a door banged, there was the click of high heels, and Lubka swept on to the stage. Behind her, walking slowly, came her mother, Praskovya Egorovna. The chairman said something inaudible to them, probably telling them off. Lubka moved her chair forward and sat down, almost completely shielding her mother with her body. She took a blue scarf with red poppies from her head, took out a small mirror and calmly began to adjust her hair.

A little hum passed round the room. The chairman announced the opening of the proceedings, introduced the judges and began reading the victims' statement.

Everyone stared at Lubka, they all knew why Lubka had been late. She'd been making herself beautiful. And how! A solid stack of dark ginger hair, obviously dyed; her eyelashes glued together with black, concealing the eyes themselves; her lips smeared a greasy red and her fingernails silver. She was wearing a new flared coat so short as to be ridiculous. She'd got herself up as if for a party. She'd better be careful it didn't turn out to be her funeral! The silly girl would have done better to have washed her face and worn something dark, not flashed her bare knees. What about stockings – was she wearing any? Goodness me, she really should have thought about where she was coming. After all, she was the accused. She really did have a nerve. And she wouldn't change. She deserved everything she got.

So thought many in the room. The majority. Their angry thoughts seemed to gather in a dark cloud filled with spite, to hang over Lubka's head.

But Lubka didn't notice this storm cloud. In a way she

liked sitting there on stage, as if she were in a play. As if she were an actress. It would be nicer still to stand up, walk and turn, like they did in the fashion houses. A manikin, no a meakin, oh, well a model! Even sitting down she was posing, now lifting, now dropping her head, moving her feet in their fashionable high boots with gold decoration. Of course she wasn't posing for these old women filling the room, nor for those behind them, her friends, who knew her so well. No, she was posing for him, that one who didn't seem to be looking her way at all, who sat with his eyes lowered. But she'd noticed that he would appear not to be looking her way and then would suddenly screw up his eyes and have a peep. A-ha!

The neighbours' claims against Lubka and her mother were laid out in the Tenants' Statement, written by the experienced hand of Virepnikov. It talked of the incessant disturbance in the Sapozhnikov's room which annoyed the other residents of the flat, amongst whom there were many of declining years and on a pension, as well as others who were still carrying out their working duties and who needed peace at night as well as at other times of the twenty-four-hour day. The statement was very detailed and listed all the excesses committed by Lubka and her guests in the flat after drinking.

At first the public listened with interest to Lubka's escapades but gradually their attention wandered as they stumbled mentally across incomprehensible words and the idiosyncratic, extravagant style of the statement. Zalomin felt at times that he'd lost his place and was re-reading what he'd already read.

Lubka didn't listen to the Tenants' Statement. She already knew from her preliminary talk with the chairman what she was being accused of. She had admitted that everything written about the noisy gatherings and drinking was true. But nothing about the fellows that were meant to have spent the night there was true. Who had seen them? When? Let them prove it. She felt secure in the knowledge that they couldn't.

When Zalomin got to point 'F' and read:

'. . . some of the guests lock themselves in the bathroom, thus creating obstacles for the proper use of the bathroom for sanitary-hygenic purposes by the basic contingent of tenants . . .' there had developed a soft humming in the room as people conducted their own conversations. Zalomin gazed at the public. The only people paying him any attention were in the first two rows. And even this attention was not concerted. The dark curly head of a young boy and the coloured, woolly hats of two young girls stood out amongst the grey heads and modest hats.

The dark-haired boy had a swarthy face, dark eyes. He seemed uneasy, appeared to find it difficult to sit still and listen. Nevertheless it was vital that he listen carefully. Mikhail Konnikov had been sent here by the Komsomol committee of the light-bulb factory where Lubka worked. The Komsomol organisation had given Mikhail wide ranging powers: if Sapozhnikova was being accused of something serious he was not to fight for her; but if it turned out to be nothing too depraved, then he could plead for her. At first Mikhail had been very attentive, but then, as he was looking at Lubka, his heart suddenly jumped. Now he was trying not to look at Lubka and was concentrating on the toes of his boots which he'd not yet managed to exchange for civilian ones – he'd only recently completed his army service. It was so difficult for him not to look at Lubka that he had to clench his teeth, making two veins stand out on his cheeks which gave his face a cruel look.

The girls in the coloured hats were also rather inattentive, although they'd been invited by Zalomin personally in their capacity as the positive younger element to counter-balance Lubka's evil horde. He hadn't said anything specific to them, but had just ordered them definitely to be there, not to let him down. They couldn't refuse.

The girl wearing a red beret, short haired, pretty, with a dimple in her chin, was staring hungrily at Lubka. Zhenya would have come here even without being invited because she was so interested in this dreadful Sapozhnikova. In her flat they told awful stories about Lubka: she drank, got mixed up with young boys, didn't study and didn't work. She'd been called bad names. The girl was interested in finding out whether this was slander or whether Lubka really was like that. And it wasn't idle curiosity. Zhenya was a serious girl, interested in sociology. Apart from which she had a personal interest in discovering whether a woman could enjoy full sexual freedom.

Zhenya did not intend being a witness. What could she have said? She lived below Lubka's room. She heard Lubka's gramophone thundering out. The tramp of the dancers made the chandelier sway and bits of the ceiling fall down. Sometimes shouts and crashes could be heard – preliminaries to a fight. Neighbours had run to them several times and asked them to call the police. But Zhenya wasn't going to say any of this – let the older ones speak.

She didn't know Lubka and didn't yet understand her. She'd met her a few times on the stairway. Lubka's walk always surprised her: it was pretty and proud, controlled. She held her head high. Swaying slightly, stepping softly. She walked as if dancing. As if she was proud – but of what? Though her figure was excellent, her face was very ordinary, uninteresting: her nose like a button, her eyes small. Or were they just stuck together with mascara? Her legs were slender; they were lovely.

The girl in the red beret gazed calmly at Lubka, steadily, as if looking at an exhibit, and didn't even hear what Zalomin was reading.

The girl in the blue hat sat depressed and timid; she was unattractive with a long nose. Zalomin had said to Ira when he'd invited her: 'Maybe you'll do.' And she had shyly asked what for. Now she was waiting in fear and trembling: suppose they suddenly asked her to come up and say something about herself? Her school reports, her acceptance by the institute. An example to Lubka. They'd gone to the same school, you see, but Ira had stayed on whereas Lubka had left. But she couldn't stand up in front of Lubka, she knew nothing about her, nothing about why she'd left school or what she'd done afterwards. And the girl tried to remember Lubka at school, but couldn't.

Zalomin had finished his reading of the Statement and turned towards Lubka's co-tenants: 'Has anything in this situation changed substantially over the last month?'

Virepnikov got up and said that things were bad. 'You can see,' he said, turning to the judges, 'what kind of people they are. One rarely sees the mother sober. Even now, although in a public place for which one might think she would have a certain respect, she is sleeping perfectly peacefully, quite unconcerned about the threat to her daughter . . .'

Lubka nudged Praskovya gently with her elbow. Praskovya lifted her head and forced her swollen eyes open.

'As for the daughter . . . the daughter, hmm, well, just look at her general appearance, her dissolute character is there before us, for all to see.'

Virepnikov sat down, nudging Rosa Iosofna with his elbow: it was her turn. Lubka was frowning.

'I'm addressing the court, both in a personal capacity and on behalf of the tenants as a whole, in order to say,' Rosa started off boldly, but then suddenly stopped. She'd forgotten. Virepnikov began to prompt her so loudly that everybody could hear: '. . . in order to say – let us henceforth be spared . . .'

But Rosa Iosofna only breathed out three words which were not in the text: 'It's a nightmare!'

Before Rosa had even sat down Old Motya turned round and hissed: 'It's really, honestly, I mean, it's quite disgraceful . . .' Virepnikov coughed – this interjection was not part of the programme. Still, Old Motya would get it right in the end, she knew what she had to say, even if she said it in her own way:

'It's quite disgraceful. My bed is behind their wall, you know. Well, all night there's these bangings and thumpings, you can't get to sleep at all.'

'But she sleeps the whole day anyway,' said Lubka involuntarily.

'That's none of your business,' said Old Motya angrily. 'If I'm retired now, I've earned it, and I have the right to sleep all day *and* all night if I want to. But you always make such a noise—'

'You made enough noise in your day too, Motya, don't be jealous!' shouted out an old man sitting by the gangway, banging his stick maliciously.

Laughter, noise. The young people on the back bench roared appreciatively at this old wit. The chairman banged the top of his carafe furiously:

'Citizens, this is not a circus. You are hindering our work.'

Effalia got up unexpectedly: 'A lot of the people in our flat are noisy, and the television's on well past our bed-time, deep into the night, so it's not just the Sapozhnikovs who annoy people.'

Old Motya tugged at Effalia's coat and sat her down forcefully, whispering hotly into her ear: 'You're sticking up for Lubka! You should be attacking her, not supporting her. Tell them about the chicken.'

'And as for Lubka Sapozhnikova,' continued Effalia calmly, 'well, she gets up to some fine tricks. She often goes too far. For example, she fed my chicken to the cat. That's worth something, half a chicken.'

'Do you mean she stole your chicken?' asked Fedorchuk, forestalling the chairman.

'No, I don't. I mean that she took it out of the pan—'

133

'I didn't,' Lubka jumped up, 'I didn't take it out, I just took the lid off, and the cat did the rest.'

'And who does the cat belong to?' asked Fedorchuk briskly.

'It's hers,' Lubka nodded towards Effalia, 'but she doesn't feed it.'

'So, the chicken was yours and so was the cat,' clarified Fedorchuk, getting into the spirit of legal elucidation.

There were guffaws from the back bench. Once again Zalomin banged his carafe.

'There is too much noise in here,' he said gloomily. 'I would like to point out that the investigation we are conducting here is not at all a matter for levity. It is a very serious matter. It is a question of a young girl's incorrect behaviour. Her life is aimless and thoughtless. Your life is a real mess,' he turned to her, 'it is not at all a pretty sight.'

'Well I think it's very pretty,' muttered Lubka through her nose, but only Rogacheva heard her.

'And your companions, who take part in your all-night parties, they have all abandoned you in your hour of need. Believe me, an older man –'

'Why do you bother trying to convince her,' said Virepnikov angrily, 'She should be hounded out of Moscow and not chatted to like this.'

Zalomin knew that Lubka's life as it now was must come to an end. It was his duty to stop her ruining her life. He was an old worker and a party man; he had been brought up to believe that a Communist will find an answer to everything. He must do something. But what?

The people here expected him to help them by getting rid of Lubka from this apartment block, which meant sending her away from Moscow, far away, uprooting her. Should he fling her out? He could see that people were fed up with the uproarious behaviour of girls like her and wanted nothing more than to get shot of them. He also knew that exile would

134

not save Lubka. In fact she would be lost for ever if she were only to have the company of empty-headed, drunk old women. Zalomin wanted today's investigation to help Lubka understand the seriousness of her position. He had already spoken to her. She'd agreed readily with everything he had said, but he had no doubt that she'd forgotten their conversation just as easily.

Perhaps a judgement by all these people here today, a judgement on Lubka's life, would shake her up a bit and make her think. Zalomin was sorry for her. He was a father and a grandfather, he had daughters and grandchildren. As an old front-line soldier he thought it significant that Lubka was the daughter of a soldier's widow, a woman who seemed permanently scarred by the war, an unmarried mother.

Zalomin wanted to get through to these people. He wanted not only the angry co-tenants to speak, but all those who knew Lubka and her mother. And let her listen to what they said. Furthermore, if anybody had anything positive to say, well and good, let them speak too. Perhaps it would touch some nerve in her, shame her, appeal to her conscience or her pride. So, Zalomin turned to the public and said:

'Comrade Konnikov, who comes from the light-bulb factory where Lubka Sapozhnikova works, will now speak,' and he nodded to Mikhail.

Mikhail got up. He didn't really want to speak. The more he heard, the Statement, the things said by the co-tenants, the more he was convinced that there was no point in trying to defend her. But something prevented him criticising her. Perhaps it was a feeling of his own power, his own firm principles, a feeling of well-being, and the contrast with Sapozhnikova, this ragamuffin, this ignoramus. And then there was her mother . . . Her mother whose head was now resting on her chest – not even anxiety could keep her awake. You had to feel sorry for the girl, even if she was a lunatic.

Zalomin indicated the rostrum. Mikhail drummed out a

few steps – an old habit from his army days – and stopped. He addressed the judges over Lubka's head, without looking at her.

'From the factory's point of view, we have no criticisms of Lubka Sapozhnikova,' Mikhail began. Although his voice came out quite normal and even, he found he had to overcome a strange nervousness. 'She carries out her appointed work satisfactorily, one could even say that she attempts to do it well.'

The last bit was not true. Even Lubka looked at him in amazement. She didn't try at all. As she was unused to getting up early she was lethargic in the morning, tired quickly, and hardly managed to last till lunch-time. After lunch she was good for an hour or two, no more. Then she would begin yawning, stretching her arms, having breaks for a cigarette. Mikhail had been told plainly and flatly to give her another month to see if she got any better. If not, she would have to go.

Confused by his lie, Konnikov added: 'She's only been working for us for three months, a rather short period . . .'

'Does she participate in the factory's social activities?' shouted a woman with a big nose in the front row. Her name was Kukshina and she was an active participant in the comrades' court. She was annoyed with Zalomin for not nominating her as one of the judges in this interesting case; there were so many people present, but she was stuck down below where nobody could see her new fur coat of imitation seal-skin bought in the second-hand shop. And, in addition, and more importantly, she was not able to stop Zalomin from making repeated and obvious mistakes.

'She does not yet participate in our social programme but we are hoping to draw her in.'

This was said with a bit more vigour: Kukshina's brusqueness evoked a desire to contradict and to argue. But to himself Mikhail thought: 'How could you draw someone like her in?' He looked up at Lubka and met her gaze. He saw mockery in her blue, mischievous eyes, but it seemed to caress him, so he was not hurt by it.

'We have a House of Culture for amateur theatricals and all sorts of different groups, Lubka can choose according to her own particular interest.' Mikhail smiled at Lubka and her eyes flashed in return.

'She should go to evening classes, not amateur theatricals,' said Rogacheva sternly. 'After all, she left school at fourteen.'

'We also have a school for young workers. And the Komsomol will undertake to follow this up in relation to Sapozhnikova,' said Mikhail, exceeding all his plenary powers.

'You should take her under your wing yourself,' said Fedorchuk softly; like all women she liked to match-make.

Lubka shrugged. She looked at Mikhail and, catching his eye, poked her pink tongue out at him, and then withdrew it. Mikhail was embarrassed.

'Our girls have already discussed the matter of guidance and we will organise it,' he muttered.

This was not true either. But Mikhail decided that when he gave his report to the Komsomol he would definitely put this point to them.

Zalomin thanked Comrade Konnikov and said that he was free to go. But Mikhail didn't leave. He returned to his seat. Beads of sweat had formed on his forehead. He wanted to get out a handkerchief but he noticed Lubka looking at him and decided not to. She would laugh at him and wonder why the defence was getting all steamed up.

Rogacheva now turned to Lubka. If you leave school early you can expect the worst. Everybody knows that. Rogacheva threw angry questions at Lubka: how was it possible she had not even acquired a standard education? Everybody else had diplomas, training, at all levels, and what did she have. Why had she left school? She must explain.

137

Why? Lubka fluttered her eyelashes. What could she say? She couldn't find the right words . . .

'I didn't want to learn, that's all,' and to underline this she added, 'I can't, I'm thick.'

The back bench hooted approvingly – one in the eye for them!

'It's the teachers who decide what can and can't be done, not the pupils, that's why we have marks and reports. If people fall behind they can be helped. But if you, out of childish stupidity, left school, why didn't your mother do anything? How could she have let you leave school before you'd even finished the third form?'

Lubka glanced at Praskovya who had fallen asleep again and said loudly: 'Wake up! They're asking why you let me leave school.'

Praskovya's cheeks wobbled as she chewed sleepily and said 'What?'

There was laughter in the room. Somebody shouted out: 'Wake up, Mum, or you'll lose your daughter.' Someone else responded, 'She's already lost her.'

Rogacheva continued to talk about the benefit of study, the need for enlightenment and the correctness of the law on universal general education. The talk was highly beneficial for the auditorium, especially for those sat on the back bench. Rogacheva was always generous with words.

Meanwhile Lubka remembered how she had come to leave school.

It was true that she'd found school difficult. Especially in the third form. She couldn't seem to grasp mathematics, physics and chemistry. She couldn't concentrate. She would lose the train of thought and then wouldn't be able to understand. The mathematics teacher wasn't too bad, she would explain after the lesson if some people hadn't been able to solve the problems. And though the physics teacher was really spiteful, still she wasn't the worst. The chemistry teacher was the real pain! An old witch. Terribly pernickety. She persecuted Lubka because she hated her. And she never ever helped her. She would ask her to answer questions more often than the others and set her very difficult problems on purpose.

Then the scandal! It wasn't even really about chemistry. They had a free period near the middle of the day. They were told not to make any noise or disturbance and not to leave the school. Some read, some did their homework, some played at noughts and crosses. Many just wandered round the school.

Lubka left the classroom. Was it because Kolya had left? Did she want to find him – by accident? And she did find him: on the far staircase, the name they gave to that part of the second staircase between the third and fifth floors, shut off from above and therefore unused. He was sitting on the stairs holding a book and pencil.

She was in love for the first time in her life, with Kolya. It was a secret, nobody knew about it, not even him. Lubka's heart raced. She went up to him and stopped. 'What do you want?' he said, irritated. But she wasn't rude, didn't turn on him as she would have done with someone else. She was quiet and sad. 'What are you reading?' she asked softly, 'Show me.' He closed the magazine and showed her the cover: *Science and Life*. My goodness, he was so clever it was frightening. But he laughed, he wasn't reading it, just trying to get out of the labyrinth. 'Out of what?' the word was unfamiliar to Lubka. Kolya moved up, 'Look', and he showed her the drawing: in the centre of a spider-web was a man with a question mark over his head. He was lost and couldn't find the way out and he, Kolya, hadn't found it yet either. Lubka got interested. 'Let me see,' she said, and in three minutes she'd led the man to the exit. Then they looked at another picture: you had to find a hunter, a fox and a wolf in the forest. Lubka did this before Kolya as well. But he solved the crossword. She couldn't get the words at all, she didn't know half of them anyway. Then they found another interesting picture. There were three thieves hidden in a park and the question was, which one would the detective at the entrance to the park find first.

The young girl and boy bent over the pictures. Her soft light-brown hair tickled his cheek. They looked at the pictures for a long time until Kolya's ears and Lubka's cheeks were beginning to burn. Then they heard a shout which made them both jump:

'Why are you hiding here?'

It was the chemistry teacher on school duty.

Lubka and Kolya descended the stairs and stood dejected before her, like accused prisoners.

'Why do you look like that? What have you been up to here?' Kolya showed her the magazine and said that they had been looking at it.

'Looking at the pictures?' The chemistry teacher screwed up her eyes maliciously, 'Well, my little ones, show me.'

All this would have been bearable if she'd left it there, but for some reason she took them to the classroom, opened the door and said: 'This is where you should look at pictures, not in dark corners!'

There were several children in the classroom and they laughed and gossiped about them. The next day somebody had drawn a cartoon on the blackboard of Lubka and Kolya kissing, hiding behind a chemistry textbook. Kolya began to avoid Lubka, turning away from her when their paths crossed and averting his gaze. Lubka was hurt and annoyed. It wasn't her fault. Then she started to tease the boy, looking slyly at him from under her lashes. She would twirl in front of him, sniggering. 'You're behaving like a baby,' he would mutter through his teeth as he passed her. 'So what,' she'd answer, challengingly.

She developed a perfect hatred of the chemistry teacher and of chemistry, along with physics and mathematics. And then Senka from 3A turned up. This Senka was really repulsive, lanky, with a prominent Adam's apple and hands that were always sweaty. He was re-doing a year. At first he just looked at her, then he began to spout rubbish about her being the prettiest girl in the whole school, that he'd met her class when they were leaving the gym and had been bowled over by her figure, that she was a real Brigitte Bardot, that all the lads in the class were in love with her. He blethered on and on, his Adam's apple moving up and down – it was amazing. Lubka stopped avoiding him and began listening to what he said with pleasure. She stopped thinking how horrible he was. 'So, I'm a baby am I,' she said to herself, 'well, I treat this one really badly, but he still keeps coming after me.'

It ended badly. Senka had somehow persuaded her to go to a party. There were five boys and four girls from the third year. The fifth was Lubka, Senka's partner. The girls bought fruit juice, but the boys had wine. They drank, danced and played forfeits, with bottles of wine as prizes. Senka always chose her. And then they found themselves in a small room where they'd left their coats. The room was dark, cramped and stuffy. Senka pressed Lubka's lips to his and squeezed her so hard that she couldn't move. At first she tried to push him away, to get away herself, but then she relaxed, moaned softly and weakened.

So Senka became her 'first'. He would make excuses to come and see her, saying that he'd help her with her mathematics, waiting for the chance. She never loved him. On the contrary, he always repulsed her.

One morning Lubka woke up filled with such hatred that she found herself saying aloud: 'Damn you, damn you!' She decided there and then that it had to finish. She would never give way to him again, she wouldn't see him any more. She didn't go to school, but he came to see her after school. She sent him away: 'Don't ever come back again. I hate you. You haven't a hope. I hate you, do you understand? I H-A-T-E Y-O-U!'

But he did come back. She shouted at him, snatched a plastic breadboard from the table and flung it at his face. She broke his nose. She wanted to kill him. 'You'll be sorry,' he honked, and ran off.

Soon whispers started in school. Whispers and jokes. The whisperings encircled Lubka like flies. They were born and multiplied. They buzzed in her ears, rustled behind her back and under her feet like dry leaves.

Then one sunny winter's day as Lubka was leaving school with her friends, some older boys, Senka's mates, showered her with streams of foul abuse and obscene jokes.

Lubka choked with anger: she went up to the boys and lifted her satchel to hit them. She didn't know which one of the three she was aiming at, she wanted to knock out all three. They guffawed; two of them got hold of her hands while the third seized her satchel and shuffled round the room with it, hunched up and repeating in a squeaky voice: 'Don't hang around with boys, don't hang around with boys, or your Mum will give you what for . . .'

The boys went on jeering at Lubka while she pulled and kicked, now surrounded by other boys and girls, all standing as if rooted to the spot, just staring, until a loud voice shouted:

'Stop that this minute.'

It was the P.E. teacher, moving menacingly towards the boys. They chucked Lubka's satchel onto the stage and ran off. She stood there, dishevelled, pathetic. The teacher approached her and said something. His lips moved, he spoke, but she didn't hear a word. Then she started to run. Somebody shouted something behind her, someone tried to catch her up, to give her back her satchel, but she rushed on headlong, without seeing or hearing. She ran all the way to her block, up the staircase to the flat, along the corridor to her room. She crept under the bed and lay pressed to the wall, like a beaten dog, for a very long time.

She didn't go to school the next day, nor for two days

142

after that. Then she was called there, together with her mother. Lubka said to Praskovya:

'You can beat me to death, but I'm not going, I'm not going to school any more.'

Praskovya didn't insist: school learning seemed to her a difficult wisdom, she herself had only had one year of secondary education.

'Maybe Lubka takes after me,' she thought, 'why force her?'

And thus Lubka's 'learning' came to an end.

Rogacheva had finished. Zalomin asked if anyone else wanted to speak.

'What for? Let's finish now,' squeaked an old voice. Zalomin remembered that this was a sitting of the comrades' court and not a general tenants' meeting.

'Well, I'm asking if anyone has anything else to say about Lubka Sapozhnikova? I would also like to hear the views of our younger comrades.' Zalomin looked at the girls in the front row, but they lowered their eyes.

'Lubka Sapozhnikova is good,' cried out a young boy's thin voice from the back bench.

People turned round, laughter broke out, somebody whistled. The back bench squeaked as those piled on top of it pushed forward a small youth of about fourteen. He stood there, bullish, his fur hat pressed to his chest, his cheeks flushed.

'Shut up, Puziryev,' shouted Lubka, standing up, 'I didn't ask you to –'

'What's his name?' Zalomin asked Lubka.

'Yury Puziryev. He's just a child,' said Lubka, as if excusing the boy's behaviour.

'Well, Yury Puziryev, if you want to say something to the point say it but come over here and speak loudly and clearly, so that everybody can hear.'

'Why should we listen to him,' somebody grumbled, 'he should be sent home.'

'Well, I think we should let him talk, and then send him home.'

'I'm sixteen years old,' Yury interrupted, coming up to the stage.

'All right, all right, we're waiting.'

'I said that Lubka is a good person.'

'All right! We've heard that already. Give us some facts.'

Zalomin felt uncomfortable at having dragged the youth to the front. Of course it was irregular. But having just invited young people to step forward and speak he didn't want to frighten them away. He heard Kukshina's spiteful rumblings: 'This isn't a kindergarten . . . He doesn't know how to keep order . . .' But Zalomin wanted some extenuating factors for the girl. If these did exist, then let everybody hear them, including, most importantly, the girl herself.

Yury coughed and began, now losing his thread, now searching for the right word:

'She's good, she cares for people. It was winter time and freezing. Thirty degrees below. She let me stay the night—'

Laughter erupted in the hall.

'She found a fine one to spend the night with!' wheezed the old man with the stick through tears and coughs.

Zalomin got up and banged the carafe angrily. He noticed that Lubka looked distressed now, tense and pale.

'My father had flung me out of the house,' continued Yury. 'It was late evening. I wanted, well, I wanted to die. Not because he'd flung me out, but because . . . because it's so bad at home, because of certain things . . . Well, so anyway, I sat at the entrance, on the staircase that leads up to Lubka's flat and I thought about what it would be like – dying I mean . . .'

Again giggles. Again Zalomin rang the carafe top.

'It was night-time, everybody was asleep. I wanted to ring

144

Lubka's bell, but I was scared of the other tenants, they're very nasty. Then suddenly Lubka came up the stairs with—' Yury stumbled and was silent.

'Go on, go on,' said Zalomin encouragingly.

Lubka, frowning, turned to Puziryev and hissed something.

'– with Avanze. That's Avanze there,' Yury waved his hand towards two handsome dark boys of identical face and height, twins, sitting behind him. One of them said something inaudible and spat.

'And Lubka sat beside me and comforted me. And then she said: "Come into the flat, you can spend the night there. You'll freeze to death here." She sent Avanze away. And then she gave me something to eat and made me a bed on the floor. And the next morning she gave me five roubles and said: "Give this to your stepmother, but make sure your father's there when you do it," so the trouble at home blew over, because of that five roubles . . .'

'When are you going to shut up!' groaned Lubka.

'You see, she's really good,' Yury finished, almost inaudibly.

'There you are! There you are!' Virepnikov jumped to his feet, 'She brings men home to her place, she spends the night with them—'

'I never ever spent the night with her!' shouted out the dark boy from the back bench.

'Maybe you didn't, but others did,' screamed Virepnikov, and turned to Zalomin: 'You see the corruption that is taking place? This deserves immediate exile from Moscow in accordance with article . . .' Virepnikov began to fumble in his pocket, looking for the necessary paper, but Zalomin did not let him continue and called for order.

The dark boy who'd shouted that he'd never spent a night with Lubka sat down muttering 'cretin!' through his teeth.

This was aimed at Puziryev. Really, why go into all these drivelling stories here, of all places?

What was the point? They would get her under a certain article and then hand her over to a real court. His father had said so; he was here, by the way. The first time they'd rowed he'd said that this court wouldn't be able to deal with Lubka and they would have to transfer this case to a people's court in order to be able to send her off to the tundra. And this would have to be done quickly, while she wasn't working, before she gained certain rights – he was sure of this, and so was someone more powerful than himself, he'd said to his mother – Avanze had eavesdropped on their conversation by mistake.

Avanze had rushed to Lubka and told her what he'd heard. His father had discussed it with a lawyer, so that meant that it was definite.

Lubka had taken his news calmly: 'So what? I'll go to the tundra then. It'll be interesting. I'll see the keepers riding the deer. I'll fall in love all covered in furs.'

Avanze didn't want Lubka to go away. It was the beginning of summer. He and Lubka were starting a love affair. He'd been jealous of his brother, Archik, and had ordered Lubka to be faithful. But she had just laughed, deliberately teasing him. At parties she would kiss Archik and say: 'Oh, dear, I keep getting you two mixed up.' Lubka would drive the passionate Avanze to wild fury. She would go around, covered in bruises, laughing. And you never knew with her what was real and what was just a game.

And then everything ended. Lubka moved on to another fellow – Pashka the boxer, strong as a horse and with a face like a gargoyle. There was no point in moaning; according to Lubka's rules, if you didn't like it, cheerio, you needn't come to her parties any more. Archik made fun of him, 'Haven't you got over her yet?' Archik was right, you don't fall in love with people like Lubka. So, hiding his love he overcame those

146

stupid feelings and continued to go to Lubka's parties. There was no point in depriving himself of all the fun. 'Well, do boys spend the night at her place or not?' thought Maya, a slim girl and part of Lubka's circle, listening to the screams and yells of Virepnikov and Avanze. The answer would appear to be in the affirmative: they did spend the night there, but there was no absolute proof. 'Did they spend the night there or not?' It was not only a question of Maya's burning curiosity about the unknown, the tempting, it was also about something else: Maya understood perfectly that the fate of Lubka's parties depended on the clarification of this question, and she was very well disposed towards these parties. Not only because of the boys, not only because of Archik, with whom she thought she was in love, but because she was interested in Lubka. Lubka was always thinking up extraordinary things to do. So, although Maya's parents had strictly forbidden her to visit Lubka, she went there, secretly, all the same.

And the parties . . . Lubka's game of lottery, for example, where the boys raffled girls or girls raffled boys. Or the fortune-telling with a saucer: the saucer really did answer questions, well, of course, it wasn't really the saucer that answered but the spirit which they called up, the spirit of a famous dead person – it had to be a real person, not someone thought up. Maya believed in the spirits because what they said came true. They had proved it already. They had called up the Empress Catherine the Great, and she had forecast that Maya would get a beating. Maya had never been beaten in her whole life. But her father had come home drunk and her mother, stupidly, had blurted out that Maya had been to Lubka's. Her father had taken off his belt and carted her off like a small child, although her mother had grasped his arm and shouted out at the top of her voice, 'Murderer!' So, it had come true. And Lalka's had come true as well. General Kutuzov had forecast that something improper would happen

147

to her, and it had, in the queue at GUM's* when she was waiting for some boots. One of the great Russian writers, Maya had forgotten which one, had forecast that gipsies would steal Lubka away. This, of course, hadn't happened. Lubka wasn't a child, and, anyway, gipsy bands no longer existed. But this mistake by one of the spirits hadn't shaken Maya's confidence in them in general – they shouldn't have asked a writer anyway, it was well known they all lied.

A pale hand was raised in the middle of the room. An old woman stood up, her head trembling. In a weak voice she asked permission to speak from her place:

'I would like to say something about this girl. I am a former teacher. I use the same entrance. Well, in summer, not this summer, but in general, every summer, for many years in a row—'

'She's confused,' thought Zalomin, 'what does she want?'

'– every summer, in the burning heat and dust, when I went out of the building I would see this girl, playing on the pavement. First when she was little, then as she gradually got bigger. With a doll, toys, or drawing with chalk. All the other children were away at dachas, in the country, or at pioneer camps, but Lubka was always there, on the hot asphalt . . .' And the old woman sat back on the bench without having said anything at all relevant. Not many people had heard what she'd said, and those who had didn't understand: what had summer, asphalt and the heat got to do with anything?

'May *I* speak, please?' Kukshina cried out furiously, as if she'd been trying to say something for a long time, 'I would like to clarify one important point.' Kukshina pointed her index finger at Lubka. 'Answer me this, please: *we* are building Communism, what are *you* doing?'

*GUM: 'State Department Store' – the biggest department store in Moscow, where you can get almost anything, located in Red Square.

148

Lubka looked confused and shrugged her shoulders: 'Well, I'm not stopping you building Communism. Go ahead.'

Voices rang out from the floor:

'What do you mean, you're not stopping us? The point is precisely that you are!'

But Kukshina heard neither Lubka's reply nor the other responses: 'So we build while people like you – you just want everything on a plate.'

Zalomin interrupted Kukshina – it was an incorrect formulation, he said, it was demagogy, it was quite wrong to use Communism to frighten people. Furthermore, it was a red herring. Kukshina, growling with frustration, sat down.

Those on the back bench responded vigorously to every utterance and were openly enjoying themselves. Only Valka took no part in the general uproar, made no witty asides, no guffaws, no digging his pals in the ribs. He constantly looked at Lubka, sometimes listening, sometimes not. He didn't know exactly what this court could do to Lubka, but he had heard that it threatened her and he was afraid. Supposing they really did fling her out of Moscow and sent her to the North?

If Valka had been healthy like Pashka, or handsome like Avanze, he would have been neither afraid nor sad. Then, if they made her go away he could have followed her, 'I ask for your hand and your heart and in return I will give you my whole self,' or something like that. Or more simply, from his heart: 'I cannot live one day without you.'

But Valka was a freak: he was lame, he stuttered and his ears stuck out like the handles of a sugar bowl. His face had no redeeming features. In Lubka's company he was strong, he was respected because he was a musician. He played the accordion and the guitar, and he could play by ear and even compose words himself.

He'd never touched Lubka in his life. He suffered silently

when the boys played with her or when, teasingly, she kissed them, one after the other.

Valka knew that he would never be burned by Lubka's kiss. Their hearts would never leap and run together, like stars in the night sky. But he was a real, true friend to her. Perhaps she had never thought about this, but she'd admitted to him alone that she'd lied about the ballet, she had never learnt ballet, just seen different dances on television and the cinema and had copied them. She picked things up quickly. So Valka comforted himself with this friendship, for you only tell secrets to true friends.

And Valka could compose songs about her, which the others couldn't. And even here, at times, everything faded away, the benches with the old women, the judges behind their table, the words, the laughter, the noise, and music took over; a lively little song about his, Valka's, sad fate:

> Oh little Lubka I love you so,
> Did you know?
> Oh little Lubka,
> With skirts so short,
> With legs that dance
> And entrance.
> Oh little Lubka,
> With skirts so short,
> And heels so tall,
> Who will love you more than me?
> No one at all.

It was difficult for him to look at Lubka when she was dancing – with someone else. She would never dance with him. Or when she organised her 'American' performance he'd forgotten what exactly it was called. Waves flowed through Lubka's body from her neck to her toes; her hands swayed like seaweed in a river; every vein danced in her, responding to the music. She had her eyes closed, forgetting everything and everybody. They were all going crazy about her. In the end someone rushed up to her and she ran off, angry. She complained for a long time after that about the person who'd disturbed her.

And he, Valka, had had to change the records on the gramophone and direct the light on to her – now red, now yellow and now green – from the old war lantern, booty left here a long time ago by one of Praskovya Egorovna's guests.

Did the boys realise how beautiful Lubka was? To look at she wasn't particularly pretty. But when she stood up, lifted her arms . . . beautiful, beautiful! How did it go?

Short skirts,
tall heels – no laughing heels.
Vitechka chased Lubka,
Grishenka chased Lubka,
Vanechka chased Lubka,
And Valka the fool . . .
Valka could see that Lubka was beautiful – could they?

And there was Pashka making cows' eyes at that midget, Lalka-the-gun. She was blushing, all afire, jumping up, sitting down, grasping his shoulder. Archik had his eyes shut as if sleeping, but was really quietly gazing at Maya from under his eyelashes. Maya had hidden her face in her coat collar, but she knew that Archik was looking at her and she suddenly blushed, like an early dawn. Avanze was frowning, he was angry with Puziryev.

Valka-the-all-seeing, all-knowing, about everybody and everything.

Pashenka chased Lubenka,
Grishenka chased Lubenka,
And Valka, the fool . . .

And then the guitar: ta-ta-ta-tam, ta-ta-ta-tam, tam-tam, ta-ta-ta-tam. The music played inside Valka and splashed at

Lubka's feet, it washed over her and lifted her up, it carried Lubka away on its waves. Only Lubka knew nothing of this.

More pensioner-activists spoke. They condemned Lubka, said she should be ashamed of herself, tried to awake her conscience and called upon her to mend her ways. Some addressed themselves to Praskovya Egorovna: the mother was responsible for the daughter. True, the daughter was now eighteen, but everybody knew that she'd gone astray a long time ago. Where had the mother been then? Why hadn't she been looking after her?

When they spoke to her mother Lubka would nudge her gently. And Praskovya would wake up and take part in the discussion: 'Yes, yes . . . of course . . . It's your right . . . What should I do, then?'

'That shashlik shop has addled her brains completely,' thought Zalomin. She just about managed to keep afloat in her sea of troubles, but any little push and she would go under completely and without a struggle.

Well, it was time to end the proceedings, it was late. They had enough facts. Many people, not only the co-tenants, had had their say. Still, Zalomin had a strange feeling that something important had been left undone and unsaid.

When the old teacher spoke he'd remembered two things. Once, on a summer's day about three years ago, as he was passing the building where the Sapozhnikovs lived, he'd seen two young girls at an open window on the first floor. One, blonde, lay across the window-sill, her dishevelled head resting on her crossed arms. The other, small and dark-haired, sat with her knees drawn up under her chin. Both of them were practically naked. The sun beat down on them with its hot rays.

'Hey, old man!' they shouted, 'come and sunbathe with us!'

Zalomin raised his head and shook his fist at them.

152

'Oh, look how old he is!' they screeched, 'Don't threaten us, old man, we don't need you after all!'

'The cheeky monkeys,' thought Zalomin, as he went on home. They certainly were cheeky, but they amused him more than they annoyed him.

The other incident was more serious. It happened last autumn, at the end of September. The weather was still warm. He and his wife had gone for a walk before bed. It was a pleasant evening, but already getting fresher. It was about ten o'clock and the street lamps were lit. There were a lot of people out on the main street; it had become the custom for older people to have a little walk before turning in, to fill their lungs with fresh air.

Suddenly Zalomin noticed a crowd around a bench. Surely they weren't still playing dominoes? He told his wife he was just going to pop over and have a look (she walked slowly because of her legs). As he approached he saw that it was Lubka, sprawled in a sitting position on the bench, asleep; her cheek was resting on the back of the bench and she was gradually slipping off the edge. The people standing around her made many comments:

'She's drunk, you can smell the wine.'

'We should call the police.'

'Why, what harm has she done you?'

'Maybe she's ill.'

'Hey, miss, wake up.'

'Leave her alone.'

Zalomin went up to Lubka and shook her by the shoulder. She opened her eyes and sat up:

'Leave me alone! I won't go, I tell you, I won't go, go away!'

Zalomin did not leave her alone: 'Get up. Get up, it's late, it's time to go home, it's dark . . .' Lubka pushed his hand away and swore.

'Hey, leave the girl alone,' said a young man with a pregnant woman on his arm.

'You ought to be ashamed of yourself, you're old enough to

153

be her father,' squeaked a little, lop-sided old woman.

It was just as well that his wife came up and said, 'Lubka, let us help you, it's late, get up, let's go.' Lubka gave in. The two of them started to take her home, and for a long time they were followed by a shrill, irritating voice, ringing in their ears:

'They have all these children and then let them run completely wild. Then, suddenly remember them again too late and come and take them home!'

When Zalomin had first summoned Lubka, because of the Statement of the Co-Tenants, he'd reminded her of this incident. She'd said it was no big deal: she'd gone to the café with two chaps, not exactly strangers but not good friends either. They'd mixed their drinks and, of course, there's nothing worse than that. When they'd left they wanted to drag her off somewhere, but she wanted to go home. There'd been a bit of an altercation, she'd sworn at them, they'd left, and that was that, she'd got tired.

Zalomin hadn't spoken about this chapter from Lubka's life here, perhaps it had slipped his mind, perhaps he had wanted not to remember: there was enough to criticise here without that.

Lubka was tired of sitting down and tired of listening. She no longer felt like an actress on a stage – she really wanted to get up and go. But that was impossible. Only her thoughts could wander at will, and she suddenly remembered something that was nothing to do with anything, something interesting, funny.

On Fridays Lubka and Praskovya always went to the Chernishevsky Public Bath House. Praskovya loved going there and always washed herself carefully and thoroughly. Lubka had been going since she was a small child and enjoyed it too. She felt renewed on these evenings.

Last Friday, leaving the soaping-up room behind her

mother, Lubka lingered by a darkened mirror on the way to the dressing room: she looked at herself, astonished – it was her and not her. Her rosy body, washed clean till it hurt, shone with trembling, transparent drops. Her knees, feet, ears, cheeks, all burned with a scarlet flame. Lubka lifted her hand and ran it along her wet hair, drawn back from the forehead to the nape. She touched the tight bun, pinned up with two hairpins, and grinned – she looked like a real peasant. But she suddenly became transfixed with horror; goosepimples ran over her body. Beside her shining pink-and-white reflection had appeared the image of a bony old woman with wrinkled hanging breasts, bluish skin and crooked joints. Her balding grey head shook, and she gazed at Lubka with little black eyes. Then the sunken mouth opened and the old woman said in a hoarse voice: 'Admiring your beauty?' And Lubka had recognised the old bath-house keeper.

'No, because I'm not beautiful,' she had replied simply.

'Not beautiful, but tasty,' smirked the old woman, and pulled at a little cord round her neck connected to a little water-proof bag hidden under her arm. She took out a cheap cigarette and lighter:

'Doesn't your husband love you?'

Lubka was about to say that she wasn't married when the old woman added:

'You'll have an easy birth, my dear. And the first one will be a boy. You'll see and you'll remember me. But don't tell anyone, say nothing, or it won't happen. Can you keep it a secret?' She turned round then and went into the soaping-up room.

Lubka was still smiling at the old bath keeper's crystal-gazing as she went into the dressing room. And although she thought briefly: 'That's all I need, to have a baby, that would really finish me off,' this was just what everybody said, and secretly the idea of having a baby appealed to her.

When Praskovya asked, 'What is it?' Lubka answered: 'Nothing. We're nice and clean now.'

A loud, sonorous baritone brought Lubka back to the court. A portly man with greying hair, the father of Avanze and Archik Stupanyan, was talking:

'Those merry little parties in Flat No. 30 are the scourge of our life. They attract young people from the whole block, they lead them astray, make their heads whirl. That young boy, he's not fourteen yet and he's already going to her place . . .'

'She won't let me in!' cried Yury desperately, betraying himself. He was sitting on the floor, hidden from Zalomin.

'He should be doing his homework,' continued Stupanyan calmly, 'but instead he's playing at counsel for the defence, and you, Comrade Zalomin, allow him to. He should be tied to the table . . .'

'Why don't you tie your own boys to the table?' asked a voice from the floor.

'I can't restrain my boys at all, they're going to the dogs, and your children are as well. Children of eighteen and children as young as fourteen. You can hear how they're dying to get over to her place!' He turned to Lubka with a half bow, 'They're all planning to pay you a visit.'

It seemed to Lubka that he wouldn't have minded paying her a visit himself if it hadn't been for his sons. She grinned.

'There's nothing to smile at, Comrade Lubka. We parents of growing boys are tormented by anxiety. And it's easy to understand why: you are distracting them when they should be studying. And so I beg of you, Comrade Judges, to remove Lubovna Ivanovna Sapozhnikova from our housing authority area and transfer her to another, more remote part of the Soviet Union, and I hope that I will be supported by other parents in this. It will be better for her as well, she can get down to work, think things out and start a new life. I personally am ready to participate directly in the action – I have certain connections in this administration which I trust will be of some help to us.'

*   *   *

For the first time in the whole evening Lubka felt afraid. She felt a breath of cold wind, whether from the tundra or the taiga she couldn't tell. That fat old man, ransacking her with his eyes, with a kindly expression, had turned out to be evil and cruel. He was ready to fling her out like a useless object, like an old rag. He hadn't said where he wanted to send her but he obviously had somewhere in mind, and, most frightening of all, he knew *how* to get her exiled.

Lubka wanted to cry. But she was sitting her in full view of everyone, in this high place, under a bright light: she mustn't cry.

A hundred eyes looked at Lubka. And they were not kind. The pale faces turned towards her were lit by no warmth or sympathy.

Konnikov, the one from the factory, would look anxiously at her now and then. Lubka didn't know what was worrying him: was it Stupanyan's speech, her possible fate, or was he sorry that he'd been so soft?

The only warmth came from her mother's breath, smelling of wine and old tobacco smoke, on the back of Lubka's neck. But this warm breath couldn't defend Lubka as it had done when she was small, it couldn't shield her from the fierce winds. In fact the opposite was the case; the deeper her mother slept, the deeper she breathed, the more lonely and defenceless Lubka became.

And what about the back bench – her friends, her companions? No warmth came to her from that direction either, they'd forgotten her. Lalka had narrowed her eyes, her head was lying on Pashka's shoulders; Maya had hidden her face behind her coat collar, but her eyes stared fixedly out at anything of interest. Archik and Avanze were sitting with their heads lowered and their ears burning. Only Valka and Puziryev were goggling at her.

Yes, indeed, they had forgotten her. They gave her no

support. She was just entertaining them, as usual. Silently the cries came to her: 'Come on, Lubka, come on! Show us a bit of class, Lubka!'

Swallowing her tears Lubka frowned and pulled up her chin. That's right, no crying! Not here, in front of them.

The girl in the red hat put her hand up: perhaps she hadn't wanted to speak before, perhaps she'd just thought of something. She didn't know herself why she'd put it up. She'd already got everything that she had come here for. She'd answered the main question: Sapozhnikova is not the way people say she is, not in the scientific sense. She is simply a little wild and undisciplined.

She, Zhenya Gornastayeva, was self-disciplined whereas Lubka Sapozhnikova was not. But now other thoughts were bubbling inside her, bubbling inside her and raising her hand up.

'I believe,' said Zhenya firmly, 'that people have the right to dispose of their lives as they wish. Of course, I agree that they should not impinge upon the lives of those around them. But should people be harmed, should they be destroyed? Two mature men,' she looked first at Virepnikov and then at Stupanyan, 'have cried out: "Get rid of her! Remove her!" How can you? And why should your sons, two strapping lads, need saving from Sapozhnikova and not the other way around?' Before sitting down the girl looked angrily at Stupanyan.

'Well done!' someone cried out. And this was immediately answered by another voice, 'They must be pals.'

Stupanyan had noticed the young girl with the beguiling dimple on her chin earlier and thought: 'Well, of course, she's a bad lot, but quite pretty.'

Although everybody was looking at her, few saw that Lubka was terrified, that she was blinking to hold back her tears and that her lips were trembling. Only those, listening to Stupanyan with alarm, who had thought, 'That's it, the girl's done for,' saw this.

Among those few were Misha Konnikov and Zalomin.

Zalomin had just got up to say his bit and then to announce a break when an old woman in a black scarf got up from the middle of the hall:

'I would like to say something,' she wiped her mouth with the back of her hand: 'Lubka is a good girl, just a bit wild.'

The hall livened up, there was laughter. But the old woman hadn't meant to be funny. She went on:

'She *is* a good girl. She used to play above my window with her skipping-rope when she was thirteen or more; we were still living in the basement then, before they moved us. I said to her, "Look, love, you're stopping the sun coming in, move over a bit." She did. And then she bought me a bit of poplar. I said to her, "This isn't much use to me. If you want to help you can take these two bottles back to the dairy and bring me back some milk." She did. Then I said to her "Thank you my dear. You will be my lucky charm," and she said to me, I can still remember it, "I don't want to be your lucky charm, I'll be your good ferry." '

'Not ferry, fairy.' Lubka smiled at that warm, far-off day which this old woman had suddenly brought back. 'It's in the children's stories, you have good fairies.'

'Call it what you want, it means the same thing. Anyway, she ran errands for me until I got better. So, she's a good girl. Write it down, so it's there in black and white. And now, love, if you've been doing something wrong, well, pull yourself together, start again. Excuse me, if I don't speak properly.'

The old woman bowed and sat down.

Zalomin got up: 'Comrades, it's time to finish. Before the court confers while you have a break I would like to say a few words—'

He now knew much more about Lubka's life and Lubka

herself than he had before this hearing: the girl had grown up without any guidance or even supervision. Her mother was careless and irresponsible. She had not fought for Lubka to continue at school. Those surrounding her, including her co-tenants, were unconcerned and uninvolved; they'd known more than anybody else about the family situation of the Sapozhnikov's but had never intervened to help in any way. Of course, the mother was mainly to blame, but the daughter had now come of age and would have to answer for her own actions.

'When you come of age in our society you are accorded full rights as a citizen of that society,' Zalomin said, 'and you are ensured the necessary conditions for a normal, reasonable life. In return, however, the state asks its citizens to work for the common good, to live honestly and with dignity, without hindering the work of those around you, without being selfish.'

He wanted to hear what Lubka Sapozhnikova would say now. The sentence that would be passed upon her by this court would partly depend on her own attitude to everything that she'd heard here. She would have to show whether she'd understood it or not and the conclusions that she'd drawn from it.

Zalomin sat down, dissatisfied with himself. It was always the same: when you were thinking you found the necessary words, rough, biting, strong and memorable. But when you stood up and spoke they came out evenly, smoothly, ready formed, like on the radio. The right thoughts don't come out. It's not that bad thoughts do, but the words come out brightly wrapped and do not move people or touch their hearts.

Zalomin nodded to Lubka – you may speak.

Lubka didn't know what to say. It was all right for those who had practice in public speaking, but she might as well burst into song. She got up unwillingly. Well, what had she

160

understood, what conclusions could she draw? She was in a fix, and she was terrified, for herself and for her mother. It was only here that she'd realised what danger she and her mother were in.

'I don't know how to speak,' she said angrily to Zalomin.

Fedorchuk jumped to her feet: 'Surely you understand that you are a nuisance to your neighbours? Are you going to stop those parties and all the other disgraceful goings on in your flat, or not? Are you going to let older people live in peace? Perhaps you could even offer to apologise to your neighbours! Well, we're waiting for an answer!'

'We don't need her apologies,' hissed Virepnikov.

'They don't need my apologies,' said Lubka. 'Well, we won't make a noise any more – after midnight. And, mmm, there won't be anything, hmm, bad going on in the flat.'

'And are you going to stop your drinking as well?' shouted a voice from the hall.

'I don't know about the drinking . . . I can't really promise. My mother drinks.'

'Ah-ha!' cried somebody triumphantly.

Zalomin banged on the table and got up angrily. Sapozhnikova had spoken badly. It would have been better if she'd kept silent. Either she really didn't understand anything, or she was playing the fool. He announced a break and the members of the court went out through a side door into a small room to confer.

The public stirred and got up noisily moving in two streams. One, the biggest, made for the exit: the old people were tired, they wanted their supper and their bed. As for the sentence, they could find that out tomorrow. The smaller stream flowed towards the stage for better seats.

Those on the back bench got up to shake themselves, to relax noisily, to exchange a witticism with Lubka.

Lubka got up, stretching like a cat with a gentle arching of her back. She shook her mother lightly by the shoulders and went to the back of the stage.

Mikhail got up to speak to Lubka as well. He walked forward a few paces, still not sure whether to or not, but when he lifted his head he saw only Praskovya Egorovna on the stage. Lubka had disappeared.

Lubka had noticed a little passage behind the wooden wings. She slipped into it and found herself in a kind of storeroom with a table piled high with scraps of cardboard and covered in bits of old glue and paint. A jam-jar full of cigarette ends stood on the table with a matchbox beside it. Lubka perched on the edge of the table – here she was alone, out of sight. She sat swinging one leg, her thoughts wandering; well, they weren't proper thoughts, more images.

She groped in the jam-jar, found one of the bigger cigarette ends; she went through the spent matches, found a good one, struck it, inhaled once or twice, and began silently to breathe out smoke.

It would be nice to go away somewhere. Far away. Somewhere not cold, warm, by the sea. The Far East, maybe? The very furthest east. Japan would be even better. In Japan she could work as a geisha girl: she could sing, dance and play. They didn't know here how she could dance; how she could shake her shoulders and chest like a gipsy, or smoothly twist her head from side to side, like an Indian dancer . . . She imagined the Japanese women with their narrow eyes, towers of hair, coloured like butterflies in their elegant, strange robes. And all around there would be little trees, flowers, small houses, like toys. You would sit in that little house and wave a fan to cool yourself. Lubka had seen all this in old magazines a long time ago which had lain in heaps in the larder beside the kitchen when Rosa Yosefna had a dentist's work-room. Lubka would take piles of them to her room and look through them, breathing in the smell of dust and yellowed paper.

No, she couldn't go anywhere. How would she leave her mother? Who would undress her and put her to bed each night after she'd staggered home from the shashlik café? She ended her shift there near midnight. When she'd cleared away the mountains of dirty dishes she could get a full measure from the dregs of the wine and brandy glasses. It would have everything in it: vodka, beer, cognac, champagne, Georgian wine, fortified wine, dry wine, sweet wine – a united cocktail.

No, Lubka could not abandon her mother. Here they cursed and laughed at Praskovya. This hurt Lubka deeply and made her very sad. Praskovya wasn't really bad. She'd never hurt Lubka, never sworn or shouted at her. She'd never punished her – well, only once. Just once.

She'd been eight years old. It was winter, already dark. Lubka had finished her homework, had put it neatly away and was playing in the corner with her dolls. Praskovya was doing her hair and putting on a nylon blouse and high-heeled shoes. Lubka knew what this meant but kept on hoping that her mother wouldn't send her out for a walk. She was very quiet in her corner and even spoke silently to her doll. Nobody went for walks at this time of night, especially when it was below freezing. Lubka really didn't want to go out.

But her mother was already saying: 'Get your coat on, Lubka love, go and get some fresh air.' Lubka pretended that she hadn't heard. Her mother brought her things to her, her little fur coat and her hat. Praskovya began to put them on her. Lubka stood there unmoving, her hands and arms stiff, not saying a word. Her mother began to get angry, to pull and tug at her. Lubka scowled and pulled her head down between her shoulders, then deliberately went all limp so that her mother couldn't put her outdoor clothes on. Her mother managed to force her into the coat but before she'd buttoned it up a man in a fur jacket arrived. He pulled out a wrapped-up bottle from his pocket and slammed it on the table. 'And who is this? Your little girl? Have a sweet, dear.' He opened a paper bag and brought out a brightly wrapped sweet. Lubka sulked; she wouldn't take it. 'Never mind, she can have it later,' her mother said, and pushed her towards the staircase.

There were no other children in the yard outside at all. Lubka stood in the snow and looked up at the bright windows. Glass lamps in shades of orange and blue burned behind them. Flowers showed green on the ledge between the double panes, together with pots and pans and milk bottles. Life continued on its quiet way behind those windows. Men and women and children would move back and forwards behind the glass panes. Mothers, grannies, even fathers lived in this block. They were warm while she was cold. Her mother didn't care about her, she'd forced her out into the ice and snow. Lubka picked up a bit of snow with her mittened hand from a ledge and began to lick it. The snow was old and didn't taste nice, permeated as it was with the soot and dust of the town. Lubka hoped she would catch a cold.

'You'll catch a cold, child!' said a woman with a rubbish bin in her hand. 'What are you doing here? It's past nine o'clock. Go home.'

'I don't want to,' said Lubka, 'There's a man with my Mummy. I don't like him.'

The woman studied Lubka silently and then said: 'Well, come to my flat then. You can have some tea and biscuits to warm you up.'

Lubka nodded and followed her. The woman lived in a flat in the same block but with a different entrance, the one next to theirs. She wore glasses and looked like the woman who'd sat next to the chairman.

Lubka's neighbour sat her at the table, poured her out a cup of tea, put three lumps of sugar in it, and placed a little bowl with biscuits beside her. Then she sat opposite her. Lubka drank the tea, smacking her lips and breathing heavily as she did so. The neighbour asked her lots of questions: where did her mummy work? Did her mummy often have visitors? And did she often send Lubka out for walks at night?

Warmth spread through Lubka together with a sense of well-being. The tea was hot and sweet, the biscuits plentiful. The lady was speaking to her as if she were grown-up, as if she were a proper guest. Lubka liked being a guest, people asked her questions and listened to her answers. She was angry with her mummy, and she wanted to please this nice lady. She exaggerated things. The lady oohed and aahed and clapped her hands. And the more horrified she became the more Lubka exaggerated.

Her mummy came home late and Lubka was left alone, hungry, all day. Her mother hid her schoolbooks and didn't let her do her homework, but sent her out for walks all the time. Her mother even forced her to go out late at night. Not long ago she had had to spend the night on the porch of their block. She was frightened of this man; he carried a knife this big! Her mother liked wine and drank it like water. She had even filled their water jug with wine. If you wanted some you just helped yourself. Her mummy was nasty. She had wrapped her up by force. Lubka had cried and cried, hadn't wanted to be wrapped up, but her mummy had wrapped her up with everything she had and then stuffed a gag in her mouth – a gag, that was a rag that you put in people's mouths when you don't want other people to hear their cries.

The neighbour was aghast. 'Where does your mother get the money for wine?' she burst out.

Lubka answered without stopping to think: 'Probably from the bank; she knows one of the cashiers there.'

When she'd eaten all the biscuits and drunk three cups of tea Lubka began to feel drowsy: her eyelids were heavy and her head kept drooping towards the table. The neighbour dressed her in her coat and hat and gloves and told her to go home.

Two days later Praskovya was called in to see the headmaster at Lubka's school. She was with him a long time. She came home breathing heavily, red in the face, her headscarf hanging wildly round her neck. She shouted: 'You devil! I'll teach you to tell lies about your mother!' She picked up a bit of the clothesline and, for the first and last time, whipped Lubka, saying all the time: 'Don't you ever tell lies again, you devil, don't ever tell lies about your mother!' Afterwards she began to cry; she fell on the bed saying over and over again: 'My life is so bitter, what life can a widow have? I am so miserable, I have no other family except for you, my poor little orphan, my fatherless daughter . . .' Lubka sat on the floor watching her mother, at first scowling, furious, then with horror. She suddenly howled so piercingly and with such desperation that Praskovya got up and took her in her arms.

She pressed Lubka to her, kissed her, muttered endearing words: 'My little daughter, my dear heart, my sweet Lubka . . .' And she rocked her and sang her lullabies until Lubka, her long legs hanging down to the floor, fell asleep in her arms. Praskovya laid her down on the bed, and herself lay down beside her. And thus they slept the whole night, fully dressed, and sobbing for a long time in their sleep.

While Lubka was sitting smoking behind the stage Matrona Spiridonovna went up to Praskovya:

'Where's your Lubka?'

'She must be in the toilet.'

'And you're still half asleep? You've slept through the whole court case, even though they're threatening to send your daughter away.'

'Wh-who w-wants to?'

'Our bald friend over there,' Old Motya nodded towards Virepnikov. 'He's been shouting "Fling her out" the whole evening. People are asking the court to resettle her.'

Matrona enjoyed the confusion and fear she saw in Praskovya's eyes, but she added, pitying her a little, 'Don't worry, they won't separate a mother and daughter.'

Muddling and frightening Praskovya still further with

these words, Old Motya went off to Rosa and Effalia.

'Praskovya says that they don't have the right, because she's the widow of a front-line soldier. She says the judges will take pity on her and her daughter. And, she says,' here Matrona lowered her voice, 'there are others in our flats who carry on with strange men, but they keep it quiet.'

And Old Motya, extremely pleased with herself, sailed towards the door which bore the inscription 'W' in lilac paint.

Praskovya was plunged into panic. Surely they couldn't send her little Lubka away? What could she do? Where could she go? Where could she get help? She was quite inexperienced in these matters, but she knew that she couldn't live without Lubka. She had no one, not a living soul, except for Lubka.

Praskovya Egorovna loved her daughter passionately. That was why she had called her 'Lubov' – 'love'. She had known that this was a love given to her for her whole life, until death itself.

The war had taken Praskovya's husband away. She had married for love when she was only twenty-two. Ivan had been three years older. She'd been slender and light then, rather like Lubka now, but her colouring had been darker. Ivan would carry her in his arms like a child. He loved her. But two months later, before they'd managed to start a child, the war came.

Ivan left. He tore her hands off his uniform by force. She didn't cry, but stood frozen. Her sister-in-law poured water over her.

She received letters from Ivan until 1944 – the last one came in October. Then the letters stopped. She waited as the months passed. She cried, lost weight, ran to the army offices to get news. But they could tell her nothing; it seemed that they themselves knew nothing. Her friends at work comforted her: perhaps he's wounded, perhaps he's shell-shocked, maybe he's been captured. He needn't necessarily be dead.

She received news of his death on the eve of Victory Day, in April 1945. She did not shriek or scream. But all joy left her, her feelings were numbed. On Victory Day she locked herself in her room and wouldn't come out. Nobody could make her. They were frightened she might harm herself.

When she did come out she seemed greatly changed. She began going out in a crowd, drinking and singing. She got involved with other men – got through three that summer alone. But everything was passing fancy, nothing was serious, as if she was acting out of spite. But who was she aiming the spite at? At herself. Her heart was sad and her body wanted fun.

Praskovya's socialising had a desperate quality; she began to drink heavily and have affairs shamelessly. Her sister-in-law criticised her: 'It would be better for you to get married again than to dishonour Ivan's memory the way you do.' But how could she get married? There were widows and old maids everywhere. Then she seemed to calm down a bit. But she thought up something else: she would rent out a camp-bed to men on business trips. Her friends tried to shame her: 'You're not an old woman, you get your wages.' But she said to them: 'It's a big room and people need somewhere to sleep.' As if she were doing it for others when, in fact, it was because she was bored alone, and the money would be useful as well.

They were mainly army men, officers – all young and merry, happy that the war had ended. They wanted to drink and have fun. Some of them were nice. Sometimes she thought she could fall in love with this one or marry that one – but nobody asked her.

In 1949 Praskovya became pregnant. She thought the father was the lively captain. She'd liked him best of all; he was nice-looking and affectionate, and he'd stayed with her for ten whole days.

The baby was a girl. Praskovya registered her patronymic

as 'Ivan' after her husband because, no matter who the father of the baby was, her husband had been 'Ivan'.

Her daughter caused her a lot of trouble. The visitors no longer stayed with her, they felt uneasy there now. She had to live on her wages alone, and they didn't amount to much. They didn't look after the babies very well in the crèche and little Lubka was often ill. She was even in hospital twice. And she recovered slowly. She was a weak child. Praskovya suffered with her and got thin and lost her looks. She no longer had any time for men, she didn't need them any more.

Her sister-in-law took pity on her: 'Leave the factory and get a job in the food trade,' she said. She set her up in a restaurant kitchen – of course they had to give a pay-off to the head cook, but they managed to get it together. Thank God Praskovya got on well in the restaurant. She worked well and quickly. She coped with everything. She was well-fed, could ensure that the child got something and, most important of all, she no longer needed to use the crèche. Either she took Lubka with her and kept her at work with her for the whole shift (she would hide her in the china cupboard, in the hall or in the buffet and the other women helped her, understanding how difficult it is to bring up a child alone), or she would leave her at home with her neighbour, the lift woman, when she was free. In the restaurant they gave the workers bones, offal and fish; Praskovya had something to give her neighbour in return. And when little Lubka got bigger she got stronger and was able to go to the kindergarten, she could be left there and she liked it.

Lubka was beautiful, like a doll. Praskovya would wash her and put her to bed, and then everyone would come to wonder at her. She had rosy cheeks, long eyelashes, golden hair and little fat hands.

Lubka grew up in freedom and blossomed like a flower.

With Lubka starting school Praskovya again became aware of her loneliness. She wanted to get married now to a

169

respectable man so that Lubka would have a good father.

A worker from the restaurant started to court her; they began meeting. Praskovya had nothing against meeting, but things didn't seem to progress: he came round to see her often enough but there was nothing said of their living together. Praskovya began to reproach him: 'It's not nice, we ought to get married.' Then he stopped coming round.

And once again love tempted Praskovya. She met the Captain again, the same one who had lived in her room. Ten, no, eleven years had passed. He was in civvies now, had put on weight, looked more important, but she recognised him. She was working as a waitress in the main dining-room and he sat at one of her tables. Her heart leapt – it was fate. She went up to him and asked sternly: 'What would you like to eat?' And when he looked at her intently she said: 'You know me then?' He laughed: 'Of course, we sang duets together.' She nearly said: 'Until you got fed up with the song,' but restrained herself. He had even remembered her name. This seemed to her a good omen and she became more friendly. She studied him closely as she served his food: did he look like Lubka or not? She thought that his smile was similar, as were his small teeth and blue eyes. The Captain poured out a second glass and pushed it towards her; 'Let's drink to our meeting.' Praskovya refused, it was not allowed at work. If he wanted, however, she would be happy to invite him round to her place that evening where they could have a little chat and she added, frightened that he would refuse: 'I've even saved a bottle for something like this.' There was no such bottle but she had decided to buy one, there was no point in counting pennies at a time like this. He smiled and asked her to remind him of the address, he'd forgotten it, it had been so many years ago . . . 'Still, you remembered me,' said Praskovya softly. 'Yes, I did,' said the Captain in a surprised voice, 'although you've changed, I recognised you. You've put on weight and become prettier, but I knew you.' And again she thought: 'It's my fate.'

170

Buying things and walking home with her purchases all her old joyousness returned, as if her heart had melted. At home she washed her arms and neck with a scented German soap – wasn't this scrap of soap from that time with him? She put on an elegant, embroidered blouse and laid the table. She asked Lubka affectionately if she'd done her homework. She didn't want to send the little girl outside and hadn't done so for a long time, but this was different, he wasn't like the others. It would be better if Lubka was not there at first. They could sit and talk and then she would show the child to him. So Praskovya said, 'Lubka, love, go to Miss Rosa and ask her if you can watch television.' Lubka left and Praskovya opened the door to the corridor a crack so that she wouldn't miss the bell. Then she sat at the table and began waiting.

Lubka returned at eleven and started to make the bed. 'Go to sleep quickly, my love,' said Praskovya, 'Somebody's coming to see me just for a little while. An old friend.' She still expected him to come. Lubka lay down, pulled the blanket over her head and peeped out of a chink in it. She didn't ask any questions: she knew these 'old friends'. But it hadn't happened for a long time . . . She peered and peered and then got bored and fell asleep.

At midnight Praskovya poured herself a full glass of sweet wine, drank it in one gulp, and took off her clothes. She walked heavily across the room, treading on her blouse which she'd flung on the floor, and collapsed on the bed, making the springs creak. She burrowed her face in the pillow which muffled her howls and crying.

And so Praskovya Egorovna had remained alone. She had nobody. Lubka was her whole joy. 'Oh that terrible war – it took your father away from us,' Praskovya would lament, 'and how can you bring up a child without its father? Oh, bitter fate . . .' She brought the child up as best she could.

*   *   *

She began to look around anxiously, and then smiled proudly and joyfully as she saw Lubka walking out on to the stage: her daughter was beautiful and good. If only she were stronger, but maybe God would grant her that as well.

The judges followed Lubka onto the stage carrying amongst their papers Lubka's sentence, her fate.

Maybe it wasn't a sentence, more a decision. Zalomin waited for silence in order to read it out.

The Comrades' Court had passed a motion of public censure on Lubovna Ivanovna Sapozhnikova for violation of the peace in a communal flat and for undignified behaviour, such as . . . There followed an enumeration of all Lubka's excesses. The court pointed out to the Sapozhnikovs the inadmissibility of the abuse of alcoholic drinks. It called upon the daughter to lead the life of a model worker and on the mother to henceforth supervise her daughter's behaviour. The decision ended with a warning:

'In the event that the behaviour of L.I. Sapozhnikova does not change and the above mentioned infringements continue we will give the papers of this present sitting, together with a petition for a re-examination of this matter to the state court . . .'

Zalomin was giving Lubka a chance to save herself. It had taken a long argument to win her this chance. Rogacheva had been against it, she had wanted the case to be transferred to the State court now. Fedorchuk had suggested entrusting the matter to the local police department: they could make observations and establish facts. Zalomin was only able to persuade them by agreeing to a definite time limit: Lubka had three months, and the present judges were charged with checking the behaviour of Sapozhnikova no later than the date indicated in the minutes.

The doors of the club swung open. The stagnant air hung around the open doors in a thick cloud. People breathed in the frosty air with pleasure. An almost spherical moon hung high

172

above the courtyard, only visible there, where there were no lights. The young people, Lubka's gang, lingered, detaching themselves from the main throng. Lubka signalled to her mother: 'You go on, don't wait.' Archik and Avanze lagged behind. Daddy Stupanyan shouted to them, 'Follow me!' and left without looking round.

'Well,' said Lubka challengingly to her friends.

The 'well' could mean anything you wanted, 'Well, how did I do?'; 'Well, did you have fun?' or, even, 'Well, what shall we do now?'

It was easiest to answer the last question and they said in a chorus:

'Let's celebrate, Lubka!'

'Come on, Lubka, let's have a drink!'

'Let's have a party, eh, Lubka?'

Lubka maintained a teasing silence. Why was she looking at them so intently like that? They didn't understand. The silence lengthened. Valka at last broke it by hitting the strings of a guitar acquired from God knows where. He sang softly and gently:

> Oh little Lubka I love you so,
> Did you know?
> Oh little Lubka with skirts so short,
> With skirts so short,
> And high heels that dance
> and heels that dance and whirl.
> Vitechka chased Lubka,
> Grishenka chased Lubka,
> Vanechka chased Lubka,
> And Valka – the fool.

The tune was lively and strong. Lubka danced little steps to this polka beat, stamping, to the gate. They all followed behind her. At the gates Valka sang the last verse:

173

Ever with his guitar, Val;
Ever with his faithful pal,
He jangles and jingles,
Jingles and jangles,
At Lubka's door.

Valka banged out the last notes with a flourish, using the
knuckles of his hand on the wood of the guitar and then
looked at Lubka, expecting a smile, a word or, at least, a
glance. But Lubka remained silent. She didn't want to sing,
she wanted to cry, and the tears coursed through her like
bitter wine. But her feet, nevertheless, responded to Valka's
merry little song. That was the way she was – whenever
music played her feet would move in time.

They went out into the alleyway. The crowd had already
dispersed. Only one young man was loitering. Lubka recognised him, it was the representative from the factory – her
defender. She smiled, that was nice, he was waiting for her, he
obviously wanted to say something to her. The gang saw her
smile and were pleased: she was smiling, Valka had cheered
her up, good!

'Hey, Lubka, shall we get some drink?' asked Pashka.

'If you want to,' she replied.

The answer was confusing: was she inviting them round
to her place or not? Pashka and Valka rummaged about in
their pockets for some money. Avanze and Archik lingered on
the corner.

'We should invite what's-his-name as well,' said Lubka
lazily. 'What is his name, that one from the factory? I can't
remember.'

'I think it's Ivanov,' suggested Lalka.

'Hey, Vanya,' cried Lubka softly in the direction of the
young man.

But he'd already gone. One minute he was there, near
her, the next far away.

'He-e-y,' Lubka raised her voice, 'Vanya, turn round!'

Lalka laughed shrilly, the rest of them roared with laughter.

Mikhail had meant to speak to Lubka but had decided not to. He didn't like that lot around her. So he'd turned and walked briskly away. His feet had frozen while he'd been waiting for her. Without turning round, without listening to the cries that followed him, he reached the corner and turned it.

'Well,' Lubka stretched and yawned loudly and sensuously. 'Time to sleep, boys. Ta-ta!'

The boys shuffled their feet. This was odd: one minute she seemed to be inviting them round, the next she said it was time for bed. They followed her through the alleyway, walking on the night snow, not yet cleared. Lubka seemed to be walking through the deepest snow drifts on purpose.

She nodded curtly in farewell to the diminished company – Maya and the Stupanyan brothers had already disappeared – and faded into the entrance of her block.

Praskovya was already asleep. It was hot and stuffy in the room. Lubka opened the little casement window, undressed and lay down. She was so tired she was sure she would fall asleep immediately.

Her mother was breathing heavily, snoring in her sleep. 'Like an animal,' thought Lubka in sudden fury. Everything in the room seemed repulsive to her, and dirty. Everything in her life!

Why had her mother let her leave school? Lubka looked at herself as a girl from a new, grown-up angle. She should have been moved to another school; she might not have got top marks even there, but still . . . In gymnastics and P.E. she would have got top marks. If she ever had a daughter she would definitely send her to dancing classes or gymnastics.

But the bright picture of a daughter brought in its wake new, bitter reflections.

Who was her father, then? Her mother had always told her that her father had died in the war. In her non-questioning way Lubka had not thought 'which war?' But now it was clear to her that he couldn't have died in the war as she had been born after it. So where was he? It never occurred to Lubka that Praskovya would have difficulty in answering the more important question of *who* he was. 'He was probably some petty thief,' she thought. 'My mother a tramp, my father a good-for-nothing, my home . . .' She couldn't begin to describe her home. As for herself, she was beyond contempt, 'a stupid fool'.

She sat on the bed, hugging her knees. And her friends? They had turned out to be selfish, worthless cowards.

Only Valka loved her, but he was lame, and Yury Puziryev, but he was only a boy.

That old man, the chairman in the court, was right. He was a bore, of course, like all old men, but kind. She really was all alone in the big, wide world.

With this bitter thought she fell asleep, well after midnight. But when sleep had already nearly overwhelmed her, weighing her body down and confusing her mind, something warm passed over her, hardly touching her. What it was she couldn't recall, and she fell asleep.

She got up still tired and in a filthy mood. She rushed out without even a cup of tea and still hungry from the previous day. Because she was in such a bad mood she got on the wrong tram, was late for work and got a telling-off. Her mood got even worse.

It was then that Lubka discovered that anger creates strength: she worked harder that day than ever before and her usual lethargy vanished.

Returning from the dining room after the lunch break Lubka met Mikhail. He stopped her and asked: 'How are you, then?'

Lubka smiled; there was nothing you could say to such a question.

'Why did you run off yesterday?'

Mikhail was embarrassed. He didn't know what he wanted to say: did he want to say 'goodbye' to her then, or did he want to go out with her now? They stood dumb for a few seconds and then both said: 'Well, see you,' and they parted.

Lubka's gang lay low for quite a long time.

But one day, two weeks later on her day off, Lubka met Yury Puziryev on the stairs. He'd obviously been waiting for her. He asked timidly, embarrassed: 'Lubka, is it all right to come round to your place now?'

'All right for whom?' asked Lubka. 'You're not allowed to.'

'Not just me, all of us. They wanted to know how you were getting on . . .'

Lubka didn't say anything. Puziryev was getting more and more embarrassed. He said frantically, sniggering: 'What's the enemy situation like, then, any ambushes?'

'So, they've sent you to spy out the land, have they?' said Lubka, 'As the bravest one?'

'No, just to find out whether we can pop round, what we should bring . . .' mumbled Puziryev.

'Oh, well, come round then,' said Lubka listlessly, without any interest at all, 'but keep it quiet.'

Half an hour later Valka with his guitar, Puziryev, Lalka the Pistol, Pashka the Boxer and Avanze appeared. They brought with them wine, biscuits and wafers.

Lubka, putting the glasses on the table, asked Avanze, 'Is Archik coming?'

'N-no,' muttered Avanze, 'Mm, I don't know, I don't think so.'

'His Daddy told him not to,' sniggered Lalka.

'His Daddy told him and Avanze not to,' added Pashka.

Everybody laughed except Lubka and Avanze. After the trial his father had warned his sons: 'You go round there again and I'll give you a hiding neither of you will forget. And I'll personally kick your beauty out of Moscow. I won't wait three months like those old fogies at the trial.'

Avanze had been too ashamed not to come to Lubka's when everybody else was coming, too ashamed to just fade away. But he'd been terrified on the way here, coming a very circuitous route along the back streets, and he hovered by the entrance until he was sure the coast was clear before dashing in. How could he tell Lubka that he wouldn't be coming any more because he was afraid of his father? And afraid for himself and Lubka? No, he couldn't say it. So he sat, sullen, shrinking at every ring on the bell – suppose his father came after him?

'It doesn't look as though Maya's coming either,' said Lubka, and removed yet another glass. 'Drink up, lads.'

But the wine didn't help, the previous gaiety did not materialise.

> At Lubka's we are partying,
> Singing, drinking danci-ing.

. . . sang Valka, strumming on his guitar, but he couldn't think of any more, so he was silent, just fingering the strings.

Suddenly Lubka jumped up and shrieked out a verse:

> We're drinking wine and all,
> With Lubka we don't care,
> She's headed for a fall,
> But we must still come here.

Valka grasped the dance rhythm and Lubka moved to it, tapping her heels loudly, angrily. Lalka caught the tune and sang:

> Lubka is a beauty,
> She won't get into trouble,

Her heels tap out their duty,
And all fall into rubble.

Everybody laughed. Lubka cheered up. They got the gramophone going and the music thundered out.

Nobody noticed Avanze leaving. Only Effalia saw him as she stood near Lubka's door, and Virepnikov, who wrote in his exercise book:

'On Friday there was once again drunkenness and debauchery at the Sapozhnikov's. There were two men and two women. One of them left early.'

Mikhail and Lubka did not meet again for a long time. They would see each other from far off, nod and hurriedly go on their way. The other girls often talked about him, they liked the young fitter. He was a great lad, lively, sang well and he played the guitar. He was handsome, he was a gipsy. That was why he could sing and play the guitar.

'He's not really a gipsy, is he?' asked Lubka.

Several girls answered her at once, contradicting each other:

'He is a gipsy, but he's quite steady.'

'He's not a gipsy at all, just dark-skinned.'

'No, his grandfather was a real gipsy.'

'He's a country boy, how can he be a gipsy?'

'His grandfather was a gipsy, he was the village blacksmith, he told me so himself.'

'Well, if his grandfather told you so himself it must be true.'

'Gipsy or not,' said the forewoman, a tall woman with a dark moustache, 'he'd make a nice bridegroom.' And she sighed, regretting, perhaps, that she was already married.

'I'm not right for him,' thought Lubka, 'he's the steady sort, I'm not.'

Mikhail wanted to talk to Lubka very much; he wanted to

know more about her. Sometimes, in passing, he would ask Lubka's forewoman: 'How's our Sapozhnikova getting on now?' as if it were part of his official duty; after all they had sent him to court for her. The forewoman would answer that Sapozhnikova was steadier now and had lost her former slackness, but still showed no perceptible interest in her work.

Mikhail was astonished at himself: what was the matter with him? Why did this girl make him shy? A lively, light-headed young girl and he could only look on from afar. So much time had passed already since that trial. Spring had come, the snow had melted. It was warm and you could even see the green grass breaking through here and there. Sparrows were chirping away everywhere. Maybe he would run across Lubka accidentally on his way home? Although she wasn't really on his way.

Once Mikhail lingered by the works entrance and then went slowly to Lubka's tram stop. He waited there, but without success. Then he wandered further, along unknown streets. As he walked he thought of only one thing. He couldn't invite Lubka round to his place or go round to hers – what would she think of him? He would just have to carry on like this, walking, wandering, and hope that one day he would meet her.

He hadn't noticed, because he was thinking so hard, that he'd walked into a square. Old people were sitting on benches, women were rocking prams with babies in and children were running around.

Then he understood. The thought came to him straight from his heart, not even properly formed into words: Lubka didn't need to be taught, she just needed to be loved. He didn't ask himself whether he loved her or not. If he had, the strict answer would have been 'no', but he thought about her constantly.

Leaving the square he came across a kiosk papered with posters. Why hadn't he thought before of buying tickets and inviting Lubka to the theatre?

A middle-aged woman with a pleasant smile was sitting in the kiosk. Mikhail hadn't the slightest idea what tickets he wanted, what theatre he wanted or what performance he wanted. He would be with Lubka the whole evening, that was enough. Although, of course, she must find whatever it was entertaining, she must have a good time. He asked the kiosk lady for two good tickets to a good performance.

The kiosk lady glanced at him and guessed, by the look in his eyes, that this was very important for him. She took two tickets out of a drawer for the Musical Theatre.

'*My Fair Lady* – is it a suitable name? It's a wonderful musical. And I can let you have another two tickets for *Ivan and Vanechka*, another wonderful play, and in a marvellous theatre, the best in Moscow.'

The next day Mikhail lay in wait for Lubka at the works entrance and they walked together.

'Hullo, Lubka, I haven't seen you for ages. How are things?'

Lubka's reply, 'I'm surviving,' was not very encouraging. But there was no retreat. Lubka was prickly: she'd been waiting a long time for Mikhail to speak to her and then had given up. And now he thought he could just turn up like this.

'I want to ask you to come to the theatre with me.'

Lubka laughed, 'Just like that! Is your girl sick?'

'What girl? I got these tickets for you and me. You're my girl.'

Lubka looked carefully at him for a long time and he saw how pinched and sullen she looked. He wanted to calm and reassure her: he took her hand in his. She didn't withdraw it but her fingers were impersonal and cold, so he released them.

They walked, exchanging empty words, and then fell silent.

They stopped at the entrance to her block of flats. Mikhail took the tickets out: 'Do you like musicals?'

'I don't know, I've never seen one. I've heard them on the radio.'

'They're good seats and it's a good show. It's called *My Fair Lady* . . . Will you come?'

Again Lubka looked at him for a long time, thoughtfully. Then she asked sharply: 'Tell me honestly, what do you want from me?'

Mikhail was confused. He nearly answered angrily: 'I want to go to the theatre with you, and that's all!' Lubka's question and the allusion it contained was offensive. But Mikhail also heard fear, distrust and perplexity in her question. It was difficult for her now, difficult for both of them. He felt that one false word or movement and the fragile, diffident feeling that was growing in her would be destroyed.

Without thinking, as you would jump in to save a drowning person, he said: 'Lubka, marry me.'

She looked at him, stunned, frightened, and saw his face, also frightened, like a reflection of her own.

They were both silent for a minute, transfixed and petrified. He held her hand in his. Her fingers were the first to come to life, she stretched them gently but did not withdraw them completely, as if testing her freedom, and she sighed and said with mocking affection:

'And when did you think of this?'

'Quite recently.' He was no longer scared, he was smiling now.

'And suppose I say "yes"? What will your mother say?'

'I have no mother. I have a grandmother in the country who's very nice.'

'Then I must stand in for your mother. Perhaps you didn't hear enough bad things about me in court?'

Lubka looked at him, narrowing her eyes slightly. She pulled gently on her fingers, but he held her hands harder and would not let them go.

'I heard all sorts of things, bad and good. Let's not

remember the bad. I like you, I can't help it.'

He pressed her fingers lightly; still she did not withdraw her hand. Mikhail pulled her gently to him and kissed what his lips found, her forehead between the eyebrows. A warm wave flowed through them both; they separated and moved a little away from each other.

Lubka looked at him gently, although there was once again mockery in her words:

'Let's try the theatre first. When did you say it was? Good, I really want to go to the theatre.'

She wanted to say 'go with you' but was being a bit careful. She liked him a lot but didn't want to think about what might happen in the long term. Nevertheless this unexpected proposal, the first in her life, delighted her.

She turned quickly and ran up the stairs. She didn't want to talk now.

And that very same day Lubka began her preparations. She would appear in the theatre looking absolutely wonderful. She would astonish Mikhail, he would be thunderstruck by her beauty. As for marrying him, well, he was probably already regretting what he'd said – who knows?

First of all Lubka washed her hair with a shampoo dye, which gave her fair hair red highlights. Then she began to consider the rest of her appearance for the theatre.

Oh, if only she had a long dress that reached down to the floor, or elegant trousers. But there were no such luxuries in Lubka's wardrobe. So, it would have to be the suede mini-skirt and the green skinny sweater. There was nothing else. But she had a lot of jewellery, a whole box-full of glass beads.

And so the long-awaited evening came. Lubka entered the theatre with her best walk: a gentle, soft, cat-like, almost lazy, step. Mikhail was already there, waiting. Their eyes sparkled as they met, and they hurried into the auditorium. Lots of people looked at Lubka, or so it seemed to her – too many, even. She glanced at a mirror in passing: her hair-do, gleaming with lacquer, was holding steady; the blue-green mascara lengthened her eyes and gave them the necessary mysterious look; a shiny necklace livened up her jumper; 'diamanté' clip-on earrings sparkled dully in her ears; even the 'turquoise' in her bracelet was still right-side-up. Everything was OK. The only thing was that in the mirror she looked older than Mikhail, but she had no time to think about that: they were already in the auditorium, the light was fading, the rustling and sighing dying down in the half-light. The curtain was raised and Lubka was completely enthralled. It was the story of a flower-girl and her transformation from a small, ragged scarecrow, a frightened, little creature, into an exquisite beauty, and of the love that envelops the two main protagonists, and their fight against it. And all this with singing and dancing and music – my God, what music! Lubka was deeply moved.

Her cheeks flamed; her own, natural scarlet colour, knowing no bounds, crept out from under the yellow-brick blush colour of her light tan make up.

When she saw herself again in the foyer mirror beside Mikhail, so serene and simple in his grey suit, Lubka gasped. 'I'll be back in a minute,' she said and hid herself behind the door of the Ladies. There she rubbed off all her rouge with a handkerchief, removed some of the mascara from her eyelashes and placed all her adornments in her handbag.

'The light's bad at home,' she said to herself in justification, 'the ceilings are all smoky and the light bulbs are useless.' But she knew really that it was nothing to do with light bulbs. She decided that tomorrow, Sunday, she would change everything in the room, turn it all round.

Mikhail looked at her happily: 'We're too late for the buffet, my fair lady, I bought you some chocolate.'

But Lubka didn't want the buffet or chocolate. She hurried back into the theatre.

When they left the theatre Mikhail asked her whether she'd liked it.

'Yes, very much,' said Lubka warmly.

She didn't have the words to say more, and he squeezed her hand. They were silent. Then he noticed that she was stealthily wiping her eyes.

'Lubka what's the matter? It was a happy story.'

'You know, I love dancing . . . I always thought that I would be a dancer, but I know now that it's too late.'

And she talked and cried like a child. Mikhail wanted to comfort her: she could dance – there were special evenings at the club and in the summer there was dancing in the square in the park.

Lubka pulled her hand away from his: 'You don't understand! I can't ever become a professional dancer, like a ballerina. You have to start training when you're still a child. If my Mum had sent me to classes when I was small I could have been a ballerina, or a dancer in a group, or a figure skater . . .'

Mikhail felt sorry for her. He hadn't expected the theatre evening to end this way, in tears and regrets.

Strangely enough it made him like her even more.

Mikhail drew her to him, pressed his face to her hair – and recoiled instantly: her hair was as rigid as wire, like glass fibre.

'Lubka, what have you done to your hair?' he asked. He shouldn't have.

She broke away from him and ran up the stairs. He shouted: 'Where are you going? Wait!' But his only answer was the slamming of a door.

Mikhail suffered for the whole of his two days off, but comforted himself with the thought that when he saw her at work he would say to her: 'I'm sorry, I really don't know anything about those kind of things, hair-dos, fashions, and perfumes. Please don't be angry with me.'

185

But Lubka wasn't angry with him, she was angry with herself for shooting up the stairs like a rocket. She should have simply said:

'I've got some lacquer on, maybe I overdid it a bit . . .' Well, from now on she would do her hair differently, she would let it hang down to her shoulders.

To make Monday come more quickly Lubka started cleaning. She wanted to give everything a thorough cleaning, to change everything round, to turn her home upside down and inside out.

By Sunday evening the only thing left to do was to shine up the fresh polish on the wooden floor. Lubka, in an old cotton housecoat and worn-out slippers, was cleaning a brush full of hairs over a newspaper. It was at this moment that her gang turned up: Pashka, Lalka, Valka and Puziryev.

They seemed to appear out of nowhere. They stood in the doorway and Pashka said cheekily:

'Now you've finished the tidying-up you can look after your visitors.'

Lalka sniggered: she thought that anything Pashka said was funny. Pashka walked straight in, all over the clean floor, and sat down. Lalka rushed in after him on her tip-toes. The other two, with more natural inhibitions, stayed put at the open door. Lubka looked coldly at them all and said frostily: 'We're closed for repairs.'

'The repairs are finished. Now we can open the café-dancehall.' Pashka held out his hand for the brush: 'To work, lads! Puziryev, do the polishing.'

Lubka put the brush behind her back, 'No. We're closed for good.'

'Flinging us out, are you?' puffed Pashka threateningly, standing up.

'She's only joking. You're joking aren't you Lubka?' Lalka put her arm round Pashka's shoulders and sat him down again. 'What's the matter? Tell us.'

'Nothing's the matter,' said Lubka in a bored voice, 'I'm just getting married.'

Pashka guffawed violently; Lalka's beads broke behind him and Puziryev laughed uncontrollably.

Only Valka stood sadly in the doorway.

'You are joking, aren't you Lubka? Aren't you?' persisted Lalka.

'Maybe I am,' said Lubka, 'but you'll still have to leave. I've got to finish polishing the floor.'

A
Delicate Subject

The heavy iron gate clanged open; from the depths of the garden a dog responded. Zoya Tikhonovna knew that the dog was chained up and was only unleashed at night towards the end of summer, when the apples ripened. There was a straight path from the gate to the house, bordered by ginger nasturtiums, honey mignonettes and pink and lilac petunias. The path cut across the dark, loose earth where bushes of blackcurrant had been planted in rows, and apples and cherry trees, their trunks painted with lime, grew in strict chess-board formation.

Zoya Tikhonovna could see the large figure of her landlady through the open terrace window. Alevtina stood bowed, her plump, bare arms moving backwards and forwards over the table. 'She's cleaning berries,' guessed Zoya Tikhonovna. As she approached the door she smiled pleasantly, if a little ingratiatingly – she was afraid of Alevtina Pavlovna.

Yesterday they had met at the lower well, where everybody went for drinking water, and Alevtina Pavlovna had said: 'Come and see me tomorrow afternoon, we have a rather delicate matter to discuss.' Zoya Tikhonovna was flustered. She thought, 'She won't wait any longer.' She owed Alevtina Pavlovna five roubles, and had owed it to her for a long time, since last summer, when they had had to pay for the injections, and she couldn't seem to pay it back, could only apologise when they met and promise to pay it soon. And although Alevtina Pavlovna always answered, 'Don't worry, take your time', it was probable that finally she had become annoyed.

Zoya Tikhonovna had taken a five-rouble note with her and it was now folded over three times and clasped in her left hand.

This money was taken from her last ten roubles on which she, Igor and Galya would have to live till pay day. She didn't want to repay the debt now, but if the situation had become critical she would have to.

Alevtina Pavlovna was indeed jam-making. On the table, covered with an oil cloth, was a mountain of berries; a little pool of pink juice seeped from underneath them. A basin, already half-filled with washed wild strawberries, was placed beside them, while at the other end of the table a full wicker basket waited its turn. The sun warmed the terrace; wasps buzzed above the fragrant wild strawberries. A big, black fly banged itself repeatedly against the glass.

'Ah, you've come,' said Alevtina Pavlovna. She flung a handful of small strawberries on to the plate and, with the back of her hand, adjusted the glasses that had fallen down her nose. 'Sit down.' With her leg she brought a stool out from under the table. 'I'll just go and rinse my hands.'

She crossed the terrace, walking heavily, and stepped down from the porch. The sound of her voice together with the metallic chink of the wash-basin could be heard as she gave instructions to her grandsons, working in the garden.

Zoya Tikhonovna sat and watched a wasp. It was attracted by a ripe strawberry, almost tumbling out of the basket. It settled on it and, its yellow-black belly trembling, drank in the juicy softness voluptuously, drawing out the sweet juice. Zoya Tikhonovna suddenly felt a terrible craving for strawberries. She swallowed and, averting her eyes, looked out the window.

The garden was filled with languor under the hot, July sun, and the sparse shade of the young trees provided no relief. 'Her own garden, her own dacha,' thought Zoya Tikhonovna. 'The children always have fresh food. It's good for them, for their health, their growth.'

'Well,' said the landlady, settling down into a wicker chair and wiping her reddened hands on her striped apron, 'I asked you to come because I wanted to talk to you about—'

'I've brought what I owe you,' interrupted Zoya, unfolding the five-rouble note in her hand.

'What? Oh, good, put it on the table. Well, I wanted to say that your daughter, Galina, she's up to no good.'

'Wha-at?' said Zoya Tikhonovna. Her voice quavered, her faded blue eyes, surrounded by a fine net of wrinkles, opened wide in fright.

'Facts have come to light that reveal she is setting a trap for Alexey Ivanovitch.'

'What do you mean, "setting a trap"?' said Zoya Tikhonovna, even more frightened than before, 'That's impossible. Galya wouldn't do anything like that.'

Before her flashed the image of her daughter, pale, thin, worn out by work, her studies and adversity, and the handsome, solid, well-dressed Alexey Ivanovitch, and everything that she now heard seemed to her so absurd, so comic, that a weak smile pierced her fright and gently touched her lips.

'It's no laughing matter,' said Alevtina Pavlovna sharply. 'So, you don't believe me? Well, I might as well tell you that people have seen them.'

'Where have they seen them?' asked Zoya Tikhonovna, again weak with fear. For some reason 'where' came out, when she had really wanted to ask 'what', 'what had they seen?'. 'Where did people see them?'

'They saw them in Moscow Street.'

Moscow Street had once been the name of the main street of this green little town, famous for the beauty of its surroundings and its ancient architectural monuments. A famous writer had once lived here. Now the name of Moscow Street had been changed to that of Gagarin Prospect. All the shops, the post office and the bus station were on this thoroughfare; all the public transport went along it.

Zoya Tikhonovna was soothed by the fact that 'it' had taken place in such busy, noisy surroundings. She tried,

191

inconspicuously, to do some deep breathing to calm the beating of her heart.

'Listen to this. On Monday morning your daughter was going to the bus stop and my son-in-law happened to be driving to Moscow. She saw him and, would you believe it, she waved to him, just like that, as if she knew him well. And he stopped. Immediately. She ran up to him and shouted, for the whole street to hear, "Good morning!". Well, then, would you believe it, he opened the door for her and actually waited for her. And she sits down in the car just like that. And they drive off together . . .'

'But what's wrong with that, Alevtina Pavlovna? He gave her a lift because they were going in the same direction . . .'

'Excuse me – you're changing the subject – we are not talking about my son-in-law, but about your daughter. *She* waved to *him*, *she* got *him* to stop and then *she* ran up to *him*. Not he, she, she – do you understand? And people saw all this, they're beginning to talk already.'

'Who saw it?' Zoya Tikhonovna heard herself saying, although again this wasn't what she wanted to know.

'Ah-ha! So you do believe me! All right, Nura from the tobacco kiosk saw it, and Matrena Feosevna saw it as she was coming out of the dairy—'

'Matrena likes to gossip,' Zoya Tikhonovna interrupted timidly.

'You're changing the subject again!' Alevtina's voice had become shriller, her rosy face was darkening, 'We – are – talking – about – your – daughter – and – her – behaviour.'

Alevtina Pavlovna spat out the words one by one, as if reciting a rule to a non-comprehending pupil.

'But what was so improper in Galina's behaviour?' asked Zoya Tikhonovna as gently as possible. She wanted to calm Alevtina but she must also defend her daughter somehow.

'It is extremely improper to run after a married man and to use his car as if it belonged to her. Don't you see? She waved her hand and he braked immediately.'

'But all he did was give her a lift. He knows her. We've all met several times over the last three years. So he gives her a lift once, what's wrong with that?'

'Once? You think it was just once? Oh, no, it seems that it wasn't the first time she'd had a lift with him.'

Zoya Tikhonovna remembered now that Galya had mentioned something about a lift to Moscow. Maybe it had been twice, or three times. She couldn't remember exactly what Galya had said. At the time she had been pleased for her daughter – let her have a little comfort, her life was hard enough, it was nicer in the car than on the train.

'So that's your attitude. You think there's nothing unusual in your daughter being alone in a car with a married man, and, obviously, you're not at all worried about how it all might finish. Well, I – am, and – I say – that – this – scandal – must – stop!'

'Please don't shout, Alevtina Pavlovna. There really isn't any scandal. You're jumping to conclusions—'

'No scandal? You don't call it a scandal? When a debauched young woman stops a car, sidles up to the driver and says: "Take me where you want . . ." '

'Alevtina Pavlovna, how can you? What do you mean, "where you want"? Who heard that? What are you saying? And how can you call her "debauched"?'

Zoya Tikhonovna wanted to add that after all it was with her son-in-law and not a stranger, but Alevtina's furious face stopped her.

'Of course she's debauched. Anyone who has a child from a stranger must be debauched.'

'A child from a stranger?' Zoya felt cold from indignation and from the insult. Her lips trembled as she spoke: 'How can you say that? You know what a hard time Galya has had.'

193

'If it's not from her husband then it must be from a stranger, well from someone else, anyway,' Alevtina Pavlovna said, correcting herself. 'In any case, she's a single woman, and with a man like him around . . .' Alevtina Pavlovna straightened herself, flung back her shoulders and lifted up her head. Her whole bearing demonstrated that her son-in-law was the kind of man who would be welcome anywhere: '. . . still young, kind, with a professional's salary, all that creates an impression on young people. And, of course, he's got his own car as well . . .'

'Stop it! That's enough.' Zoya Tikhonovna got up and put out a hand, as if trying to stop the stream of ugly words from touching her. She couldn't talk, her lips were trembling and her eyes were full of tears.

'Sit down!' Alevtina Pavlovna slapped a chair with such force that frightened wasps flew off the strawberries. 'Listen to me until I've finished. I will not allow anybody to come between a man and his wife, even if it weren't my own daughter and my son-in-law. Your daughter likes my son-in-law and has taken advantage of the fact that his wife is on holiday. Please don't interrupt! Let me finish. As her mother you must understand that it is your duty to control her. So, let there be no more of these occurrences. I don't like scenes, I try and avoid them. It's much better to talk things out quietly and calmly. But, if you ignore what I say, if I ever hear or see anything again, I'll make such a scene that you'll wish you'd never been born.'

'All right. I'll tell Galya not to go in your son-in-law's car again.'

Zoya Tikhonovna got up, bowed her head silently in farewell and went towards the door.

'Please don't take it personally. I have nothing against you.' Alevtina Pavlovna got up and pointed towards the berries: 'Take some strawberries for little Igor.'

But Zoya Tikhonovna was already stepping down from

the porch. She may not even have heard these last words. She walked evenly to the gate, shut it firmly after her and, with the same even pace but a little faster, she walked along the narrow strip of stones laid on the grass and sand. Then she turned into a little pathway and walked to their rented dacha. She entered the little hut, as small as a toy, that stood behind their landlady's house, and lay down on the bed without even taking off its white cover. She was shaking and her temples throbbed – her migraines always began this way: 'Please let Igor stay a bit longer with the landlady,' she thought dully, and then she was seized by nausea.

When Galya got home that evening Zoya Tikhonovna's migraine was already receding. Her head was tied in a scarf, her face was white and her eyes sunken. Galya put her mother to bed and gave her some strong tea. Then she took care of her little son. He had spent almost the whole day sitting in the landlady's kitchen.

Zoya Tikhonovna told Galya about her conversation that day after her daughter had got into bed and turned out the light. She left out the rude, hateful words and did not describe how Alevtina Pavlovna had been trembling with malice.

'Go to sleep now, Mum. Good-night. Don't worry, you sleep now,' said Galya.

Early the next morning, as usual, Galya started to get ready for work. Zoya Tikhonovna was awake, but still in bed. She watched from under lowered lids, the light still hurt her eyes, as Galya got dressed. 'She's so thin and pale,' she thought, 'it's hard for her, working and travelling. Well, in autumn little Igor will go to the kindergarten and I'll find myself some work, we'll have my pension and my salary. It'll be easier then. There's no work here at all . . .'

Galya had already got to Gagarin Prospect before the cherry-coloured Moskvitch car caught her up, hooted and braked. She looked round at the noise but didn't stop.

'Hey, Galya, what's the matter?' shouted an astonished male voice.

'She stopped, 'Thank you, Alexey Ivanovitch, I don't need a lift.'

'Aren't you going to Moscow?'

'Yes, but I'm going on the bus from the station.'

'I don't understand. You mean you don't want to come with me?'

'That's right, Alexey Ivanovitch.'

'I see. We're a bit haughty today, aren't we? What am I to deduce from this strange behaviour?' Alexey Ivanovitch tried to conceal the anger in his voice with a playful tone. He sat there, with the door half open and one foot on the asphalt road: fresh, sweet-smelling, with hair damp and dark from his morning shower.

'Are you annoyed about something? Have I upset you?'

'Oh, no, it's nothing like that. Please don't think that you, or that I . . .' Galya got confused and fell silent.

'Well, please tell me what's happened then,' he said, and his dark, straight eyebrows knitted.

'You'd better ask your – ask Alevtina Pavlovna', said Galya, her face suffused with red, which seemed to give her a bloom that made her look quite pretty. She turned round so sharply that her pleated skirt unfurled like an umbrella and her light, flowing hair danced down her back. She ran to the bus stop where her bus was just drawing up.

'Well, well, so that's what's going on,' thought Alexey Ivanovitch, carefully steering round the broken asphalt at the crossroads. 'My mother-in-law is widening her sphere of influence. She now decides who I can give lifts to. Well, suppose I don't like driving by myself? Suppose I get bored? Supposing I like having someone to talk to? Too bad, my mother-in-law thinks it's wrong so it must stop.'

He felt a deep anger. Was he a bad husband? Or a bad father? He loved his wife and children. And if he had deceived his wife two or three times during their fifteen years of marriage, they had been fleeting affairs. He had known how to cover them up. And this girl meant nothing to him. It was laughable. She aroused no emotion in him at all, he was not attracted to her in the slightest. Well, maybe he felt sorry for her, he wanted to protect her, maybe surprise her a bit . . . He remembered Galina's grey eyes and how they changed expression as she listened to him, now cloudy, now clear and shining. She was always quiet. If she said anything it was always in answer to questions. She was a very good listener. It occurred to him also that she was very shy. And he suddenly saw before him her fine hair, spiralling like smoke in the wind.

Yes, this evening he would definitely talk to Alevtina Pavlovna. He would ask her what the matter was, what precisely she was worried about. He saw before him the portly, upright figure of his mother-in-law, her dark hair still untouched by grey, oily-looking, her eyes drilling into him and her sharp, shrill voice.

She was an amazing woman. There was no corner of their life into which she had not poked her nose, no corner and no matter. A lot of things depended on her, she was the main cog in their domestic machine. She checked the children's lessons, made jam and stewed fruit for the winter, she stretched every rouble to its limit in order that they might save for something worthwhile. She freed them from worries, from rush, and, thanks to her, they were able to work and rest fully.

Alexey Ivanovitch braked and stood in line behind a level-crossing barrier.

'No, no,' he said aloud, and sighed.

No, he wouldn't ask his mother-in-law anything. He couldn't possibly say anything to her about this girl, it would only confirm Alevtina Pavlovna's absurd imaginings. Then she would feel it necessary to talk to Nina about it, and his wife was so jealous. It had long ceased to amuse him. Collective jealousy was just what he needed right now! Ridiculous.

197

'Never mind, we'll manage,' he said aloud again, and lit a cigarette. He really did feel like talking.

The train passed with a loud shriek, the barrier lifted and the cars started up. Alexey Ivanovitch let out the brake and the cherry-coloured Moskvitch trundled after the others, keeping to the speed limit, in line, one of the many hurrying links to Moscow.

The
Woman with the Umbrella

After lunch they sat in the summer-house and looked at the lake with its low shores, its bays stretching far into the horizon, and its islands. They looked at the old trees in the park and at the other holiday-makers.

The people moved in two streams: one hurriedly making for the restaurant, the other, in a more leisurely way, gradually fragmenting, in search of free benches in the shade. It was hot.

Every now and then they would exchange a lazy sentence in the summer-house.

'Isn't our lake delightful?' said a plump blonde with a new rosy tan.

'Not bad, Yarva, not bad at all,' replied the solid, ginger-haired man in the open-necked shirt.

Professor Duzhin didn't like the sensitive enthusings of his young wife. He would sometimes mockingly call her 'Dushechka' or 'Dushenka', a play on their surname and an obvious reference to the Chekhov short story about the woman who wore her heart on her sleeve.

The Professor thought of nature as something good for one's health, but didn't particularly like looking at it. He devoted the whole of the pre-prandial period to playing cards with other devotees of the game, with his back to the lake.

'There are very few fish in the lake,' a youngish man said; he was burnt black by the sun.

'There are some near the other side of the lake, you could fish from a boat,' said his wife.

The Fishers, Moscow lecturers, were amazingly alike,

199

both straight, dark and unemotional. They wore the same shorts, tee-shirts and plimsolls. They even had identical hair-cuts. They alternated the lakes that they fished in and knew more about the reservoirs around this small Estonian town than the inhabitants themselves. They would hang their fish out to dry in the sun in the yard of the house where both couples had rented rooms and which was also used for the communal supper.

'I can't see anything interesting at all,' sighed a young man, mixed up in the straps of his camera, his rucksack and his binoculars, through which he monitored the opposite shore of this narrow inlet in the hope of photographic booty.

The photographer was one of Mrs Fisher's postgraduate students. He had come here on holiday on her advice, but her guardianship and her shorts, revealing her hairy, straight legs, made him feel uncomfortable. He felt quite at ease with 'Dushenka', but really wanted to meet a young girl, perhaps like the one sitting here in the corner of the summer-house bent over a book. He hadn't managed to get a good look at her yet, but could tell by her slender neck and her thin, dark arms that she was young.

However, even while glancing sideways at the girl, he continued to hold the binoculars to his eyes.

'Oh-ho, I see a heavenly apparition on the horizon,' he said.

Everybody livened up immediately: 'Where?' 'What?' 'Show us'.

The girl tore herself away from her book. She tossed back her dark hair and looked at them severely. They were pre-venting her from reading. Then she too glanced in the direc-tion indicated by this smart, even handsome, young man.

A tall, thin woman in a white dress that reached almost to the ground was moving slowly along the lake-side path. One of her arms was stretched out in front of her carrying proudly, as if it were a battle flag or banner, an opened, black umbrella.

It did not shield her from the sun, for it sailed in front of her, but on her head she wore a ragged white veil, the ends of which fell down her back.

Now Dushenka had the binoculars and Mrs Fisher was stretching out her hand impatiently.

'The poor thing, I feel so sorry for her, she's obviously deranged.'

'She's walking in a very funny way, as if she's on a tight-rope,' Igor said.

'Don't mock the unfortunate,' said Dushenka.

Mrs Fisher looked at the woman. She confirmed that she was mentally ill and said that she appeared in the park in this strange dress from time to time and so had been given the nickname of 'the bride'.

'It is your opinion then, gentle ladies, that a long dress and a black umbrella is proof of madness?' mocked Duzhin.

'But it's such an odd umbrella,' said Dushenka, with wide, frightened eyes, 'it's edged round with white lace. Probably the poor woman lost her fiancé in the war, and that's why they call her "the bride".'

'My dear, don't let's invent things. The charm of life lies in enjoying real pleasures.' And the Professor kissed his wife's hand.

Dushenka picked up the binoculars again. Why are we so fascinated by mad people? We want to look inside their dark world and both long for and fear the unknown.

'Where is she? I can't see her.'

The woman in white had, indeed, disappeared. In vain Mrs Fisher and Duzhin aimed the binoculars at the shore. The woman had vanished like a ghost, as suddenly as she had appeared, as if she had flown away, borne aloft by her strange umbrella.

The postgraduate photographer relinquished the binoculars and abandoned the company. Leaning slightly in the direction of the book which the girl was reading he said softly, half-whispering: 'Is it a detective story?'

'Yes,' she said angrily, turning the book round and showing him the title.

' "Crime and Punishment," ' he read, and smiled. 'You're absolutely right. It is a detective story, and one of the most interesting.'

'Have you read it or just seen the film?'

'So that's how you are . . .'

'How?'

'The sarcastic kind. Did *you* read it before the film?'

'No, to be honest. I started but couldn't get through it. Now I can't put it down.'

'You've grown up. Are you a student?'

'Are you?'

They had a hushed conversation. Then Igor turned to his friends, 'I would like you to meet Ira.'

'Pleased to meet you,' Duzhin stood up and looked condescending: quite pretty, face a bit too narrow, nose a bit too sharp, but not bad at all. Long legs. A sweet girl.

'Nice to meet you,' Dushenka stretched out her arm and touched the girl's shoulders. And she thought, 'Igor's bored with us, let him have his fun.'

Mrs Fisher looked silently at the dark, shining hair and at the skimpy summer frock and golden tan. 'She's showing all her bones. It didn't take them long to get to know each other. Everything happens more quickly these days,' she thought.

Mr Fisher nodded to the girl. He thought: 'A nice little thing, like a small bird.'

The conversation had stopped abruptly. There was a long, awkward silence.

Suddenly Mrs Fisher's sharp voice cried: 'Another one, look, look! Another mad woman. She's moving very fast. And an umbrella.'

'Another umbrella,' rumbled Mr Fisher, 'it's no longer original.'

'The umbrella, her umbrella—' Mrs Fisher could no longer speak for laughing and thrust the binoculars at Dushenka, pointing towards the meeting point of two avenues.

Everybody turned their heads.

It was there that a little, winding path left the main avenue. It skirted the rose garden, led up towards the summer-house, passed it and became lost in the depths of the park. The woman with the umbrella had turned into this path. She was a strange figure, who became even stranger the more you looked at her.

She was walking hurriedly, nearly running. She was almost bent double with her umbrella held before her like a shield. A bare knitting needle stuck out from the middle of the umbrella, which hid the whole upper half of her body. Only her thin, strong legs, pulling her skirt tight at every step, were visible underneath it.

Following the path the woman approached them. She passed the summer-house and they could see her profile clearly.

'She has a good head,' said Duzhin, 'Her nose is rather large but it has a noble shape.'

'Her right shoe is worn down at the heel,' observed Dushenka, lowering the binoculars.

'I like it when women wear their hair in buns,' said Mr Fisher, 'it looks nice.'

'There's still something odd about her, even if she does wear her hair in a bun and have a noble nose,' Mrs Fisher said to the men. 'Where on earth is she going in a tearing hurry like that? There's absolutely nothing that way except the overgrown shores of the lake and the forest.'

'Why must she be odd? She's just down-and-out,' Professor Duzhin pronounced this description with satisfaction, 'A down-and-outer. Such an umbrella could only be carried by a tramp.'

All five of them laughed.

'Stop it!' Ira jumped to her feet, slamming her book shut.

'You're making fun of her and you don't know anything! She teaches at Moscow University, I've seen her there, she's a professor, she's got a – a . . .'

The young girl was jumping from one foot to another in agitation. Her cheeks were red and her eyes dark.

'What's her surname?' asked Mr Fisher.

'I don't know. She's a Doctor, a professor . . .'

'My dear, don't get so worked up. You've made a mistake. This woman probably looks a bit like that – that professor,' said Dushenka, trying, as always, to calm things down.

'Like the story of the old woman whom everybody thought was the lavatory attendant, but turned out to be the head of the department of quantum mechanics,' said Igor amiably.

Ira hadn't heard this story before, but everyone else must have for they laughed companionably. Ira frowned.

'Well, I'm telling you that she is a professor. But it doesn't really matter who she is.'

'She's no professor,' said Mrs Fisher. 'A professor in an institute of higher education wouldn't go around with a broken umbrella. She would have bought herself a Japanese one long ago. I'm positive that you are mistaken.'

'Look, she's sat down on a folding chair and is looking in her bag. Pensioners are always fumbling around in their bags for things. She's a typical pensioner,' said Dushenka persuasively.

'And she's probably an old spinster too! An old spinster who's a bit eccentric,' said Duzhin repetitively.

'No, she's a professor, and I'll prove it. Let's go and ask her. Come on, Igor, let's find out her surname,' Ira grabbed his hand.

'That's being a bit pedantic . . .' muttered Duzhin.

'Hang on, Ira, that could be a bit awkward. It'd be better if I went on my own.'

204

Dushenka shook her finger threateningly at Igor: 'Don't be silly, stop playing tricks.'

Mrs Fisher nudged him gently, 'Go on, Igor, and don't forget to find out whether she's a spinster or not.'

Igor leapt out of the summer-house crying: 'Follow me with your binoculars. And wait. Wait, Ira!'

The summer-house crowd quietened down. They spoke politely about other things, thus emphasising their non-involvement in these youthful antics. Nevertheless, the binoculars were passed from hand to hand. Only Ira kept on reading her book. She read the same page over and over again. The other four watched the silent scene through the binoculars, providing a commentary on it.

Igor went up to the woman, bowed and said something. He smiled. She lifted her head and answered. She looked stern. She pulled out a book and glasses from her bag.

Duzhin: 'It seems that the interview with Lady Tramp is over. Igor slips the camera strap off his shoulders and squats. She stretches her arm out in front of her, palm upwards.'

Mrs Fisher: 'A forbidding gesture: "I need no superfluous glory." Igor takes up his notebook and pen. Sits on the ground. Asks. Waits respectfully for an answer. She talks. Laughs. So does Igor.'

Mr Fisher: 'Talks took place in a friendly, relaxed atmosphere. Igor puts his notebook away. Gets up. Bows. She extends a hand.'

Dushenka: 'Look, look! Charming Igor has tamed her. Igor picks up the open umbrella from the ground, twirls it and studies it closely.'

Mrs Fisher: ' "Please tell me from where you obtained this treasure." Igor does something with the umbrella. Lady Tramp looks on with interest. She takes an object from her bag and offers it to Igor, who is concentrating hard on the umbrella.'

Dushenka: 'Oh! The umbrella opens and closes and the knitting needle doesn't stick out any more. Lady Tramp talks. Smiles. Gives a nod of her head. Puts on her glasses. Reads.'

Mrs Fisher: 'Igor is a TASS reporter, conducting an interview with Miss Umbrellason. He runs back laughing.'

Igor: 'She is a most interesting old gentlewoman. At first she tried to chase me away. She said: "I'm on holiday, no reporters please." She really is a Doctor of Biology. Sofia Levovna Kerotskaya. A professor at Moscow University. When I mended her umbrella she said: "Now I respect you." '

Duzhin: 'And then you asked whether she was a spinster or not?'

Igor: 'Yes, well, not quite in those words. I asked her if her husband was the artist, Nikanor Kerotsky. She said she wasn't married.'

Mrs Fisher: 'There you see, the Professor and I were right.'

Mr Fisher: 'Who wins?'

Igor: (grasping Ira by the hand and pulling her to her feet), 'Ira.'

The girl pulled herself away angrily. 'I know you're meant to enjoy yourselves on holiday, but I don't like your idea of fun.'

'It's only a little joke,' Dushenka said gently, 'don't get angry.'

'As Ivan Andreyevitch said in one of his fables, it's no crime to laugh at people who seem funny,' said Mrs Fisher, looking challengingly at Ira.

'It was Alexander Sergeyevitch who said it, Griboyedov Alexander Sergeyevitch.' Ira turned and walked away from the summer-house deeper into the park.

'Ira, wait!' shouted Igor.

They could see now that the girl was really beautiful when she moved. She stepped lightly, swaying gently as if to some inaudible music, with the free, almost angular grace, of a fawn.

'Enough of this squabbling, ladies and gentlemen, it's time to go.' Professor Duzhin stood up. Everyone else got up as well, and they resumed their conversation:

'Do you want to come with us to the cinema?'

'We're going to Lake Yusus, do you want to come, Igor?'

But Igor had gone, chasing after Ira.

The company was quiet then until they got to the main avenue.

'Maybe she *is* the head of the department of quantum mechanics, but she's still got a screw loose,' said Mrs Fisher.

'*And* she's a spinster,' said Duzhin.

Evening came, the sunset hour. The sun was setting behind a wooded hill, its rim swimming between the dark teeth of the fir trees. The last rays, rising into the canopy of the sky, lit up the feathery clouds. They burnt with a bright, exulting light and then darkened into a silver pink.

The oval-shaped lake called Yusus changed colour as it reflected the sky. Now its surface was a rosy silver, but one could see through this live, floating silver to the black, unmoving depths. The western edge of the lake had clumps of trees and was darker and thicker than the open, sparkling, eastern side. The edges of the mirror lake reflected the tree branches. Nearer the middle was the upside-down pointed church with its slender cross. This far-off church, invisible from this point, seemed an underwater fantasy.

Sofia Levovna stood for a long time on the steep banks of the Yusus. She was transfixed by the silence, the play of light, the mysterious mingling of the sky and the lake, the awesome awareness of depth and the cold darkness.

Every time she visited this little town she always came in

the evening to Lake Yusus to stand for a long time on its eastern shore. Her love rested here, in this lake. There was no other place where she could visit it. The house where they had led their short communal life no longer existed. There was no grave, she didn't even know roughly where he was buried. But she told herself that here, in this quiet lake, in its far depths under the weightless burial cross, their love was at peace, and there was no place more holy or more solemn to her than this.

Their first summer together they had lived close to Lake Yusus. There had been a small village then on the south shore and on their walks they had asked one of the small-holders to rent them a little hut. The owner had put in it an ancient wooden bed with a drawer underneath, filled with fresh hay, a table and two stools. The wind carried in to them the smells of the lake, cut grass and wood-piles through the glassless window. The timbered walls oozed tar in the heat of the day. At night time small forest creatures scampered under the floor. Food was prepared on a metal stand under which they lit chips of wood and brushwood. Their meals were simple: fish soup, buck-wheat porridge and potatoes, but the smoke made them taste good.

Sofia Levovna had been young and light then. When she tired on their long walks her husband would lift her up and carry her on his shoulders. He was strong and had great endurance, accustomed to walking and carrying loads. He was a geographer. He was a man of the forest. He loved nature directly, without sentimentality. He understood its hidden language.

Every day, at sunrise and sunset, they would come to the lake to swim, to get water and to fish. And while he sat fishing she would wander quietly round the lake, or stand and wonder at it as she did now.

Many years had passed since that summer. Much had changed. There was practically nothing left of the little village. The barn and cow-shed were dilapidated and overgrown with weeds. Their little hut had disappeared. Only its foundations remained, made from dark-grey stone and overgrown with nettles.

Even the lake had changed during these years, its shoreline had moved and had become overgrown with thickets of cane rushes. The dam which had allowed the lake to renew itself fully every springtime had rotted and sunk. Now a little stream flowed from the lake, constantly draining it and making the lowlands boggy, so that even in summer the paths sighed under one's feet. The old willows looked sickly and leaned wearily over the water.

Yes, that summer had been a long time ago.

Their life together had been short: two years, then goodbye, a parting, forever.

It was strange: she remembered clearly how they had torn her away from him, dragged her off him. She remembered how they had forced her hands to loosen their grip and her fingers to unbend. Why did she remember it this way when it hadn't been at all like that?

Her grief had turned her to stone, she had been restrained, frozen. She had not flung her arms around him when they had said goodbye, had not flung herself upon him and held tight to his shoulders as it now seemed to her. She had stood and looked numbly at him. He had stepped towards her and she had lifted her wooden face to him and had given him her cold lips to kiss.

He had left without her farewell kiss – forever.

Since that time she had been alone. There had been no one else. No one else that she could have loved. She could have remarried, but without loving, and for her that would have been pointless.

But that time was also past. It had been a long time ago and was over now. For many years now she had lived only for her work. Well, for her work, her friends and her students, although, of course, her students were part of her work. Her students, her postgraduates. Thank God, there were always a lot of them, a never-ending stream.

They gave her a lot of trouble, of course: they deceived her, they tried to justify their laziness and lack of talent, they asked for higher marks than they deserved, they took books and didn't return them, they sometimes even took her money. They would come to her home for a tutorial and a meal at the same time, they would weep out their sorrows and their anger before her. She had to comfort them, defend them to the dean, find a place in a hostel for someone to live, find a pass for the library for someone who had lost theirs.

And they liked her, of course. They had organised a wonderful birthday party for her in spring. She had rejected an official birthday celebration. She had wasted enough time in her life on these boring official functions. The students had turned up at her home with harlequin masks on, in fancy costumes, and making a terrible cacophony with flasks, measuring vials, harmonicas and combs. They enacted witty scenes, parodies of official ceremonial speeches from various institutes and societies delivered humorously. They had gone to a lot of trouble to present her with these lively performances.

It was good that she had them and that when they left they were replaced by others.

But the years were racing by, she was already sixty years old. A day would come when she would leave them. It upset her to think about it, especially it upset her when she thought about it here, on the banks of the Yusus.

Sofia Levovna glanced at the darkening water, at the sky in which the rosy colour was melting, and at the first light mist hanging over the darkening shores. She said: 'It's late, time to go.'

She said this aloud. She often spoke out loud to herself when she was on her own. She smiled wryly, once you start

talking to yourself it's time to go. She recalled some funny
little verses:

> As I walked by myself
> And talked to myself . . .

She walked along the empty shores on the well-trodden
path that wound round clumps of nettles, that passed the
deserted house, and as she walked she whispered the verses to
herself in time to her feet:

> . . . And talked to myself,
> Myself said unto me:
> 'Look to thyself
> Take care of thyself
> For nobody cares for thee.'
>
> I answered myself
> And said to myself
> In the self-same repartee:
> 'Look to thyself,
> Or not look to thyself,
> The self-same thing will be.'

Suddenly there was a rustling and hissing in the reeds. Two
dark figures appeared in identical belted raincoats, identical
glasses and, in their hands, identical fishing rods. Their sex
was indefinable. A man's voice cried: 'A bite – pull it in.' A
woman's voice answered: 'My worms have all gone, fling me
the box.' Then they started to leap and skip in the grass as
they tried to grasp the mutinous fish on their lines. Two fish
landed with a smack at Sofia Levovna's feet, throbbing and
twisting as they suffocated in the air. She stepped back and
bumped into a bucket full of fish rustling in the sultry gloom.
She stepped to one side and almost trod on some slashed
carcasses, surrounded by fish scales and pink innards.

Sofia Levovna sniffed fastidiously. She made a detour

round the fishing place and hurried away, walking faster and faster, as if cutting through the air with her head. Soon she disappeared into the smoky dust.

For supper Dushenka prepared baked fish with dill and tomatoes and cucumbers. Then they drank tea and talked. Igor sat by himself, flicking through a magazine. He didn't join in the conversation, he was thinking of Ira. The Fishers talked of their meeting by the lake. The Duzhins interrupted them with questions:

'We looked and saw that it was the Tramp Lady racing by, marching and muttering, nearly singing aloud – some sort of march, tam-pa-pa, pa-pa-tam, some sort of rubbish: "I myself, to myself" – some sort of verse . . . Of course, she had her umbrella with her. Suddenly two fish landed at her feet – she jumped up and rushed away! But first she stopped and swore.'

'You mean, she actually swore?'

'Yes, she did, and she growled, and she stepped back on to a bucket of fish and gave such a roar!'

'Yes, she bolted like a runaway horse.'

Duzhin laughed, 'So everybody's right: she is a professor and she is mad, our Tramp Lady.'

Suddenly Dushenka yawned loudly and sweetly, 'Excuse me!'

'Well, ladies and gentlemen, time for bed. We're all tired. Who's going to tidy up? Igor – we worked while you played. Your turn.'

Duzhin took a flowered apron from a chair, put it on Igor and pushed him towards the table.

The days passed. Summer was ending, so were the holidays.

Ira returned the Dostoevsky to the library unread. She sailed, walked and went to the far lake with Igor. They were both interested in photography. 'They're tracking down views,' said Duzhin. This interest stopped them quarrelling, even drew them together.

Igor was attracted to the girl. He was always trying to put his arm round her shoulders, to hold her hand, to kiss her. But she kept her distance. At first she repulsed him gracefully and good-naturedly. But she began to get more and more irritated. In the end she said: 'You're just like a fly at a honey pot.'

He was hurt. He spent three days in hiding, alone from morning till night, but he couldn't keep it up. Their walks resumed. Ira asked him to teach her photography, she developed from being a pretty model in the background of a snap to a keen student.

They found the nature here unusual and offering many interesting possibilities for slides. They could see far-off lands from the high hills. Green meadows alternated with yellow fields and brown hay-making. Blue and slate-grey patches of lake were dotted everywhere, sloping heights were replaced by steep ones, shaped like Easter bread and wearing dark fir-tree crowns. Everywhere there were scattered boulders smoothed by glaciers.

When they looked at all this from high up, when they saw the sky with its swollen clouds and the earth with its fleeing shadows of these clouds it seemed to them that they also flew. They would run shrieking down, jumping and slipping on the grassy slopes.

Once they went to Lake Nupol. Igor took Ira by a way he knew well, along a long forest path. He said it was the best way.

They climbed a hill.

'There'll be a clearing soon, a window opens and through it you'll see a wonderful "photograph"!'

They came out into the clearing. In front of them was blue sky. The firs alternated with alders. They saw a hazel grove. Igor turned into an almost imperceptible path. A hundred feet further on and the path would squeeze through a young spruce grove and then, suddenly, his 'window' would appear: a gap in the trees, a sharp incline and an old willow tree, unusual so high above the water line, one of whose two trunks lay on the ground. Through the willow was the view of the lake.

Igor was as excited as if he was going to show Ira a painting he had done. His heart thumped and he squeezed Ira's hand. Surprisingly she did not take her hand away.

And here it was: the window onto Lake Nupol. The lake was shining full of patches of sunlight, gradually darkening as it stretched towards the far hills. The grey branches of the half-dead willow gave depth to the picture, lightly framing the wild light.

Sofia Levovna was sitting on the horizontal trunk, her hands clasped in a closed circle. She was leaning back looking into the distance.

Igor was filled with such anger that he nearly said, 'Look, the Tramp Lady got here first!' But he restrained himself in time. When he was with Ira he didn't use this nickname. They stopped a little way away. Koretskaya did not see or hear them.

'Shall we go a bit nearer?' asked Igor softly, 'You can see the near shore with its boulders from there, and, in a way, I know her. Let's go closer, I can ask whether her mended umbrella is still all right.'

'No, we shouldn't disturb her.'

Igor frowned, then made a circle with his hand and looked through it: 'You know, it would make a nice picture, against the light, a woman's silhouette. She's outlined clearly against the old willow. Shall we take a picture?'

Igor unstrapped his camera, but while he was setting up the exposure and distance Sofia Levovna disappeared. They could just make out a silvery thread in the grass leading down to the lake.

They sat on the prone willow and were silent for a long time as they looked at the view. Then Ira said: 'She did have a husband, I knew but I didn't want to say anything then. It was a long time ago. He died.'

'During the war?'

'I don't know. I don't think so. But it was some kind of terrible death. She's been alone for a long time.'

'Didn't she have any children?'

'I told you: she's alone, on her own.'

'Do you think she's alone because, all these years, she's been waiting for him?'

'Waiting for him? I don't know. She just couldn't forget him. It's good to have a love like that: once in your whole life and for your whole life.'

Igor didn't think that that kind of love really existed, it was only found in books. But he didn't want to argue.

Again they were silent. Igor got up to assess their surroundings. He chose the point for the photograph: Ira – she looked so nice lying on the lower trunk.

'Don't move – I'm taking a picture.'

The Zenith snapped. Igor went closer for a snap of Ira without the background, without the branches rising above, alone on a willow trunk, as if floating on a flat-bottomed boat.

He approached her and bent down to lower his camera to the earth. She suddenly put her arms around his neck.

Igor flushed, surprised and breathless in the long kiss.

The dry smell of pine needles, dead leaves, grass and mint rose from the hill in the warmth of the sun. The hot air shuddered and wound in thin streaks above the earth; it seemed that this living, trembling light was the breath of the lake.

It was a cold, dismal day. The wind chased the low, ragged clouds, and then the rain came pouring down.

After lunch the Duzhins and the Fishers decided to go for a walk in the park. They went to the summer-house and looked at the lake with its wind-driven waves. They were about to go back when Igor and Ira appeared.

'Where have you been hiding?' asked Dushenka, 'We were waiting for you at lunch.'

'We went up the big ski-jump,' they said together.

'Weren't you frightened in weather like this?'

'Petrified, and elated. It was marvellous '

The big ski-jump was a recent construction. It was as high as a five-storeyed house. A narrow staircase without railings led to the top.

'And supposing the wind had blown you off?' Duzhin gazed at Ira through her transparent raincoat: in trousers and a sweater she looked good enough to eat.

'We weren't blown off. We ate in a café on the way back,' replied Igor.

'It looks as if it's going to last a while,' said Mr Fisher, studying the movements of the black clouds.

'It doesn't matter now,' said Dushenka, 'We'll be leaving soon.'

They were to leave in a few days time. They all had their tickets.

The Fishers gazed silently at the path and then asked: 'Where's the Tramp Lady got to?'

'Careful!' said Duzhin, widening his eyes in mock fright, 'You should say "Incidentally, I wonder where the Lady Professor is".'

'The Lady Professor has left for Moscow,' Ira said calmly, 'We saw her yesterday at the bus station.'

'Did she leave on the Tartu Express?' asked Mr Fisher. 'Were there many people on it?'

'She left in a taxi. She had a bit of luck: the car was returning from Tartu, I managed to stop it,' said Igor.

Duzhin: 'Aha. Correspondent Umbrella did not forget his acquaintance.'

Igor: 'We met by chance. I helped her with her suitcase.'

Mrs Fisher: 'I hope she didn't forget her umbrella?'

Ira: 'She threw it away.'

Dushenka: 'Why do you think she threw it away? She might have just forgotten it.'

Ira: 'We saw: as the car turned onto the main road an umbrella flew out of it.'

Igor: 'She aimed so expertly that it landed on a tree.'

Dushenka: 'It seems a strange way to get rid of unwanted things.'

Duzhin: 'I'm sorry, but she's definitely a bit odd . . .'

Ira: 'You've forgotten to add: *and* she's a spinster.'

At
Her Father's and Her Mother's Place

In the cold January frosts of 1923 Talya moved to her father's place. It only took seven minutes from there to school whereas from home it took forty. Her father had a spacious, light room with windows that looked out on to three corners of the world. From the eastern facing window she could see along Spiridonevka Street as far as the Nikitsky Gates. The window was made of one single large pane of glass and was so transparent that it seemed not to exist.

Looking through this window they parted and they met: the one staying behind would stand by the window, the one leaving would look back and wave a hand. The one being met could see from far off that someone was waiting and would begin to smile while still some distance away. Talya liked this window.

There were a lot of books in the room: on shelves, on the writing table, on chairs and even on the floor. Beside the table hung a photograph in a wooden frame. It was of a large group in the hospital where her father and mother had once worked a long time ago. They were very young then: he was tall and beardless, wearing his army uniform and a hat with a little cockade in it, an army doctor; she was on the other side of the group, slender, in a long dress with a white apron and a nurses' kerchief tied firmly round her round, pretty face with its straight eyebrows.

Talya liked living at her father's: it was a happy, carefree and relaxed life, like a continuation of the school holidays. In the morning together they drank the aromatic coffee that her father made on the little hot-plate in his room. Then she would get ready for school and he for work. Talya left first, while her father was still in the cotton dressing-gown he used for tidying up. She would laugh at him and he would play the fool – wave the dishtowel at her, pretending to be a servant, and call her 'your grace'. Before she left her father would pull a handful of silver coins, whatever he happened to have, out of his pocket. If he pulled out a lot he would say, 'A rich day', if less 'A poor day', but there was always enough for her to eat breakfast in the milkbar at Nikitsky Gates, in the building where the walls still retained the trace of words that had been erased: 'Chichkin' and 'Blandon'.

Talya would return home and read, lying on the divan. Or she would go through a heap of old magazines, looking at the pictures. Then she would do her homework.

Her father came home towards evening. She would keep watch for him at the window. At last his tall figure would come round the corner. He walked unhurriedly, his shoulders slightly hunched and his head bent. He would raise his hand while still far off and she would wave a magazine or exercise book in answer.

Talya liked her father: he was handsome, with a soft, chestnut-brown beard, a high forehead and clear, brown eyes.

He knew everything in the world: the names of the stars that they saw through their window in the evening; about the lives of the gods on Mount Olympus; about Michelangelo and Raphael, Galileo and Copernicus; about the flood and Noah's Ark, and where storks and swallows fly in the winter time. He could describe any country in the world as if he himself had lived there many years and had seen everything with his own eyes.

In the evening they read, separately or aloud, together. Her father knew a lot of poetry by heart. He would read Heine to her in German, lightly rolling his 'r's' so that you hardly heard them at all. Or he read her Balmont or Blok.

Her father drew well. When he was describing something

to Talya he would make quick little sketches. She would listen to him, kneeling on a chair, her chin resting in her folded arms, following intently the lines that his pencil was making, trying to guess what he was drawing.

They had another game: to draw from memory any animal or bird of Talya's choosing. They sat at different ends of the table. Talya drew slowly and hesitantly. She often stopped, craning her neck to try and see what her father was drawing in his notebook. Her drawings were clumsy; her horses were like those made of gingerbread, her father called them cart-horses. Their feet and joints were all at the wrong angles. Her father's horses were light, fast and impetuous. They raced or, at the very least, cantered along. Talya's drawings made them both laugh.

Then they would drink hot, sweet-smelling tea, brewed in a particular way, with delicious sandwiches made out of soft, rich buns. If Talya had difficulty with her maths or physics homework her father would readily help her with it. He explained everything simply and clearly, using anything that came to hand for his graphic illustrations: a thermometer, a triangle or some little copper scales with tiny weights that were once a necessary part of a medical man's baggage.

Then they would pull the two low armchairs together and Talya would make up her bed and lie down in it, covering herself with the chequered blanket that smelt of tobacco and medicine. Her father would turn out the main light; only the old lamp on its metal stand and its shade at a perpetual angle stayed on. Her father said that Hans Andersen had written his stories by just such a lamp. Her father would sit in the light of the old lamp and the squeak of his pen and the rustle of his papers could be heard deep into the quiet night.

From her corner Talya would look at her father, at his balding head, his long, slender fingers with which he pulled at his beard and think how nice it was here with him and what a shame it was that they didn't all live together.

221

'I'll definitely ask him why he left us tomorrow,' she would decide as she fell asleep.

But another day would pass without her asking.

One Saturday evening her father prepared a surprise for her: when they sat down to their afternoon tea she found a watch under the napkin on her plate. It was a man's watch with the word 'Mozer' inscribed on its handsome flat face, surrounded by clear figures. It also had a slender, fast second hand. Talya shrieked with joy, shook her chestnut curls and clapped her hands, but this wasn't enough to express her feelings, so she jumped onto the sofa and did a somersault, pressing her head on her father's bony knees and flinging her legs high in the air. He laughed: 'Bravo!' He pulled her to him. She was a typical thirteen-year-old, skinny, with long legs, and her brown eyes were just like his.

'So you like it, my lambkin?' And he helped her to put it on which entailed making another hole in the strap and he said how difficult it was to find good watches these days and to find small ones was quite impossible.

On Monday this happy, carefree life came to an abrupt end. Talya came back from school and flopped onto the sofa, then she got up to do her homework. She noticed a torn, violet-coloured envelope in the middle of the writing table. It had her father's name on it. There was also a sheet of paper of an identical violet, folded in four beside it. She picked up the sheet of paper with distaste and it seemed to unfold reluctantly. She read: 'I'm in love with you like a young girl.' She continued to read although she had realised immediately that it was a shameful letter. Her ears and cheeks burned. The letter ended with many kisses and was signed 'Rita'. Then Talya read the letter from the beginning, she read it again and again as if wanting to prolong the pain that it caused. She was particularly upset by the sentence: 'I can't wait until you'll be on your own again'. But even more hurtful was a sentence which she didn't immediately understand. She studied it for a

222

long time for its hidden meaning: 'Oh, when will the magic lamp light up our window once more?'

A feeling of utter weariness swept over Talya. She lay down on the sofa, curled herself up and shut her eyes. She lay like that for a little while. Then she jumped up, tore a clean strip of paper from the letter and wrote on it clearly in pencil:

I'm going home. Here's your watch, I don't need it.

Talya

She began to hurriedly take off the watch. It was nearly time for her father to arrive. She tugged at the strap but couldn't undo it. Suddenly she heard the bang of the outer door. It was him. Panic-stricken she stood motionless for a few seconds, then she stuffed the original letter under the blotting-pad, crumpled up her note in her fist, and flung herself onto the sofa, her eyes shut tight, burrowing into the pillow in an effort to bury herself as deeply as she could.

'Are you asleep, my little lambkin?' he asked.

Talya said nothing. Her father moved away, then came near again. Every nerve in Talya's body felt stretched to breaking point. She could feel the tears tickling her nose and she was terrified of making any noise.

'Don't you feel well?' her father asked anxiously.

'No, I've got a pain in my tummy,' she said, groaning mournfully, already believing in this pain.

Her father was worried. He asked her what she had been eating, where precisely the pain was; she must stick out her tongue, she must turn round and undress so that he could examine her.

'Look, lambkin, I'm a doctor, please don't make a fuss.'

'Leave me alone!' shouted Talya, 'Leave me alone!' Then, like a small child, she cried, 'I want my mummy, I want to go home.'

Her father thought that he understood. Perhaps, after all,

it was better for a young girl to live with her mother.

'All right, let's go. I'll take you there.'

She didn't want him to come with her. She didn't want him to help her pack her things or to help her on with her coat, hat and boots. She pushed his hands away, frowning and furious and silent.

He took her home to Plushik Street by horse cab. Normally she enjoyed this sleigh-ride but today she sat woodenly, her head lowered, her eyes fixed on the hole in the blanket that covered their feet.

Her mother wasn't home yet. The stuffy room smelt dusty. Unwashed dishes stood on the table. Her father didn't want to leave her by herself and asked how he could help. He told her to lie down.

'I don't need anything. I'm all right, I'm all right!'

The cabbie was still standing by the gates outside. Her father returned home with him. It was only when he was getting ready for bed that he found the crumpled ball of violet paper on the sofa. He straightened it out with some difficulty and read Talya's note. Then he understood everything. Rummaging about on the table he saw the letter under the blotting paper. 'It's all so stupid,' he thought angrily. Then he re-read the letter and smiled. He half moved to fling it into the waste-paper basket, but changed his mind and opened the drawer of his writing table and placed it with the other letters.

Talya sat on a chair, waiting for the door to bang behind her father. Now that she was home she wanted to cry again. She raised her head to prevent this: if the tears stay in your eyes then you can't call it crying. The dark, cracked ceiling trembled and became waterlogged before her gaze. She blinked and the tears really did disappear.

'Why is everything so horrible at home?' she thought.

The iron stove, the 'bourgeoiska' still stood in the middle of the room exhaling an aroma of lukewarm paraffin although radiators had long been providing the heating. An unpainted iron bed along one wall and a wooden bed, with a grey flannel blanket along the other wall, met in one corner. Cups, an empty sugar-bowl and a plate with some stale bread on it stood on the square, newspaper-covered table. The curtainless windows looked out on to blind brick walls. Two boxes, one on top of the other and covered in a kind of stripey material, served as a wardrobe. Beside them were heaped a waste-paper basket and two suitcases . . .

Talya got up and opened the small casement window. She took the crockery into the kitchen and tore the newspaper off the table. She crumpled it into a ball. She reached for the brush but changed her mind and brought a bucket and cloth in from the kitchen.

She remembered a conversation that she had had once, long ago, with her mother. 'Why don't we use a tablecloth every day?' she had asked on some special occasion. 'Is a tablecloth important?' her mother said, answering one question with another. 'Does your happiness depend on something like that?'

At the time Talya hadn't thought about these words, she had just decided that because her mother was so seldom home she didn't care. But now she said to herself: 'Mum doesn't like it here because Dad doesn't live here.' She remembered another home, not this one on Plushik Street, nor the one by the Nikitsky Gates, but a third one – the far-off, sunny, warm home of her early childhood.

Her mother always went to work early in the morning, before Talya was properly awake. She was a nurse in an infirmary attached to a large factory. She had a lot of other things to do as well, besides her work. She'd be at a Party branch meeting, at a general meeting, engaged in the political education of the women's section, called to the district committee, or doing voluntary public work on a Saturday. Even on her days off she was busy: somebody was having trouble placing their children; somebody was waiting to be allocated a larger room, somebody needed a loan.

Talya knew about her mother's work. They always told each other where they were going and when they would be back. Her mother would tell her about many of the things that she had seen during the day: 'Just imagine,' she would say, distressed, 'a little boy, that big, had to stand on a stool to make the key fit in the door so that he could open it to me. There was a little girl, still a baby, sitting on the floor, and he was meant to look after her while his mother was at work, to feed her from a bottle. It was terrible.'

Her mother's work would follow her about. Women in distress, old and young, would come in search of her, in urgent need of her advice. Sometimes her mother would ask Talya to go into the kitchen and read, sometimes she herself would go in there with her guests. They talked in hushed voices and, as her mother saw them out she would say loudly something like: 'Don't give in now, you stick to what you've decided,' or, 'Once we hear from the lawyer we'll be able to do something,' or, 'Don't you get depressed now, you hang on there.' Talya didn't ask questions. It was obvious to her that people needed her mother and that was why her mother gave them all her time. She rarely arrived home before nine or ten in the evening, and then she would have to wash, sew and cook. 'That's your tablecloth for you,' said Talya to herself as she wiped the floor with a wet rag.

Nevertheless, when she had washed the crockery and had even cleaned the old enamel kettle with its broken spout, Talya opened a suitcase and took out the blue tablecloth which was their one household possession. She covered the table and then put on it the cups, the clean, sparkling sugar-bowl and the kettle, full of fresh, boiled water.

She took a handful of vermicelli from the kitchen table and cooked it with salt. There was no butter anywhere, but she found an unopened packet of tea. After she had eaten half the tasteless food Talya drank freshly made tea without sugar. By now it was after ten. Talya tore a page out of her exercise book and wrote:

Mum, what's happened to you? I've missed you, but I can't wait any longer. I've got to go to bed. Don't leave tomorrow without waking me first. A hundred kisses.

Talya.

Supper is on the table.

The young girl fell immediately into such a sound sleep that she didn't hear the click of the door as it opened a few minutes later.

Her mother took off her fur hat, flung her coat on a chair and, peering into the room, took off her felt boots before entering. She padded to the table in her stockinged feet, read the note and smiled. Then she went back to the table and tasted the cold vermicelli. 'Absolutely horrible,' she whispered, and laughed softly. She had missed her daughter so much, but she hadn't realised how much until now.

Then she took the pins out of her fair hair that had been in a tight roll on the nape of her neck. She shook her head, unravelling her hair. She pulled off her dark blue jumper and her black cloth skirt. Her eyes were half-shut from fatigue. She sat on the edge of her wooden bed and wove a long plait. She wore a linen shirt with a low round neck that revealed her strong white throat. Then she waited a minute, as if gathering her strength, before going to the light switch and turning it off.

In the morning Talya was awakened by her mother tickling her face with the end of her plait. She sat up in bed with her eyes still shut and put her arms around her mother. They fell back on the pillow together.

'Talya, wake up,' said her mother, 'it's late.' Talya woke up instantaneously.

'But I asked you to wake me up early. And why have you still got your hair in a plait?'

'I've got the day off today.'

'Mum! The whole day off! Mum, say I don't have to go to school today, ah? I've missed you so much.'

Her mother laughed. 'You've found a fine excuse for missing lessons. Come on, up you get. When you get back from school we'll have a proper meal together, and let's go and see a film shall we? I'll have a real day off.'

Talya got ready quickly. Her breakfast was on the table: bread, butter and sugar. Her mother brought in the kettle.

'You came so unexpectedly, Talya. I've borrowed all this from the Alexandrovs. But today I'll go out shopping and you'll have a proper meal. I've just got to prepare an important report for tomorrow.'

Talya laughed. She knew her mother's 'days off'. And she also knew what her 'proper meals' were like. She would make a soup thick enough to stand a spoon up straight in and would say: 'There you are, first and second course in one.'

'Are you going to wash your plait, Mum?' That's what Talya called the washing of her mother's long hair. Her mother would have cut it short a long time ago but Talya had begged her not to and always helped her with it.

'Oh Talya, it does need washing, I must wash it.'

'There's something else I want to know.'

'What is it?'

'Why do we live in such a mess?'

'A mess? What do you mean?'

'Everything's so dirty, and we're so poor.'

Her mother looked round the room. 'Maybe you're right, but it's up to us, Talya. Let's give it a good clean, then.'

'Yes, we'll get rid of the stove and whitewash the ceiling.'

'Well, yes, we can get rid of the stove, but we'd better leave the ceiling until spring. We'll do it together one

Saturday. But as far as being poor goes, I don't think you're right. Is there anything you have to do without?'

If her mother had asked her what she wanted, Talya could have named a great many things without difficulty: a knitted beret with a pom-pom, just like Luda Cheshnakovaya's; woollen gloves, a grey pleated skirt, a jumper and scarf . . . To say that she actually *needed* something was more difficult. But she found something – proper ice-skates! Her mother was astonished. Tanya went skating in her ordinary boots with blades tied on to them. Why would a person need two pairs of boots? As soon as she'd said this it seemed to Talya that a second pair of boots would indeed be a bit much.

'Well, Talya, we can discuss our poverty some other time, but I would like to say something to you: in our country now many people have very hard lives; they lack the most elementary necessities, they never get enough to eat. We must arrange our common lives so that everybody has a good life, do you understand? We Bolsheviks must think of ourselves last. Now, off you go.'

Talya had her hat with the ear-muffs on, together with her coat, and her books, tied up with a strap, were in her hand, she was already at the door when she asked:

'Mum, why don't we live with Dad?'

'Not again, Natalya!' A hard line appeared between her mother's fluffy eyebrows. 'How many times have we discussed this before? I told you, he left us when you were five.'

'But you haven't answered my question,' said Talya stubbornly, 'I really want to know, and you must tell me this evening. I'm not a baby any more.'

'I thought we were going to the pictures,' said her mother in a kind of yearning, childish voice, but her face had lost its softness and her eyes were cloudy. She said angrily: 'I don't want to discuss this, do you hear? Once and for all! I don't want to talk about it and I don't want you to bring it up unless I mention it first. All right? Is that clear?'

'All right, all right!' Talya leaned against her mother. 'Don't get angry. I won't talk about it. Look, Dad gave me a watch.'

Her mother's agitation did not lessen. She glanced briefly at the watch and continued: 'It's a lovely watch. Talya, your father is a good man, do you hear? You must believe me, he's a fine man.' Her mother turned Talya round to face her and pressed Talya's cheeks hard with the palms of her hands. 'He is a good man, and you must love him, you must.'

Talya thought that her mother was going to cry. It was unusual and frightening. She tried to pull herself free. 'All right, Mum! Now I must go, I'm late.'

'Off you go then,' her mother pushed her towards the door and shouted after her into the corridor: 'Mind the trams.'

Tram number 15 went from Plushik Street to the Nikitsky Gates. Talya sat in the half-empty, frosty-white car. The tram went slowly, creaking and groaning from the cold. There was a little round transparent hole in the window which must have been made by somebody's warm breath. Talya, frowning, with eyebrows as fluffy and straight as her mother's, concentrated on rubbing it, but she did not look out of it.

Everything outside the window was well-known to her, from her home to the big, rose-red church on Arbat Square where, with a jangling of iron, the tram turned into the tree-lined avenue, to the yellow house with columns where she got out.

She was thinking about her mother and her father . . . They were both good people. Her father as well, of course. She loved them both, her father as well, in spite of yesterday's letter . . . But her mother . . . The way she had talked about him today . . . So her mother still loved him very much. But did that mean then that her mother was . . . unhappy? But the two words just didn't go together. She saw her mother,

her brisk step, her swift movements, her infectious, ringing laugh, and her eyes, always brilliant, always changing colour, from grey-blue to sky-blue. Unhappy people didn't have eyes like that – did they? How could he have stopped loving her? What had happened?

Talya took off one of her mittens and scratched the hoar frost repeatedly with her finger, making a crooked furrow that looked like a question mark. Through the little icy opening she could already see the yellow house with the white columns – her stop.

About the Author

Natalya Baranskaya was born in St Petersburg (now Leningrad) in 1908. Her parents were both committed revolutionaries and much of their time was spent hiding underground from the Tzarist police until they were finally forced to the West with their young daughter. In 1915 Natalya Baranskaya returned to Russia with her mother and they settled in Moscow. She studied at Moscow University and married in the mid 1930s. When her husband was called up for service in the Second World War, she and her two children were evacuated to the Altay region. After her husband's death on the Western Front, Natalya Baranskaya returned to Moscow where she remained until the end of the war. She never remarried, and women living on their own, with or without dependent children, is a recurring theme in her work. In 1958 Baranskaya began working at the Pushkin Historical Museum in Moscow as deputy curator where she remained for eight years. Only on her "retirement," then aged fifty-eight, did she begin her writing career.

Natalya Baranskaya has written many books, among which are *The Color of Honey* and *Yaksina Kuzminichna,* based on her experiences of the Second World War. *A Week Like Any Other,* her best known work, created a sensation when it was published in Moscow where she still lives.

About the Translator

Pieta Monks was born in London in 1946. She studied Russian at Sussex University and has travelled extensively in the USSR. She lives in London where she now works as a freelance translator and teaches Russian.

International Women's Writing from Seal Press
Selected Titles

WORDS OF FAREWELL: *Stories by Korean Women Writers* by Kang Sok-kyong, Kim Chi-won and O Chong-hui. $10.95, 0-931188-76-8.

THE HOUSE WITH THE BLIND GLASS WINDOWS by Herbjørg Wassmo. $9.95, 0-931188-50-4. The story of a young girl's struggle with incest by one of Norway's most important authors.

EGALIA'S DAUGHTERS by Gerd Brantenberg. $8.95, 0-931188-34-2. A hilarious satire on sex roles by Norway's leading feminist writer.

TO LIVE AND TO WRITE: *Selections by Japanese Women Writers, 1913–1938,* edited by Yukiko Tanaka. $9.95, 0-931188-43-1.

TWO WOMEN IN ONE by Nawal el-Saadawi. $7.95, 0-931188-40-7. A novel of sexual and political awakening by a well-known Egyptian writer.

ANGEL by Merle Collins. $8.95, 0-931188-64-4. A vibrant novel from the island of Grenada.

NERVOUS CONDITIONS by Tsitsi Dangarembga. $8.95, 0-931188-74-1. A novel of growing up in Zimbabwe by a brilliant new voice.

SEAL PRESS, founded in 1976 to provide a forum for women writers and feminist issues, has many other titles in stock: fiction, self-help books, anthologies and translations. Any of the books above may be ordered from us at 3131 Western Ave, Suite 410, Seattle WA 98121 (include $1.50 for the first book and .50 for each additional book). Write to us for a free catalog or if you would like to be on our mailing list.